# THE FAMILY BY THE SHORE

An air-mail letter and wallet of photographs from Hong Kong bring unexpected — and shocking — news for Laura Robbins and her younger brother and sister at Spryglass, the tall old family house facing the seashore on the wild Lancashire coast. Their seafaring father's startling revelation from overseas changes everything forever. As well as great happiness, the months ahead hold heartache, conflict and tragedy for the family by the shore — not least for Laura, loved by two men but uncertain of her own feelings or future . . .

*Books by June Davies*
*in the Linford Romance Library:*

IN DESTINY'S WAKE
THE APOTHECARY'S DAUGHTER

JUNE DAVIES

# THE FAMILY BY THE SHORE

*Complete and Unabridged*

**LINFORD**
*Leicester*

First published in Great Britain in 1994

First Linford Edition
published 2015

A catalogue record for this book is available
from the British Library.

ISBN 978–1–4448–2442–1

Published by
F. A. Thorpe (Publishing)
Anstey, Leicestershire

Set by Words & Graphics Ltd.
Anstey, Leicestershire
Printed and bound in Great Britain by
T. J. International Ltd., Padstow, Cornwall

This book is printed on acid-free paper

# 1

'So I won't see you tonight?' Laura Robbins couldn't hide her disappointment as she glanced up into David Hale's tanned face.

David was working hard to establish his market garden. Laura had a part-time job at Monk's Inn in the village, and looked after her younger brother and sister. In their busy lives, sometimes family tea at the Robbins' house was the only time they had together.

It was early morning. Sunshine flooded the cheery kitchen, lighting up the bowl of daffodils in the middle of the table. David had popped in on the way to the local market and now they sat finishing their mugs of coffee.

'Don't look at me like that!' David protested, reaching across to squeeze her hand. 'Or I'll forget all about the stall and take you off into the country for the day.'

It was a tempting prospect.

At twenty-six, he was nearly six years older than Laura, but he'd never been in love as deeply. Laura had captured his heart from the very first moment he saw her on that dusky December afternoon.

She was on her hands and knees on the snowy village green, wrestling her woolly scarf from a small grey dog that looked as if he, too, had been casually knitted. At the same time, Laura was trying to dodge a barrage of soggy snowballs thrown by her young sister.

To this day, David blessed his good fortune that Becky had such a rotten aim with a snowball. The icy missile had whacked him squarely on the ear. Laura had scrambled to her feet, concerned, anxious, offering apologies. Then, somehow, they'd both started laughing. Becky had shyly joined in. Smokey, the dog, trotted off with the woolly scarf and David, quite naturally, walked along with them to the edge of the village.

They'd parted at Sandford church and he'd watched Laura and Becky racing down towards the snow-dusted shore. When they'd finally disappeared from sight, David turned and headed home to Riverside Mill. He already knew he wanted to see Laura again . . .

'Even if it's late, couldn't you still pop in?' Laura began hopefully, carrying the fresh vegetables David had brought through into the cool pantry. 'After I've put Becky to bed, we could have supper together.'

'Best not.' David's voice was regretful. 'I've still got to fix those cold frames. With any luck, I'll have enough glass left over to do that pantry window for you. James has offered to lend a hand, so we should get it done over the weekend. While I'm at it, I'll take a look at the porch roof. Is it still leaking?'

Laura nodded bleakly and sighed. 'Spryglass seems to be falling apart,' she replied, following David into the vestibule of the narrow Victorian house. It stood midway along the sea-facing crescent, with tall evergreen hedges and a gnarled apple tree just unfurling new leaves. 'I wanted to have the outside woodwork painted before Dad got home, 'specially now he's coming ashore for good, but . . . ' Laura shrugged. Lately it had been hard enough just making ends meet.

'I can go to that DIY place in Liverpool for some paint and a couple of brushes. And I know where to borrow a long ladder.' David grinned. 'James and I'll soon have the old place looking as grand as the day the cotton merchants built her!'

'Some chance — but thanks!' Laura opened the heavy front door for him, letting the sharp, salty air come rushing in. 'I just want the house to look nice and clean and comfortable for Dad, the way it always did when Mum was alive.'

'Laura! You're doing a terrific job — caring for James and Becky and this house!' exclaimed David. 'And there's nobody prouder of you than your father.' He paused in the open doorway, drawing her around to face him. 'Except me . . . '

Tenderly his lips sought hers, but Laura coloured with embarrassment. She was trying to wriggle out from David's embrace as the garden gate creaked open.

'David! The postie!'

'Let Ted Tattersall find his own girl,' David murmured, insisting upon a final kiss before setting Laura free. As he strode down the uneven path towards his van, he grinned at the postman.

''Morning, Mr Tattersall!' muttered Laura self-consciously.

'Not much today,' the postman commented morosely. 'Bills. A card from the music shop in town — they've got some Beethoven thing James ordered. And a packet for you from your dad.'

'Oh, good! We haven't heard from him for ages.' Laura took the bundle of mail, then looked at the postman inquiringly. 'Only the one letter from Dad?'

''fraid so. I thought it a bit peculiar myself, so I had an extra look round the sorting office,' Ted replied. 'But there was nothing for James or Becky. I see your dad's in Hong Kong again. There before Christmas, too, wasn't he? And before that, Lisbon and Port Said? Sailing the world — that's the life!'

'Mmm, Dad does love the sea,' Laura commented absently, studying the slim air-mail package. 'But he always says he'd rather stay at home with us. He would have come ashore sooner if he could have found a decent job.'

'Well, I hope he knows what he's doing,' Ted sniffed doubtfully, starting back down the path. 'I'd hate to take up teaching at his age, even if the pupils are grown men at college!'

Laura couldn't help smiling as she returned to the kitchen. But it *was* odd Dad had written only to her. He knew how much James and Becky enjoyed getting their own letters from him.

★　★　★

Humming softly, Laura propped the bulky envelope up on the dresser, wanting to save it until later when she could share it with James and Becky. She began breakfast and started to fill the lunchboxes, though her gaze kept wandering to the dresser. Dad often included a cassette tape with his letters, sometimes even a video for Becky. They helped the little girl understand where Ken was when he was away from home.

Laura chewed her lip thoughtfully. This time, Dad hadn't sent any tapes. And why only the one letter? Addressed to her?

Taking the crockery from the dresser, Laura picked up the air-mail packet as well. Still hesitating, she slit it open. A wallet of photographs slipped out onto the table. And three sealed envelopes.

Becky's name was printed on one in large multicoloured letters, with a matchstick drawing of Ken racing from his ship towards a fat red pillar-box.

Despite her increasing apprehension, Laura smiled.

Quickly, she opened her own envelope. As usual, Dad began by asking after everyone. Laura . . . David . . . James, Becky, Gran and Granddad Jessup. Aunt Helen and Uncle Alex and their children, Diane and Ashley.

Laura could practically hear her father's voice . . . Unfolding the pages, she pictured Ken sitting in his cabin, writing in fits and starts, with all the noise and bustle of the huge cargo ship going on all about him.

But this was quite unlike Dad's usual cheerful, newsy letters.

*Have I ever thanked you for all you've done these past five years?* he wrote. *When your mum died, even though Gran and Granddad came to live at Spryglass, I saw you grow up all at once. And later, after Granddad's stroke, when they had to move into the flat, it was you who kept our family together, Laura.*

8

*I don't know what I would have done without you. But I'd do anything for you not to have given up so much.*

'Oh, Dad, you're so wrong!' Laura cried aloud in the empty kitchen. 'I *wanted* to leave school and help! I love being at home with Becky and James. There isn't anything I'd rather be doing!'

*Never a day goes by when I don't miss your mum,* Ken's letter went on. *I'll always love her. I want you to know that* . . .

Laura's eyes swam with unexpected tears. When Mum died, she and James and Becky had had each other, and Gran and Granddad Jessup. But Dad had had to do his grieving far away amongst strangers.

He wasn't the sort of man who could easily show his feelings, and it touched Laura's heart that he'd done so now. She could only guess at the pain and sadness that lay behind her father's carefully chosen words. His handwriting blurred before Laura's misty eyes as she looked through the rest of his letter.

*Coming ashore to start at the college is a huge step for me. It's one thing being a hands-on engineer aboard ship, but a different prospect entirely to be teaching in a classroom. I did have some second thoughts, but now I'm convinced it's the right decision. You'll be able to start living your own life at last. Maybe even settle down with that young man of yours!*

*I just don't know how to tell you this, Laura. I wish I could talk to you face to face! Perhaps it would be easier if we were sitting in the kitchen together, as we always do when there're things to talk over. You see, I've met someone very special. It was in the little curio shop where I bought that jade dragon for Becky's last birthday. For a long time we were just friends.*

*Alison is a dressmaker here in Hong Kong. When I got cold feet about accepting the college job, she encouraged me, made me believe in myself and my ability to succeed. So I accepted. I'd started making arrangements to come home before it hit me. After this trip, I'd probably never go back to Hong Kong. Never see Alison again.*

*I suddenly realised how empty my life would be without her. Then I found out Alison felt exactly the same way! We didn't want to be separated, not even for a few weeks.*

*Alison is a lovely woman, Laura. Kind and gentle. She's bright and clever and she makes me feel I'm alive again . . .*

Laura broke off, feeling a growing alarm. What was Dad trying to tell her? The handful of words on the final page sprang out at her. Laura read them over and over, disbelieving. It couldn't be true. Just couldn't be!

11

*Laura, love,* Ken Robbins concluded simply. *Alison and I have decided to get married.*

* * *

When James came downstairs a short while later, he expected to see his sister bustling about the kitchen and the table laid and ready for breakfast. Instead, he found Laura just sitting, staring into space.

'Laura? Are you all right?' he began, then saw the air-mail packet and the scattered pages of a letter. 'Is it Dad?' asked James quickly, a note of panic entering his voice. 'Has something happened?'

'No! No, nothing like that,' Laura reassured him at once, gathering up the contents of the packet. 'It is from Dad, but it isn't bad news. At least, I don't think so. What time is it, anyway?'

'It's OK. I'm up early.' James turned as he opened the fridge and poured a glass of orange juice. 'I want to get to school early because there's extra music practice. I can fix my own breakfast.'

'You'll do no such thing!' Laura spread the cloth across the scrubbed square table. James had matured so much, especially during the last six months, and she knew he was trying hard to be the man of the family while Dad was away. 'Sit down and drink your juice,' she told him as she finished setting the table. 'Breakfast won't be two ticks.'

'Thanks.' James did as he was told. 'You didn't wait to open your letter from Dad?'

'Er, no,' Laura answered awkwardly. 'They all came together in the same packet.'

James looked even more surprised as Laura handed over the envelope addressed to him. He made to push it into his schoolbag. 'I'll save mine for teatime.'

Laura turned from the stove. 'You'd better read it, Jamie.'

Everything James thought, and felt, always showed clearly on his face. Laura watched his expression change as he read the pages.

'Married?' he burst out impulsively, looking across at Laura in consternation. 'I've never thought about Dad getting married again, have you? And to someone we don't even know — ' James broke off abruptly. He avoided Laura's eyes, striving to get a grip on his emotions. He mustn't be weak now. He had to be calm for Laura's sake.

Being the eldest, and a girl, she'd been closest to their mother. What must she be feeling now? Now another woman — a stranger — was coming to take Mum's place? Coming to take *Laura's* place!

'I wonder what she's like?' James distractedly pushed a hand through his fair hair.

'Dad sent some photographs!' exclaimed Laura, suddenly remembering.

James pounced on the paper wallet,

emptying the photographs onto the table. A Chinese junk crossing Silvermine Bay at sunset, a picturesque island inhabited only by nesting seabirds, a hundred and eight oil lamps burning to celebrate the festival of Star Gods.

'Here!' He snatched up a picture of Ken standing before a sun-washed shrine, a slim, dark-haired woman close to his side.

Brother and sister stared at the photograph. Alison was dressed in a simple cream linen suit. Her face was shadowed by the wide brim of a matching cream hat with pale coffee-coloured flowers trimming the crown.

James threw himself back against the chair in exasperation. 'We can't tell anything from that! Not even what she looks like. Or how old she is.' He indicated Laura's letter. 'Does Dad say anything in yours? How they met? Who she is? *Anything?*'

'Just that she's a dressmaker in Hong Kong,' Laura replied numbly. 'Apparently they've known each other a while,'

15

she added flatly. 'Been friends. Then they realised . . . ' Scraping back her chair, she got to her feet, mechanically serving her brother's breakfast.

'It'll be good for Dad to have someone,' James ventured tentatively. 'And it'll be nice for you. You and David can get married now.'

Laura raised an eyebrow. 'He hasn't asked me!'

'Only because he knows you wouldn't leave us, and because there isn't enough room for him to live here,' James declared stoutly. 'I bet David proposes as soon as he knows you're free to say yes!'

'There's no point thinking that far ahead,' Laura answered with a smile. 'What else does Dad say?'

'Oh, you know. How much he's looking forward to our going fishing together. I loathe fishing, Laura! And about helping me train for the football team. You know how he feels about *that*!' James couldn't keep the despair from his voice.

'Oh, Jamie!'

Laura's heart went out to him. Her gentle and considerate brother was strong and well coordinated, but he possessed neither the aggression, nor the competitive streak, to be the kind of sportsman their father wanted.

'Football's OK for fun,' James went on earnestly. 'But Dad still treats me like a little boy, making plans and decisions for me. Why doesn't he take me seriously? What if he won't let me go on with my music?'

'It's too early to think about *that* either!'

James nodded, with a resigned smile. 'So, when are we going to tell Becky? About Dad and — what's her name again — Alison?'

'I'll do it,' Laura replied, 'when I go up to wake her.'

'Do you think you should play the whole thing down?' James spoke gravely. 'Becky's been pretty unsettled lately, with Miss Briscoe leaving and this new teacher taking over her class.

17

Perhaps we shouldn't make a fuss in front of her.'

'Now we're over the shock, there's nothing to make a fuss about,' Laura said sensibly. 'Dad says Alison is a fine woman. She must be nice, or he wouldn't be marrying her. Everything will turn out for the best,' she added optimistically. 'You get off to school now, and have a good day. Don't worry about football, A-levels or anything else!'

* * *

Laura climbed the stairs to the attic bedroom she and Becky shared and pushed open the low door. 'Breakfast in bed!' she called softly. 'It's a special morning!'

'A letter from Daddy!' Becky squealed in delight, spotting the envelope propped against her beaker of milk.

'You don't need to wait until teatime to open it.' Laura perched on the edge

18

of the bed. 'There's some very exciting news inside!'

Becky's face lit up at the gaily coloured drawing with which Ken had illustrated his letter. Then her eyebrows knitted with intense concentration as she struggled to make out the simple message, stumbling over even the shortest words.

Laura stroked Becky's fair curls, gently prompting and encouraging. Even though her sister didn't remember Mum, Laura was surprised the little girl accepted the news without query.

'If Dad and Alison are married,' Becky remarked, scrambling out of her nightie, 'I'll have a mummy — like everyone else in my class, won't I?'

'Yes, pet.' Laura swallowed the sudden lump in her throat. 'Why don't you write a letter to Daddy — to Daddy and Alison? We can do it tonight, after school. Now hurry up and get ready.'

While Becky was dressing, Laura picked up the telephone and dialed Riverside Mill. She listened, without surprise, as it rang and rang.

David worked hard and long hours; even so, money was woefully short. The profits from the fruit and veg stall at the midweek street market helped, though Laura was keenly aware how desperate the struggle was. Her job at Monk's Inn had taught her book-keeping and she was glad there was something useful she could do to help him — but it meant she had no illusions about David's prospects.

'Oh, David!' she whispered, reluctantly replacing the telephone. 'I need to talk to you so very much . . . '

A few hours later, as she shopped in the village, Laura's thoughts were still whirling as the reality of Ken's remarriage — and the many changes it would bring to her family — began to sink in.

'Laura!'

Absently, she glanced around. Then her face broke into a warm smile when she spotted Dan Jessup emerging from the library. Her grandfather limped now, and he was much thinner than before his stroke. When he'd negotiated the final step, he waved his stick triumphantly. 'Couldn't have managed that a few months ago!'

'Granddad!' she reproved gently. 'Behave yourself! You should be taking things easy.'

'You sound just like your gran! Don't fuss,' growled Dan. 'I'm feeling better than I've done for ages.' He paused. 'You won't mention this to your gran, though, will you? It'd only upset her. But that flat's driving me mad!'

'I thought you liked it there?' queried Laura in surprise. The Jessups' ground-floor flat was modern and compact and conveniently situated at the edge of the village.

'It's nice enough,' Dan responded indifferently. 'Grand when I was poorly and couldn't get about. Now, though . . . ' He shook his head. 'I miss having a garden. Oh, I potter about up at your Auntie Helen's, but it's all coloured chippings and glazed

21

planters. Not a proper garden at all, really.'

Dan's blue eyes twinkled as he paused for a breather outside the post office. 'I was hoping to bump into you,' he confessed. 'I met James on his way to school. He didn't say much but, well, I could tell from his face that something was going on.'

'We've had a letter from Dad.' Laura hesitated, before adding evenly, 'He's getting married in Hong Kong.'

'He never is! Why, that's grand!' Dan was clearly delighted. 'Good for Ken! Who is she?'

'Her name's Alison,' Laura replied, taken aback by her grandfather's joyful response. 'We don't know much else about her.'

'I hope they'll be happy,' Dan went on sincerely. 'Ken deserves it. Shall I tell Gran? Or do you want to?'

'I'd like to.'

'Smashing!' Dan nodded enthusiastically. 'Have you time to pop in now? She'll be at home . . . '

* * *

Nancy Jessup was having a satisfying day.

She liked to keep busy, and thoroughly enjoyed helping run the cottage hospital shop. Many of the patients were elderly and long-stay, and Nancy made a special point of spending time with them. She was thrilled when one of her elderly ladies had given her a thank-you gift that morning.

'Just a little something from my fruit garden, Nancy,' frail Miss Pendlebury had said, smiling. 'I always do my own bottling, and this was the last batch of blackcurrants before I broke my hip and landed in here! I asked my great-niece to fetch it from my larder.'

Once home in her own tiny kitchen, Nancy set to baking. The blackcurrants would make a delicious tart, and Dan would be hungry after his walk. Nancy frowned as she rolled the pastry. She worried about Dan whenever he went out on his own. Was he trying to do too much too soon? He'd always been an active man, and now he was beginning to feel better . . .

The sound of his key in the front door broke into her thoughts.

'I'm home, Nanny!' Dan called. 'And look who I've brought to see you!'

'Laura!' Nancy hurriedly wiped flour from her hands so she could hug her granddaughter.

When she heard Laura's news, she could scarcely believe it. 'But Ken's never breathed a word. He's never even mentioned he was considering getting wed again!' she gasped. 'When is he — are they — coming home?'

'They're travelling part of the way on Dad's ship,' Laura explained. 'Then flying the rest. They'll be home by the end of the month.'

'Is she — Alison — from Liverpool?' Nancy asked.

'I'm not sure. Dad didn't say — '

'Is she single?' went on Nancy hurriedly, her mind racing ahead to the possible consequences of Ken's remarriage. 'Or divorced? Or widowed perhaps, with children of her own?'

Laura stared at her grandmother blankly. The possibility Alison might have a family hadn't occurred to her!

'Ken would've said,' Dan put in calmly. He saw Nancy was troubled, and wanted to ease her growing anxieties. 'Now, how about a cup of tea? What've you been baking?'

★  ★  ★

To Laura, the day had seemed endless. Putting the saucepan onto the stove to heat milk for Becky's bedtime drink, she turned wearily to the kitchen table where James was engrossed in his homework.

Becky had spent the whole evening laboriously writing to her father. Laura folded the sheets into an air-mail envelope, hesitating only a few seconds before addressing it to *Mr and Mrs K. Robbins*. By the time Becky's letter reached Hong Kong, Dad and Alison would be husband and wife.

'Why don't you go over to the mill for a while?' suggested James, glancing up at his sister. She looked worn out. 'It'd do you good to see David.'

Laura couldn't argue with that. 'But aren't you going out?' she asked. 'It's your football night.'

'Even if I wanted to spend three hours training — which I don't — I've half a century of European history to catch up with. You get off. I'll see to Becky's cocoa and read her story.'

'Are you sure?'

'Laura!' he said loudly. 'Go!'

Laura was soon cycling away from the coast towards open fields, where horses and cattle were beginning to settle down for the night. Presently she heard the burble of the river, which gave David's market garden its name of Riverside Mill. Only the dilapidated, slate-roofed mill-house still remained, but Granddad had told them how once, long ago when he was a boy, a working grain mill had stood on the bank, drawing its power from the fast-flowing river.

In spite of the gathering gloom, no lights glowed at the mill's small square windows. David couldn't be back yet, Laura realised. Propping her bike against the hedge, she sat down on the worn stone doorstep to wait. The nocturnal life of the surrounding woodland was waking up. Laura heard the swish of an owl's wings, and glimpsed a sleek creature moving silent and swift as a shadow across the field where David had planted potatoes.

Despite the soothing murmur of the river, Laura was feeling anything but serene. She couldn't seem to even think straight any longer. She prided herself on being a practical, capable woman, yet here she was, close to tears in the darkness and longing to rush to the comfort and strength of David's arms like a lost and frightened child.

At last a heavy vehicle trundled up the rough track and David jumped down from the cab.

'Laura!' He was delighted to see her. 'What are you doing here at this time of night? I had a flat tyre . . . Thought I'd never get home!'

As Laura felt the warmth of David's arms encircling her, the last vestiges of control gave way. She couldn't be sensible or optimistic any longer. Clinging to him tightly, she buried her face in his chest and all her bottled-up fears and doubts poured out.

'I want Dad to be happy — of course I do,' Laura concluded, as she sat with David before the crackling open fire in the mill's living room. 'But I'm so — so *angry* at him! He's turned all our lives upside down. How could he do it? Just up and marry a total stranger? How could he?' She met David's eyes miserably. 'I know it's mean and selfish, but I wish he'd never met this woman.'

'It's not mean or selfish, at all,' David reassured her mildly. 'It's natural. For years, looking after Becky and James and Spryglass has been your whole life.

You've been the one to take charge, make decisions. Now you're faced with the prospect of handing it all over. That would be difficult enough in normal circumstances, but it's harder for you because you haven't had a chance to get to know Alison yet.'

'I thought you'd understand,' murmured Laura in disappointment. She wanted — needed — David's support. 'You just don't see what this marriage means to James and Becky and me, do you?'

'Yes, I do,' David replied gently, reaching out to touch her cheek. 'It's time to let go, Laura. Time to start living your own life. Now you can stop playing mum and — ' He broke off.

He'd wanted to propose for a long time. But not here, not like this. He wanted that special moment between them to be romantic and intimate.

'You and I needn't be apart so much,' he went on more softly, lowering his face to Laura's.

Much later, after he'd taken her

home, David worked long into the night patching up some second-hand cold frames. It gave him plenty of time to brood over Laura's cool response to his kisses.

\* \* \*

Sleep wouldn't come to Laura the night before her father was due to arrive home with his new bride.

She lay still so as not to disturb Becky, but her mind buzzed agitatedly and would allow her no rest. Dawn was lightening up the sky when she finally fell asleep. All too soon, Smokey's barking woke her again. David was down in the garden. He'd brought vegetables and salad, freshly picked that morning. As soon as Laura got back from walking Smokey on the shore, she began washing and peeling. During the wakeful hours of night, she'd made up her mind to be cheerful and composed all day. It had to be a happy occasion for everyone. Nothing must go wrong.

She had the special meal for Dad's homecoming planned down to the final crumb. Gran and Auntie Helen had wanted to help, but they'd understood when she'd said she wanted to do everything herself. She was making good progress when Becky and James came down to breakfast. They were going to school as usual, but having the afternoon off.

David had offered to drive them all to the airport, but Laura had decided it would be nicer to stay at home and have a special welcome awaiting. Then Dan Jessup had tactfully suggested that only Laura and the children be at Spryglass when the newlyweds arrived.

'Best give them a while to themselves,' Dan had told Nancy and Helen. 'We'll have our chance to say hello when they come to tea on Sunday.'

During the morning, Laura gave the house one last dust and polish and made up the bed in Mum's — the front — bedroom facing the sea. Then she laid out clean towels, a new tablet of sandalwood soap — Dad's favourite — and put a posy of flowers freshly gathered from the garden onto the dressing table, after removing the framed picture of Mum and Dad together that usually stood there. Laura carefully carried it upstairs to the room she and Becky shared.

The hours sped by. She was just lifting a large saucepan of vegetables over to the stove when the front door burst open and Becky came racing into the kitchen, a bulky roll of sugar-paper in her arms.

'Wait till you see, Laura!' she cried, dancing up and down excitedly. 'It's called a frieze! I did it in class. Wait till you see — but I'm putting some glitter on first!' Becky was off up to the attic like a whirlwind.

Laura looked at James, who was silently hanging his schoolbag on the peg in the hall. 'I've been dropped from the football team,' he said bleakly. 'The coach said I've missed one too many training sessions.'

'Oh, Jamie! What bad luck!' Laura exclaimed sympathetically, adding silently, *Today, of all days!*

'I don't mind — not about the football, at least,' James went on honestly, coming into the kitchen. 'It'll give me more time for my music — and revising.' His A-levels were just around the corner. 'It's Dad I mind about. He'll be so disappointed.'

'No, he won't. He'll be so glad to be home. Would you like me to tell him?'

James shook his head. 'No, I'll do it.' He hesitated. 'Would it be cowardly to leave it till tomorrow?'

'I think it'd be tactful. And considerate,' Laura reassured. 'Give him — them — today to get settled. There'll be lots of time for talking later.'

While Laura got on with melting the chocolate for topping the celebration cake, James wandered thoughtfully into the dining room. Whenever he was troubled, James sought refuge in music. He began playing softly on the second-hand upright piano his mother had found for him when he was eight years old. Mum had always understood and encouraged him. James's fingers moved lightly over the yellowed keys. It was going to feel very strange, having another woman in the house.

* * *

Becky clattered down the stairs with the unrolled frieze draped over her open arms. 'I've finished it, Laura!' she called, hurtling into the kitchen. 'I've put the glitter on! It's for Alison and Daddy's room! Look, I've drawn Smokey and — ' She stretched her arms out even farther.

'Be careful!' Laura's warning cry came too late.

The plastic bowl toppled from the table, and melted chocolate oozed out across the floor.

'Thank goodness it wasn't hot!' gasped Laura with relief, kneeling to wipe splashes from Becky's bare legs.

'But what about Daddy's special

cake?' wailed Becky, close to tears. 'We were going to ice it. Now I've spoiled it!'

'Don't be a silly, of course you haven't!' Laura comforted her sister with a cheerful hug. 'I'll just melt more chocolate, that's all! Now, are you going to show me what you've been up to with all that glitter . . . ?'

Leaving Becky putting up the colourful frieze in Ken and Alison's room, Laura hurried down into the dining room, where James was scribbling notes on the back of an envelope.

'Will you go to the village and buy more chocolate? We've just spilled all we had.'

'Sure.' James got up at once. 'No problem.'

On his way out to the back garden for his bike, he passed by the cooker and glanced round at Laura. 'Shouldn't the stove be hot? None of these pans are . . . '

When David Hale arrived a short while later, he found Laura crouching in the cramped cupboard under the stairs, a torch gripped between clenched teeth. She felt hot and dusty and frustrated and on the verge of panic. In less than two hours, Dad and Alison would be here. And half of the meal was still standing uncooked on a cold stove!

'Hi, there!' David's face broke into its easy smile. 'You look like you're having fun!'

If her hands hadn't been full replacing the blown fuses, Laura might have hit him.

'Not only pretty,' David went on blithely, 'but a competent electrician, too!'

'Don't mention electricity to me!' Laura cautioned, backing out from the cupboard. 'Not a word, David!'

'Fine by me.' He grinned. 'I'd much rather kiss you.'

'Fool!' She struggled free, glowering at him as they went through to the kitchen.

'I came to see if you needed an extra

pair of hands.' David halted at the solidifying puddle of chocolate and the upturned bowl in the middle of the floor. 'But I can see everything's under control.'

'If you really want to help — ' Laura cast him a narrow look. ' — you could clear that lot up!'

'Right away, ma'am,' he replied, getting down onto his knees with a wet cloth. 'I knows me place.'

Laura swiped at him with a damp tea towel, crossing to the dresser and carefully taking out the best crockery.

\* \* \*

'Your cake looks fantastic, Becky!' exclaimed David admiringly, as the little girl was putting the finishing touches to the thick, chocolaty frosting. 'Can I scrape out the bowl?'

'You shouldn't really,' Becky replied severely. 'But you can, because I have to go and put my new dress on.' She pushed the bowl into David's waiting hands and clattered upstairs.

Laura had already changed into a full-skirted primrose dress. As she moved about the dining room, fussing with the table and the flowers, David couldn't keep his eyes from her. It was wonderful to see Laura back to her old self, laughing and smiling, her blue eyes dancing. David had no way of knowing the immense effort she was making to appear cheerful and carefree, nor how hard Laura was striving to quell the increasing knot of tension and anxiety.

Following her into the kitchen, he slipped his arms about her waist, kissing the nape of her neck. Her skin was soft, her hair scented with sea-spray and flowers.

'Marry me, Laura . . . ' David breathed impulsively. 'Marry me now!'

'Don't be ridiculous!' blazed Laura, her frayed nerves finally snapping as she spun round and faced him. 'How can I possibly marry you?'

David couldn't have been any more shocked if she'd struck him. 'But you

— you're free now,' he began in confusion, reaching for her again.

Laura pushed away from him. 'If I couldn't leave Becky before, how on earth can I leave her now? Alison may be my father's wife, but she certainly isn't Becky's mother! She's a total stranger. Do you really expect me to trust Becky — '

'Laura! Laura!' Becky cannoned into the room. 'They're here! They're here!'

With Becky and Smokey racing on ahead to the gate, Laura, David and James gradually spilled out from the house onto the stone steps. They were starting down the garden path as a taxi was drawing to a halt.

His face creased in a broad smile, Ken Robbins stepped out. He waved and called greetings, then swung Becky up into his arms and hugged her. When he'd set her down again, Ken helped his new wife from the taxi. 'Alison,' he was saying proudly, 'these are my children: Becky and James, and Laura . . . '

Laura's carefully rehearsed words of

welcome dried in her throat. The petite, fashionable woman standing before her was nothing like she'd imagined.

'Hello, Laura.' Alison smiled warmly. 'I am so very happy to meet you at last.'

Laura returned the greeting mechanically. She was quite unable to take her eyes from the face of this delicately beautiful Eurasian girl, only a few years older than she was . . .

# 2

Laura stared with disbelief, into the dark eyes of the lovely young woman who was her father's second wife. As the newcomer smiled hesitantly, she floundered for something to say to break the embarrassed silence. 'Shall — shall we go indoors?' she faltered at last, ushering Alison ahead of her up the path. 'I daresay you'd like to freshen up. Dinner will be ready whenever you and — and Dad — are.'

The family crowded into the hall, and suddenly everyone was talking at once. The old house was filled with noise and voices and Smokey's excited barking. David was bringing in the last of the luggage when Ken clapped him on the shoulder.

'Your turn next, is it?' Ken enquired cheerfully, oblivious to Laura's horrified glance. 'I expected to come home and find the pair of you engaged at the very least!'

'Dad!' Laura muttered with acute embarrassment, her face flaming.

'Oh, all right, Becky!' Ken good-naturedly turned away as his youngest daughter tugged on his hand. 'Let's have a look at this picture of yours.'

'Sorry about that.' Laura couldn't meet David's eyes. 'Dad didn't mean — '

'I know. He thinks you're in love with me,' David returned crisply, starting out into the vestibule. 'I made the same mistake myself!'

'David!' She ran after him, catching hold of his sleeve. 'Don't go!'

David looked down at her, stony-faced.

'I can't cope with this alone,' pleaded Laura. 'Stay for dinner. Please?'

\* \* \*

'So, after graduating from college, I started out as a dressmaker and designer,' Alison explained as they ate.

'I commenced business on the eighteenth day of the first moon, in the hope the Star Gods would bestow prosperity, wealth, joy and longevity upon my little shop.' She laughed, her dark eyes shining. 'Nonetheless, in the beginning, I *still* experienced very hard times.'

'I know all about that,' chipped in David amiably. 'Is there a lucky deity for struggling market gardeners?'

'I'm sure there is,' Alison replied with a brilliant smile. 'There seems to be one for almost everything.'

Yet another rather awkward lull descended. The mood in Spryglass's flower-filled dining room was uneasy, and Laura was inwardly willing the meal to be quickly over. The celebration dinner she had so carefully planned tasted like sawdust in her mouth. She was worried about David, too. He'd agreed to stay, but there had been no trace of his former affection. He seemed so cold and distant . . . to her, at least. However, Laura couldn't help noticing he was certainly managing to chat to Alison easily enough. Although Becky was far too shy to actually speak to Alison, the child was contentedly sitting beside her, hanging on every word, her eyes never leaving her step-mother's face.

Presently, Laura brought in the splendid cake with its sumptuous chocolate frosting, clusters of sugar flowers and glimmering candles; and while the cake was being cut, Alison turned to Becky and asked about the painting the little girl had hung in her and Ken's room. Laura frowned. Alison might be making an effort to draw Becky out, but she spoke to her as though she were another adult, instead of a small child longing for a mother. Returning to her place between James and David, Laura experienced a prickle of resentment. Only a handful of years might separate them, but she hadn't a thing in common with this poised, worldly-wise young career woman.

'Alison ran a very successful business

in Hong Kong,' Ken was saying. 'She gave it all up to marry me.'

'Darling, you exaggerate!' Alison had overheard, and looked around from her conversation with Becky. 'My shop was hardly haute couture,' she protested, leaning over to kiss his cheek.

'Is your family in Hong Kong?' James asked politely.

'My father is in Hong Kong. He has an antiques business there,' replied Alison. 'My mother's a fashion journalist. After they divorced, she returned to France while I stayed with Father in Hong Kong.' She sipped at her glass and smiled at James. 'I understand you enjoy music?'

The young man's face brightened for the first time. 'Oh, yes. I'm in the school orchestra. And I compose a bit — ' He broke off, darting a quick look to Ken, hoping the subject wouldn't turn to football. But it did.

'Music's fine for a wee hobby,' remarked his father. 'But professional football could be a real career. Jimmy

45

has natural ability and real prospects — the team coach told me so. You're going to play for England one day. Maybe even Scotland, if they'll have you!' Ken concluded with a proud smile. 'Aren't you, son?'

It wasn't exactly a question, so James lowered his eyes and said nothing. Laura knew exactly how he must be feeling and gave him a sympathetic kick under the table. How on earth was he going to tell his father he'd been dropped from the team?

Laura was grateful to finally escape to the solitude of the kitchen, only to be startled by the touch of a cool hand upon her bare arm. She hadn't been aware of Alison following her.

'That was a delicious meal, Laura.'

She received the compliment silently. Alison had scarcely touched a bite.

'Thank you so much for going to such trouble,' went on Alison with a smile. 'May I help with the washing-up?'

'Certainly not! You're our guest —

guest of honour,' Laura corrected herself. 'Do go back to the others.'

Alison smiled again, but this time it did not reach her eyes. She started back across the kitchen as David appeared in the doorway. He gave her a warm smile and held the door open for her.

'Are you going to chase me away, too?' he asked, taking off his jacket and rolling up his shirt sleeves. 'A bit sharp just now, weren't you? It was nice of Alison to want to help.'

'If I was rude, I'll apologise,' Laura returned curtly.

'I do understand this is a difficult situation for you,' he ventured carefully. 'But it can't be easy for Alison, either.'

'I suppose you're going to tell me she's the ideal wife for my father?'

'Why wouldn't she be?' David shrugged, joining her at the sink. 'Alison is a kind, intelligent woman. I like her.'

'You've made that perfectly obvious!'

'Laura, this just isn't like you!' he exclaimed in exasperation. 'Can't you even *try* to see things from Alison's point of view? She's a stranger coming to a strange country, suddenly part of a close-knit — '

'For heaven's sake, David!' cried Laura in despair, spinning round to confront him. 'She's twenty-six years old. Dad's nearly forty-eight!'

'The age difference isn't bothering them, so it has no business bothering anybody else,' David replied briskly, his patience wearing thin. 'At least give Alison a chance. Get to know her before you disapprove of her.'

'It's easy to see whose side you're on!'

'There's no question of taking sides,' he retorted tersely. 'Ken and Alison are married. Like it or not, you'll have to accept it.'

'Well, that's certainly put me in my place, hasn't it?' she snapped, hot colour rising in her pale cheeks.

'Laura, be reasonable! I'm only saying — ' David broke off abruptly and snatched his jacket from where he'd left it over the chair back. 'Oh, what's the point!'

Laura swung around, barely able to steady the tremor in her voice. 'Where are you going?'

'Home,' he answered over his shoulder, opening the kitchen door. 'Don't you realise I didn't want to argue about Ken and Alison? I wanted to talk to you about us! But it seems there's no point in that, either!'

★　★　★

When the over-excited Becky had finally fallen asleep, and James disappeared into his room to finish homework, the conversation between Laura and the newlyweds gradually faded to quietness. The couple were sitting together on the sofa in the window bay, Ken's arm around Alison's shoulder, her head resting against his chest. Laura grew more and more uncomfortable.

'Anyone for a last cup of tea?' she

said at length, already on her feet.

'Oh, no, thank you,' murmured Alison, opening drowsy eyes. 'Ken?'

'Not for me. I'm ready to turn in.' He smiled tenderly at his wife. 'Coming, love?'

She nodded, returning his smile and reaching up to kiss his cheek. Laura looked away quickly, unable to conceal her embarrassment. After they'd gone upstairs, she went around tidying up, as she did last thing every evening. Somehow, the homely rooms didn't seem quite like home anymore. Although it had been a long, long day, Laura was convinced she wouldn't sleep. Eventually, however, she started up to the attic bedroom she and Becky shared. However, when she reached the shadowy stairwell, Laura froze.

Ken and Alison were tiptoeing from the room where Becky was sleeping, closing the door gently behind them. Tears welled into Laura's eyes. She felt excluded. Shut out.

The couple paused on the landing.

Ken's hands slipped about Alison's waist, his lips touching hers in a lingering kiss.

Anger flared within Laura now. How could Dad have married someone so unsuitable? Yet even as the thought passed through her mind, Laura found herself longing for the closeness the newlyweds were sharing. Why had she let David walk out? No — why had she *driven* him out? Continuing up the stairs to bed, Laura ached with loneliness.

★ ★ ★

Although her apartment in the Peak District of Hong Kong offered panoramic views of the city and the harbour, where traditional sampans jostled for space with modern shipping, Alison had rarely given the ocean a thought.

Her first impression of Spryglass, however, was that wherever she was in the narrow old house, it was impossible to ignore the sea's nearness. The persistent sound of surging waves was always there, and the sharp, cold smell of it. Alison fancied she could even taste salt on her lips as she paused on the sand-dusted garden path with its borders of early primroses, waiting for Ken to join her.

He was going to show her around Sandford, then they were going on to the local bank. Finally, they'd pop in to say hello to Ken's parents-in-law, Dan and Nancy Jessup. Alison turned as Ken came down the steps, beaming at her.

'You look great, love!' he said, brushing her cheek with a quick kiss and slipping his arm around her narrow shoulders.

Alison squeezed his hand, glad to be completely alone with him again. Even if it were only for a short while. Amidst so much that was unfamiliar, she had needed Ken's reassurance. It was wonderful to see him looking at her like this, as he'd done when they exchanged their marriage vows.

'It's a bit misty this morning,' Ken remarked as they started through the garden gate, glancing over the miles of sea and shore, 'but you can just make out the Welsh hills across the water there.'

Alison nodded, scanning the grey ocean and the beach with its flocks of seagulls. 'I don't remember ever seeing so much empty space before!' she exclaimed, comparing it with Hong Kong's brilliant, bustling streets and constant vitality. Here, there wasn't a building for as far as the eye could see. Or another person besides herself and Ken. 'Or hearing so much silence!' she added with a laugh.

'That's because you're a city girl, Mrs Robbins.' He grinned back at her as they started away from the coast and towards the village. 'Even in the dead of night, the sea and shore are never completely silent. There's always some sound. Wait until you get used to it, then you'll know what I mean.'

The lane was broad, lined with hedges, old fences and gnarled trees whose branches met overhead in great green arches. The footpath was slippery with moss, scattered with petals from the blossom-laden apple and cherry trees. A boy on a placid-looking bay mare trotted from the deep shadows of the pine woods. He walked past the couple before cantering for the shore.

'Are there stables nearby?' Alison asked.

'Mmm, the other side of the woods. Near the river,' answered Ken. 'Not far from David's market garden. Can you ride?'

'I used to. But I haven't done much since I was young.'

'As long ago as that, eh?' He sounded good-humoured, but Alison saw Ken's expression become serious. She guessed his joke had sparked a sharp reminder of their homecoming. He hadn't said a word to her about it, but she had sensed his dismay at his children's reaction.

'They were surprised, that's all,' she whispered, reaching up on tiptoe to kiss him. 'Just give them time, darling.'

'Yes,' he said with a confidence he scarcely felt. 'You're right.'

At least, he hoped Alison was right.

He'd realised — too late — he should have told the children everything about Alison. Laura, in particular, needed to know how he felt about her. Instead, he'd shied away from the subject and avoided mentioning how much younger than him Alison was. He hadn't wanted his children to get the wrong idea. He'd been convinced once they'd met Alison, and got to know her, they'd understand. For weeks, he'd been looking forward to bringing the woman he loved home to his family.

'Is Sandford like the place where you grew up in Scotland?' Alison interrupted his thoughts as the old sandstone church came into view.

Ken shook his head, looking at the clusters of stone cottages, small-windowed, some thatched, and the horseshoe of low bow-fronted village shops.

'I was born in a pit town. Coal mining, that is,' he explained. 'It was just after the war and the pit was on its last legs. My older brothers were laid off, my father was on short time . . . ' Ken shrugged dismissively; he'd never been comfortable talking about himself. 'The mine *was* the town. There wasn't anything else. My sister and I went to relatives in the Highlands until I left school at fifteen. Not much education. No prospects. No hope of a job.

'An uncle of ours lived near Liverpool. He had a scrap yard, and three daughters.' Ken grinned slightly. 'He knew how my family was fixed, and he wrote saying he needed two strong lads to work in his yard. That's how my brother and I ended up in Liverpool.'

'It must have been difficult for you,' murmured Alison, touched by Ken's simple telling of the bleak story.

'I suppose it does seem pretty grim, looking back,' he remarked. 'At the time, it was all right. There were plenty worse off. Ewan couldn't wait to go back north, but I'd seen the sea and I knew that was the only life I wanted. I studied at night school and got a job with a shipping line,' he concluded with a smile. 'And I've gone to sea ever since.'

'Until now.'

'Until now.'

'Any regrets, Ken?' she asked, searching his face earnestly.

'Not a one!' answered Ken firmly, raising her hand to his lips. 'Staying ashore is going to take some getting used to, though,' he admitted ruefully. 'I've never really lived here. Sandford was Jeanette's home. I have to keep reminding myself that I won't be sailing away anymore. I'm here for good. It's an odd feeling,' he admitted sheepishly. 'So is starting a new job at my age.'

'The college is fortunate to get you.'

'I wish I had your confidence in me. I've spent near thirty years working as an engineer. I'm just not sure how I'll cope with teaching other men to be engineers.'

'Darling,' began Alison seriously, 'you'll be — '

'Wonderful — aye, I know!' He grinned as they strolled past the newsagent's and crossed the curving, tree-lined road to where the bank was sandwiched between the post office and the chemist.

'Sure you don't want to come into Liverpool with me later?' Ken asked. He was going to collect various documents from his former employers.

'I'd only be in the way,' Alison replied, casting a backward glance at the picturesque village as Ken held the door of the bank open for her to enter. 'Besides, I'd like to explore a little more.'

\* \* \*

When Ken had proposed to her that warm evening aboard a sampan drifting across the sun-streaked bay, Alison had accepted without hesitation, even though she knew it would mean giving up everything familiar. Family, friends, home and career would all be left far behind as she travelled half the world away to begin life as Ken's wife.

He'd spoken about his children often, showing Alison their photographs and sharing their letters with her. But still, Laura, James and Becky had remained remote, distant figures. She'd been too excited and too blissfully happy to fret about meeting the Robbins children for the first time. In fact, Alison hadn't given it a thought until the moment she'd stepped from the taxi and met Laura's cool gaze.

There had been no friendliness in her step-daughter's stiffly polite greeting — only shock and suspicion. And it had unnerved Alison. She'd tried to hide her feelings, hoping no one, especially Ken, would guess her discomfort. But now, walking at his side across the village green, Alison confessed she was concerned at the prospect of meeting the parents of Ken's late wife.

'I hope they like me,' she murmured.

'They will. And you'll like them,' Ken responded, tightening his grip on her hand encouragingly. 'Dan and Nancy have been like parents to me. My own died before I was nineteen and I've lost touch with my brother and sister.'

Alison knew Ken was trying to reassure her, however his words only increased the pressure. She was more anxious than ever now for the Jessups to like and accept her into the family. She took a deep breath as Ken rang the doorbell of the modern ground-floor flat. The door opened, and the genuine warmth of the elderly couple's greeting immediately set Alison's fears to rest.

'Come along in!' Dan was beaming. 'Let's get a look at the newlyweds!'

Ken made the quite unnecessary introductions, and Dan gently clasped Alison's hand in both his own. 'It's grand to meet you, Alison,' he said sincerely. 'I hope you and Ken have every happiness together.'

'Oh, thank you so much!' she exclaimed softly, uncharacteristic tears not far from her eyes. 'You're very kind.'

Nancy was hugging Ken, hesitating only a moment before stepping forward and shyly giving Alison a hug too.

'Welcome to the family, lass!' The elderly woman's face broke into an even broader smile as she drew Alison into the neat living room. 'Sit down and make yourself at home,' she instructed, bustling through to the tiny kitchen. 'I'll just put the kettle on.'

'I see you've done a bit of shopping,' Dan remarked as he carefully set the tray with the blue willow-patterned cups and saucers onto the coffee table. 'At Almond's, eh?' he went on, eyeing the brown-and-white-striped paper bag at Alison's side. 'Met Hilda Almond, did you?'

Alison heard Ken's muffled snort of mirth and nodded, looking distinctly shamefaced.

'Don't remind me!' she replied,

taking her purchase from the paper bag to show Dan and Nancy. 'I'd left Ken at the bank, and I spotted this instant camera in the window of the chemist. It seemed such a good idea to buy it, so I can enclose some photographs when I write to my father. I went inside and asked for the camera — ' Alison raised her eyebrows. ' — and that was when I realised I hadn't any English money.'

'You had a lucky escape there!' Dan exclaimed with a straight face. 'It's a wonder Hilda Almond didn't call the police and have you arrested!'

'Take no notice — Dan's just pulling your leg,' Nancy chipped in, seeing that Alison wasn't quite sure how to take Dan's sense of humour. 'Hilda's not a bad sort really. We were at school together. She's just . . . just . . . very efficient.'

'Efficient? The woman's nowt short of terrifying!' Dan contradicted flatly. 'Ever since I accidentally dropped a bottle of cough mixture, I haven't dared set foot in the shop. I have to ask

Nanny to get my razor blades!'

Dan was laughing now, and Alison and the others joined in.

'I felt such a fool with my handful of worthless Hong Kong dollars,' confessed Alison. '*And* guilty — Mrs Almond was very disapproving! Fortunately, Ken came to my rescue and I got the camera. After I've taken some pictures, perhaps Becky would like the camera? She might enjoy taking photographs and seeing them appear straight away.'

'That's a nice idea,' said Nancy, beaming. 'I'm sure she'll be thrilled. She's been so excited waiting for you and Ken to get home. How are the bairns?' she added, refilling Ken's teacup.

'I wish I knew.' Ken gave a perplexed sigh. 'Laura and David . . . Jimmy . . . Even Becky. I can't open my mouth without putting my foot in it. Nothing's as I expected it to be.' He looked from Nancy to Dan's concerned face. 'I feel like a stranger in my own family.'

'Time'll put that right,' Nancy reassured him. 'You've been away the best part of six months, Ken. The children are growing up fast. They're changing and so are their lives.'

'Nanny's right,' agreed Dan. 'It's like during the war. When I came home from the army, I was different and so was everybody else. We all had to get to know each other again.'

'Just take it slowly,' Nancy finished with a smile. 'It'll all work out — then you'll wonder what you were fretting about!'

'My wife's given me much the same advice,' remarked Ken, returning Nancy's smile and accepting another piece of her parkin. 'Thanks. No one can touch your baking, Nancy! By the way, how are Helen and the family? I tried to ring her earlier, but got no reply.' He turned to Alison. 'Helen is Dan and Nancy's younger daughter. She and her family moved away from Sandford last year.'

'Aye, Sandford wasn't good enough

for Alex — Helen's husband,' Dan commented with feeling. 'He always was uppity.'

'Dan!' Nancy reproached with a frown.

'Well, it's true! They moved to a new bungalow out at Ingle Green. We don't see as much of Helen and the children as we used to. You'll meet Helen — and Ashley and Diane — on Sunday, when they come to tea. Alex, too,' Dan finished, chewing on the stem of the pipe he wasn't allowed to smoke since his stroke. 'If he can spare the time to come, that is!'

After leaving the Jessups, Alison and Ken parted in the village. When he'd hurried off to catch the Liverpool train, she wandered around the village and looked with interest into the windows of Sandford's one and only dress shop, bought some air-mail stationery from the newsagent and chose a pretty potted plant as a thank-you gift for Dan and Nancy.

Despite telling Ken she could find

her way back to Spryglass without any trouble, Alison took a wrong turning somewhere near the church. When she finally arrived back at the old house, fine needles of cold rain were dashing from the brooding grey sky.

Grateful for the warmth of the kitchen, Alison peeled off her light-weight jacket. Her fabric shoes were wet through and stained with mud and grass and she kicked them off, too. Shivering, she switched on the kettle for coffee and hurried upstairs to change. She really would have to do some shopping for warmer clothes — and a few pairs of sensible shoes!

When she came down again and had made her hot drink, the afternoon was so dark she had to turn on the lights. An offshore wind was blowing and draughts stirred the curtains around the windows and whistled under the door. Cupping the coffee mug in her cold hands, Alison peered out through the window to the dripping, windswept garden. A storm was brewing. James and Becky would be cold and wet when they got home from school, and Alison wasn't sure what time to expect Laura back from her work at Monk's Inn.

She went through to the pantry, thinking about cooking the evening meal. But she didn't know much about cookery. What could she make? She didn't even know what her new family liked to eat. Her eyes slid along the well-stocked shelves, then she noticed a jug of sauce and several covered bowls. Evidently, Laura had supper already planned. Even to a bowl of carefully selected potatoes.

Alison hadn't been alone in Spryglass before. In the quietude of the rainy afternoon, she wandered inquisitively through the rooms. There was so much of Ken's late wife still present — the furnishings and colour schemes, the books and ornaments, all were obviously Jeanette's tasteful choices. Absently taking a neatly folded pile of Becky's freshly pressed school clothes from the ironing board, Alison went upstairs to the girls' attic bedroom.

What sort of woman was Jeanette Robbins? she mused thoughtfully. Had she and Ken been happily married? Alison was frankly curious. She didn't even know what Jeanette had looked like.

That question was unexpectedly answered as Alison was putting Becky's clothes into the top drawer of the tallboy. There, tucked carefully amongst the blouses and nighties, was a framed photograph of Jeanette and Ken on their wedding day.

'What are you doing with that?'

Alison started violently. The photograph slipped from her hands to the hard wooden floor.

'Laura! Oh, I'm so sorry!'

Alison bent to retrieve the jagged pieces of glass from the broken picture frame, but Laura pushed her aside. 'Leave it. Just leave it alone!' She was fighting back tears.

'I didn't mean to pry,' Alison tried to explain. 'It was in the drawer and — '

'This was Mum's favourite photo.' Laura was so distressed she was furious. 'Granddad made the frame. Now you've ruined it!'

'Perhaps it can be repaired?' suggested Alison desperately.

'Don't touch it!' Laura snatched the photograph out of Alison's reach. 'Haven't you done enough damage? Do you know why Becky hid Mum's picture like that? It was so you wouldn't see it on our bedside table and feel hurt!'

'Oh, no . . . ' Alison shook her head despairingly. 'I don't want to take her mother's place, Laura!'

'You couldn't!' Laura retorted passionately, her emotions boiling to the surface. 'You can never take Mum's place!'

# 3

The old clock on the mantelpiece noisily ticked away the long, tense seconds as the two women stared at each other in silence. Then Laura dropped to her knees. Hands trembling, she began to pick up the fragments of glass from the smashed picture frame. Mum had never enjoyed having her photograph taken. There were so few pictures to remember her by . . . This one, of her and Dad on their wedding day, was cherished. Taking a scarf from the tallboy, Laura carefully wrapped the precious photograph and broken frame.

'You don't belong here!' she blurted vehemently, holding the bundle close to her. Even as she spoke, Laura realised she was being malicious. But she still could not stem the torrent of bitter, hurtful words. 'All Mum wanted was Dad — and us — and her home. But that'll never be enough for you, will it? Since the day you arrived, you've done nothing but talk about Hong Kong and your shop and your career and your ambitions. You don't *want* to be a wife and mother! I don't know why you married Dad at all!'

Alison recoiled in shock. She'd never even suspected the depth of Laura's resentment. But there was pain there, too, raw and exposed. Alison's own anger evaporated. She wanted only to comfort the unhappy girl kneeling before her, who suddenly looked so very young and vulnerable.

'You and I — we have more in common than you know,' she began gently. 'I know what's it's like to lose a mother.'

'How can you say that?' Laura demanded incredulously. 'You don't know what it's like. You can't! Your mother is still alive!'

'That's true, but she left when I was little,' replied Alison slowly. 'I grew up without her.'

She could still clearly recall the day, soon after her ninth birthday, when her father had visited her at boarding school. Gently he'd explained that he and her mother were going to be divorced. Mimi remarried shortly after returning to France. It was almost seven years before Alison was to see her again.

'Will you tell me about your mother, Laura?' she asked tentatively, perching on the corner of the high old-fashioned bed. 'I'd like to know about her very much.'

Laura turned away, her whole body rigid. She rose slowly, turning away to open the drawer of the tallboy and gently placing the scarf-wrapped picture and frame inside.

'You may be my father's wife — and Spryglass is your house now.' Her quiet voice was unusually brittle. 'But this is still *my* room — mine and Becky's.' Tears began spilling from Laura's eyes and she kept her back to Alison so they would not be seen. 'Please go away and leave me alone!'

Alison went downstairs to the kitchen and started unpacking the things she'd bought after she'd left Ken in the village. Finally, when only the brown-and-white striped paper bag containing the instant camera remained, Alison paused. Would it be such a good idea, passing it on to Becky after she'd taken some photographs to send to her father in Hong Kong? Ken and Nancy and Dan Jessup had obviously thought so. However, what about Laura? She might not approve of Alison's giving the child an expensive gift.

Ken had brought presents from Hong Kong for all the family, but hadn't handed them out yet. He wanted to wait until Dan and Nancy came to tea on Sunday and give them theirs at the same time. Perhaps it would be wisest if the camera was just quietly slipped in among Becky's other pre-sents . . . ?

Alison frowned. She wanted to be friends with Laura. However, her step-daughter didn't even seem willing to meet her halfway. She tried to imagine how she would have felt if her own father had brought home a wife, but the comparison was quite impossible. Alison loved her father dearly, but her childhood had been very different from the close-knit family in Spryglass. Cliften Lee owned a successful and prosperous antique business. Even when Alison was on vacation from boarding school, he'd frequently be away from home on buying trips, or meeting clients or colleagues.

For much of the time, Alison had been cared for by their housekeeper. She'd had her father's love, and everything his money could buy, but she'd been deprived of his company. Sometimes, she'd felt very lonely indeed . . . She sighed, staring through the kitchen window. Rain was streaming down, gushing from the gutters and gurgling into the rainwater butt outside the back door. Alison absently turned her wedding band round and round her slim finger. She was accustomed to confronting and resolving problems, to dealing with employees and customers and business contacts . . . Nothing within her experience, however, had prepared her for coping with what was facing her now.

Yet it must not continue. Not even for another day.

Switching the kettle on for tea, Alison got out two cups and saucers. She and Laura had to talk. Alone, and now. Before the rest of the family came home. Presently, she heard Laura's footsteps coming down the stairs. The younger woman came quietly into the kitchen, her eyes red-rimmed and her cheeks unusually pale.

'I'm making tea,' Alison said uneasily. 'Would you like a cup?'

Laura nodded hesitantly and pulled back one of the chairs, then sat down at the table. 'Thank you.'

'I really am terribly sorry about breaking your picture, Laura,' said Alison as she placed the tea things onto the crisp green tablecloth.

'It was an accident,' conceded Laura, staring down at the cups. 'I'll ask Granddad if he can fix the frame.' She darted an uncertain glance across the table, finally meeting Alison's eyes. 'Please don't tell Becky it's been broken.'

'Of course not, if you feel that's best.' Alison poured Laura's tea and added milk, but merely added a thin slice of lemon to her own cup. 'Laura,' she began deliberately, 'you and I really have to — '

Laura rose abruptly from the table, her tea untouched.

'James and Becky will be home shortly.' She crossed to the sink, her slippers noiseless on the stone-flagged floor. 'I'll have to see to supper.'

Alison watched Laura wash her hands, then tie on a clean apron before going into the pantry. 'I've peeled the potatoes,' she remarked, only to observe the younger woman's mouth instantly tighten. 'Wasn't that right?'

'I'd planned on baking them.' Laura forced a polite smile. 'Jacket potatoes are Dad's favourite. I'd already done the ingredients for the fillings. Now I'll have to make something else.'

'I'll help you.'

Laura tensed. No doubt Alison meant well, but she'd be more hindrance than help. Laura had her own ways of doing things and would get on much quicker by herself. The children and Dad would be cold and wet when they came home. She wanted a hot, tasty meal ready and waiting for them. 'There's no need for you to do that, Alison.'

'I think there is.' Alison tried to keep her voice even. She was unsure exactly how to broach the subject, but was determined to say what needed to be said. 'I'm not a guest here, you know. Besides, it isn't fair for you to do all the household work. You have your job — '

'I don't mind. I'm used to it. And I love cooking,' replied Laura firmly, bustling past her. 'After you're settled in, maybe then we'll see.'

'I *am* settled in,' persisted Alison, struggling to be tactful and keep her tone friendly and casual, as though this conversation was not of the utmost importance to them both. 'I admit I've never run a house, nor been responsible for a family, or a child ... Please believe me when I tell you I have no wish to push you out, Laura. However, I am Ken's wife now. This is my home. My family. I believe it's time I started caring for them.'

She braced herself for Laura's response, anticipating another outburst. None came.

Laura was grating the peeled potatoes into a bowl. She didn't look up, didn't attempt a reply, because she knew her voice would betray her. She'd been desperately trying to cling to something which was already gone forever. Being angry and resentful was no use. It wouldn't change anything. Alison's unruffled tone and her calm, reasonable words echoed in Laura's mind. She *was* Dad's wife. Spryglass *was* hers now. *Everything* was hers. And Laura could do nothing but accept it.

She quietly got on with preparing the meal while Alison fussed about the kitchen behind her: taking dishes from the dresser, setting the table, placing the bowl of fresh flowers in the centre. Doing all of the ordinary, homely things that Laura had done for so long . . .

Smokey's sudden ear-splitting bark startled them both. The little dog rushed in from the dining room, where he'd been watching out of the big bay window. He raced through the kitchen, claws clattering, barking wildly, and began scratching at the garden door. James and Becky, followed by Ken, burst into the warm, welcoming kitchen.

'Here we all are, home from the sea!' Ken grinned, dripping rainwater as he kissed Alison's cheek. 'Or at least, home from school and town.'

'Daddy waited for us at the corner,' laughed Becky, kneeling to fuss her ecstatic little dog. 'He raced us home!'

'Is this all the post?' James asked, hardly out of his drenched school coat before going to the dresser to check the envelopes propped behind the Toby jug. 'Wasn't there anything for me, Laura?'

'Waiting for a billet-doux from Charlotte, are you, Jimmy?' Ken winked broadly at Alison. 'He's got a pretty wee lassie keen on him!'

'Charlotte and I are friends, Dad,' returned James with amiable patience. 'Just friends. And we sit next to each other at school so she doesn't need to send me letters.'

Laura was disentangling Becky from Smokey and unfastening the little girl's soaked coat. 'You're wet right through!' Giving Becky a quick cuddle, she hurried her towards the stairs. 'We'll get you dried off, then I'll make hot chocolate — '

'I'll make the drinks, Laura.' Alison was already gathering mugs from the dresser.

Laura paused in the doorway, her eyes briefly meeting Alison's. Then she

80

shrugged before turning to follow Becky upstairs. Alison stared after her, only half-hearing as Ken continued teasing James. She sensed that any reconciliation with Ken's eldest daughter was further away than ever.

★  ★  ★

Getting up early had never been a problem for James, not even when he'd had a paper round and football training to fit in each morning before school. He liked being awake while the rest of the family was sleeping. The house was quiet and still, and he could work on his music.

It was almost daylight now, and the blackbirds in the pear tree outside his window were whistling and calling. James closed his composition notebook and switched off the bedside lamp, stretching out on his back, his arms folded behind his head. To his surprise, he had realised he missed playing football. Although the season was over, the team still had to train and practise. It was that commitment he was relieved not to have.

He didn't regret being dropped from the team, except that his father would be disappointed when he found out. James stared at the ceiling and sighed. He'd been putting off telling Dad. Waiting for the right moment, he told himself. But the right moment just never seemed to happen.

James listened as the grandfather clock at the foot of the stairs chimed the quarter-hour. It was too early to get up yet. He didn't need to be at Green's Dairy for another hour. Deliveries were a little later on Sundays. It was thanks to Charlotte that James had got the job helping one of the regular milkmen on his round. Charlotte's brother, Simon, had given the job up to go backpacking in Algeria, and Charlotte had put a word in with her father. Mr Green's family had owned the dairy for generations. James hadn't received his first wage packet yet, but he already knew exactly how he would spend it.

It would be nice to be able to take Charlotte out occasionally. Not that they were going steady, as Dad called it, but they were good friends and James liked her a lot. Then there were books he wanted, and new music . . . Things he would never ask Dad for money to buy. Yes, having some money of his own would be great. Especially if his exam grades were good enough and he *did* get into music college. James swung his legs off the bed and got up. There was no point in planning, or even thinking, that far ahead. He had to get through his A-levels first. And despite having written to Manchester almost two weeks ago, he still hadn't received a reply from the Royal Northern College of Music.

James sprinted noiselessly down-stairs, leaping over the three that creaked and towelling his wet hair as he went. At the bottom he caught sight of his reflection in the tall wall mirror and grimaced. Dabbing the trickle of blood on his smooth cheek with the towel, he realised it had been a mistake to shave. It wasn't as though there'd been much in the way of bristle, but he'd managed to nick himself anyhow. Now he'd have to stand up in front of Charlotte and the entire church congregation and play a violin solo with little bits of tissue paper stuck to his face!

Hurrying into the kitchen, he tossed the towel into the wash basket. Laura must already be out walking Smokey, because his lead was gone from the hook on the back of the garden door. Of course, *she'd* have an early start today, too, he recalled. It was Laura's week for doing the church flowers. And after church, she'd be going into work for a few hours to help with the traditional Lancashire lunch that Monk's Inn served on Sundays.

James poured a glass of orange juice and cut two uneven slices of bread for toast. It still seemed odd to come down in the mornings and not see Laura moving quietly about the kitchen, the table set for breakfast and the lunch boxes packed and ready. He buttered his toast, spreading it generously with homemade gooseberry jam. Alison wasn't accustomed to early rising. She'd admitted her notion of breakfast was strong black coffee and a quick flip through the Hong Kong newspapers. He smiled, recalling the chaos of those first few days. The whole family would get in each other's way, scurrying round the kitchen at the last minute. Anything that could get burned or spilled invariably did!

Alison never got rattled, though. Somehow, everything got done in the end. And it all seemed to be working out, because mornings were pretty calm and organised now. James made himself another piece of toast. He'd noticed Laura had been keeping very much in the background lately. Cheerfully helping, but careful not to get in the way. But what was she really feeling about it all? James couldn't even guess. They'd always been so close, yet his sister hadn't said a word. James finished his juice and put on his jacket. He and Laura just didn't talk to each other the way they used to. They always used to discuss everything together when Dad was away at sea. More and more, James found himself wondering if Laura was as cheerful and settled as she appeared.

★　★　★

After church, Becky was eager to show her father the foals in McCobb's meadow. Ken turned to Alison. 'Coming with us, love? McCobb's is only about half a mile from David's market garden. We can drop in and say hello. I'm sure he'd be pleased to give you a guided tour. David's not the sort of man to boast, but he's done wonders with that old place. Not just the land, but the mill, too. According to Dan, it'd been derelict since the thirties.'

'Perhaps another day,' replied Alison, thinking it would be nice for Ken and

Becky to have a few hours alone together. 'I want to get everything ready for this afternoon.'

'We're not expecting royalty!' Ken protested with a laugh. 'Just the family for Sunday tea. Mind you, if Alex Fairbrass is coming . . . ' He glanced wryly at James as he joined them. 'Maybe you *should* give the silver an extra polish! Alex carries on like he's royalty, isn't that right, Jimmy?'

★ ★ ★

'Don't bother about what Dad said earlier,' James commented when he and Alison were strolling homewards from the village. 'Uncle Alex is OK. He and Dad just seem to rub each other up the wrong way, that's all. They never actually quarrel; they just sort of . . . of . . . '

'Annoy one another?' suggested Alison amiably.

James laughed and nodded. 'It's

Auntie Helen I feel sorry for. She's the one who usually has to smooth things over.'

'Helen is your mum's younger sister, isn't she? I'm looking forward to meeting her,' Alison remarked, pushing open Spryglass's weathered gate. 'And your cousins, too.'

'Well, Diane'll be here,' answered James, unlocking the front door and standing aside for Alison to go in. 'Even though they've moved away, she still goes to my school and she told me she'll definitely be coming this afternoon. But I wouldn't count on Ashley. He has an important job at Liverpool Museum, and he's a consultant with an auction house in Chester. Ash is away most weekends viewing furniture and paintings and so on.' He paused, waiting. Alison had stopped at the kitchen door.

'I know it's family tradition to have Sunday tea here in the kitchen,' she commented. 'However since this is the first dry and sunny day we've had all week, how you do feel about eating outdoors?'

* * *

'Eeee, this is the life!' Dan Jessup sighed contentedly. The family had just enjoyed a delicious tea in Spryglass's sea-facing sun-filled garden. 'And thank you for my present,' he went on, nonchalantly adjusting the stylish tie Ken and Alison had brought from Hong Kong. 'I'll wear this when I collect my pension and impress the postmistress. She's one of my girl-friends, y'know.'

'She won't be able to resist you in that tie, Dad!' Ken grinned and glanced up to where Alex was sitting between Nancy and Laura on the shady porch. 'Hope that Chinese paperweight was all right for you, Alex. I couldn't get a wee one.' He turned to Alison to explain. 'Alex has a factory on the old Dock Road, where the Overhead Railway used to be — Gulliver's Toys. So how is the water-pistol business then, Alex?'

'Hard. Like earning a living from any other kind of business,' his brother-in-law returned shortly. 'You'll find life ashore a great deal tougher than sailing all over the place without a care.'

'Oh, don't let's talk shop,' Helen interrupted hurriedly, giving Alison an apologetic look. 'It's so nice, the whole family being together for once. I'm only sorry Ashley couldn't be here, too. He's in St Anne's viewing a collection of military medals an old gentleman wants to sell.'

There was pride in Helen's voice, but James heard a barely smothered giggle and Diane flopped down beside him on the grass. He'd been sitting a little away from the others in the shade of the apple tree, preoccupied with budgeting the proceeds of his milk round.

'Ash is in St Anne's all right,' she whispered slyly. 'What Mum and Dad don't know is that he's taken Cindy Sharples with him! I listened in on the extension when he was phoning her to make the arrangements.'

'You would.' James sounded disinterested, scribbling figures into the back of his notebook.

Diane frowned at him, disappointed her news had met with so little response. 'Have you heard from the music college yet?' she asked after a minute. 'About getting an audition?' She now had James's full attention.

'Why not just shout my private business to the whole village?'

'Oh, sorr-eee. I didn't realise it was a big secret!' She pulled a contrite face.

'It's not a secret, it's just private!' James said firmly. 'And you shouldn't have been eavesdropping when Charlotte and I were discussing it!'

He got up, shoving his hands into the pockets of his jeans and wandered down the garden and out of the gate onto the shore fields with their tall, feathery grasses and clusters of wavering foxgloves, long-ago escapees from the garden now growing in wild profusion all the way down to the sandy shore. The tide was ebbing, quiet and smooth with barely a ripple. James narrowed his eyes against the almost harsh brightness of the late sun. Granddad was right about this fine weather only being a respite. The sky above the Welsh hills was ominously dark, a sure portent of more storms to come.

Becky was away playing in the dunes with Smokey, trying to persuade him to be still long enough for her to take a picture with her new camera. When she spotted James, the little girl waved and ran to him, pulling a photograph from her shorts pocket. 'Look — I took this of Daddy and Alison!'

'Hmm, it's very good, Becky,' James said, smiling. The picture showed the couple chatting on the porch by the honeysuckle. 'Why don't you give it to Alison?' he suggested, and seeing his sister's shy response, went on encouragingly, 'I know it'd make her happy.'

Becky still looked uncertain.

'Go on!' James gently urged.

'All right!' Becky's face broke into a smile. 'But only if you come with me.'

James pretended to catch Becky's hand, but she laughingly pulled away. She ran in front of him into the garden, where Ken and Alison were sitting together on the warm stone steps, their heads close together. When Becky got nearer to them however, she slowed down and let her brother catch up. James felt her small hand creep into his own, her fingers tightening around his as she offered Alison the picture.

'Oh, Becky, it's lovely!' Alison touched the little girl's cheek tenderly. 'Look, Ken — our first picture together since our wedding. Thank you so much.' She looked from Becky to James, her happy eyes meeting his. 'Thank you both.'

★ ★ ★

The torrential rain, driven by a gale-force wind, had finally ceased shortly before dawn. By breakfast time, only a dry north-westerly still gusted around Spryglass, tearing the remaining blossom from the trees.

Laura was relieved her father and Alison wouldn't have to cancel their planned shopping trip to Southport. Alison badly needed some warmer, more serviceable clothing. Although the two women were not the same size, Laura was loaning her a mackintosh just in case of another downpour. Clearing the breakfast dishes, Laura planned her day. She wasn't due at Monk's Inn until noon. Once Dad and Alison left for their train and James and Becky got off to school, she'd have the whole morning — and the house — to herself. Laura would welcome the peace and opportunity to quietly sort out her tangled thoughts and feelings.

A frown creased her forehead as she stacked the clean dishes into the dresser. She'd neither seen nor heard from David since their unhappy quarrel. Laura had looked out for him every morning when she'd been walking

Smokey, but he'd never appeared. She sighed wistfully, going into the pantry for flour to bake a batch of bread only to hesitate, scoop in hand. There'd been no chance for any proper baking since Alison had arrived but now she had the time, why not make a special treat for tea? Viennese plait was a firm favourite with all the family. And Laura could easily bake an extra one and pop it in to Gran and Granddad's on her way to Monk's.

She was chopping up the mixture of angelica, glacé cherries and nuts when the sound of her father's annoyed voice sent Laura hurrying into the dining room. She guessed at once what the heated words must be about. James was standing dejectedly, schoolbag over his shoulder, his attempts at explanations falling upon deaf ears.

'You had a responsibility — a *duty* — to your coach and teammates, Jimmy!' declared Ken, his sharp eyes drilling into the boy. 'You've let them all down!'

'Ken? I could hear your shouting from upstairs.' Alison swept into the room, already dressed for going out in a slim-fitting mustard suit, the mackintosh borrowed from Laura folded neatly across her arm. 'Whatever's wrong?'

'I asked Jimmy how he was coping with the milk round and his football training,' replied Ken crossly. 'Turns out he's been dropped from the team!'

'I see.' Alison's reply was calm.

Laura was faintly amused. Her step-mother obviously considered exclusion from a football team as insignificant reason for such an extreme reaction from Ken.

'And why did I have to prise the truth of the matter out of you, Jimmy?' persisted Ken angrily. 'Why didn't you come straight out and tell me what had happened?'

'I was going to tell you,' James began wretchedly.

'When? Next week? Next month?' cut in Ken sarcastically. 'You have to work to get anywhere in this life. You can't

96

afford to lose chances by being too lazy to — '

'It wasn't like that, Dad!' cried Laura, unable to hold her tongue any longer. 'James did try to keep up with the training, but he's had so much studying — '

'This is between Jimmy and me, Laura. It's got nothing to do with you,' Ken silenced her. 'Let your brother speak for himself — if he can!'

'What good will it do?' blurted James, his face taut and white as he glared across at his father. 'You never listen to me. Never! You don't hear anybody but yourself!' Turning on his heel, he strode straight-backed from the room.

Ken immediately made to follow. 'Jimmy! Don't you speak to — '

Alison laid a restraining hand upon her husband's arm. 'Why not let him be for now?' she quietly suggested. 'James and Becky have to leave for school soon and we're on our way out, too. Wouldn't it be better to talk this over with him this evening?'

Ken took a deep breath, his face grim. He nodded, though exhaling in exasperation. 'Aye, that makes sense I suppose. I'll just say cheerio to Becky, then we'll be away for our train.'

When the front door closed behind Ken and Alison, Laura went to seek out James. He was standing forlornly in the windswept garden, waiting for Becky to finish feeding and watering her wild birds.

'Jamie, are you all right?'

He nodded, still white-faced and shaken. 'I never intended to deceive Dad,' he mumbled miserably. 'Honestly, I didn't!'

'I know,' responded Laura sympathetically. 'When he simmers down, Dad will realise that, too.'

James looked unconvinced. He hated rows.

'Anyway, you go to school now.' She gave him a little push as Becky came running towards them. 'And leave me to get on with my baking!'

Working alone in the quiet kitchen, Laura's thoughts strayed again and again to David Hale. She still couldn't quite believe how keenly she was missing him. Until this past week or so, Laura hadn't even realised how much she'd come to need David and depend upon his quiet strength. He'd always been there when she needed him. Emptiness engulfed her, leaving in its wake a sense of having lost something infinitely special.

She'd been furious with David when they'd argued, believing he was not only wrong, but unfair and unreasonable too. Now, it didn't seem to matter who was to blame for the row. All Laura wanted was to see David again. Be with him. Suddenly, she made up her mind to swallow her pride and apologise. And was on pins for the next hour or so, waiting impatiently for the Viennese plaits to finish baking so she might be on her way out to Riverside Mill.

★   ★   ★

Drifts of wind-borne sand, broken branches and other debris from the previous night's storm lay strewn across the lanes. Laura had to dismount and walk her bicycle, manoeuvring between water-logged ruts of thick mud. When the mill's distinctive crooked chimney came into sight, she unexpectedly felt as awkward and nervous as she had on their first date. What on earth was she going to say when she came face to face with David? That she'd been wrong to turn down his proposal? That she loved him and wanted to marry him?

Laura's spirits suddenly soared. It was so easy, so wonderful, to imagine marriage to David. Being his wife . . . sharing a home together . . . A man who truly loved her, a home, a family of her own . . . And yet — how much of her desire to marry David was a simple impulse to escape from the increasingly difficult situation at Spryglass?

Laura sighed, heart-sore, her eyes on the rutted path awash with rubble and muddy water. She'd have to think seriously about this. And, until she did so, she couldn't accept David's proposal. Not yet, anyway. Glancing up as she rounded the stand of sycamore, Laura froze in her tracks, stunned by the devastation laid before her.

The last occasion she'd been here, neat fields were green with thriving vegetables. Now, sheets of floodwater extended from hedgerow to hedgerow. The murky surface was broken by split branches and the straggling tips of uprooted plants, and afloat with scattered seedlings torn from their protective boxes and pots. Cold-frames were smashed, their contents crushed and broken. The greenhouses David had painstakingly repaired and renovated were a tangled mass of jagged glass and splintered timbers.

Her horrified eyes at last caught a glimpse of David emerging round the side of the mill. There was a coiled rope slung over his shoulder and his face was lined with exhaustion. The relief that he was safe and unhurt almost overwhelmed Laura.

'David!'

She ran to him. David caught her in his arms, holding her tight, his face buried in her hair.

'It's all over!' he mumbled huskily. 'Finished. There's no way I can — '

'Don't even *think* that!' Laura responded fiercely, holding his face in both her hands. 'The mill *can* be saved. We'll do it together!'

David stared at her silently, the moments ticking past.

'That's impossible,' he said tightly, a note of anger edging into his voice. 'Don't you realise? It's over, Laura.'

Taking her wrists in his hands, David slowly moved Laura away from him until they were no longer touching and standing quite apart.

'It's too late. We can't get married now.'

# 4

Just take a look round!' David's eyes were filled with despair. '*Look*, why don't you?'

But Laura was unable to tear her gaze from his face. He was despondent. Broken. His hopes and dreams, all he'd planned and worked hard for, suddenly in ruins buried beneath the flooded fields and storm damage. Her every emotion, every thought, was for him alone. Nothing else mattered. Not even the devastation surrounding her. Not the embarrassment of having asked David to marry her. Or the humiliation of his blunt refusal. Only David himself was important now.

He was usually so strong and decisive, brimming with plans and ideas, and with such a passion for life and for his work that he took Laura's breath away. From the moment they met, she'd been drawn to this proud, fiercely independent man whose smile could make her feel incredibly special.

Now David stood before her, every ounce of energy and spirit knocked out of him. He was unshaven, his clothes soaked, his dark eyes underlined by even darker shadows. Had he been working the whole night through? Battling alone against the howling wind and cold and the blinding rain in a hopeless fight to save what was clearly already beyond saving? Not so long ago, Laura had depended upon David completely. Now he was defeated and vulnerable. Now he needed her.

She took a tentative step towards him, her fear of rebuff overwhelmed by her desire to comfort. Almost shyly, she slipped her arms about his waist and hugged him. This time, David did not push her away. Laura sensed some of the tension ebbing from his body and moved closer against him, resting her cheek against his shoulder.

'I love you, David,' she murmured.

David's breath caught in his throat, and she raised her face to look at him. 'That's the first time you've ever said that.' He exhaled slowly.

To have heard Laura say those words, even twenty-four hours ago, would have meant everything to him. Now it was too late. Just as her finally deciding to marry him had come too late. Suddenly David was consumed with bitterness. Drawing away from her, he started out across the flooded fields. He'd lost everything! There would be debts he couldn't pay. Orders that couldn't be filled. And what of the mortgage on the mill? Suppose it was repossessed?

Frustration and anger boiled deep within him. He'd worked hard, done his best. All for nothing. In less than an hour, the storm had wiped out years of effort and left him with nothing! No livelihood, no future. Not even a home to offer Laura.

'I'd better get back to work,' he muttered tersely, stooping to retrieve the rope he'd dropped. 'I have to get a

105

tarpaulin on the roof before the rain starts again.'

Pushing her wind-blown hair from her eyes, Laura followed him round the corner, then stopped in dismay. There must've been hundreds, probably thousands of pounds' worth of damage to the roof and upper-storey wall above the mill wheel. The round glass window with its thick, almost greenish old glass was gone completely.

'It was the window coming in that woke me last night,' David commented, adding the canvas sheath of hand tools to his burden. 'My guitar was underneath a heap of rubble. When I dug it out, there wasn't so much as a broken string,' he concluded with grim humour. 'How's that for irony?'

Laura could scarcely speak. 'David, you look terrible,' she got out after a minute. 'You're so exhausted you can hardly stand. I don't suppose you've eaten anything, either. You *must* take a break!'

'I can't!' he answered sharply. 'Maybe it's hopeless, but I have to keep trying. I can't just sit around doing nothing!'

'Don't you think I understand that?' Laura returned gently. 'But when you're rested and thinking straight, things might not look quite so bad. Please come inside. I'll make you something to eat.'

'There's no need for that, Laura,' he said flatly. 'Anyhow, shouldn't you be at work?'

'Not for a while yet,' she replied, checking her watch.

'Besides,' David was saying, glancing at the darkening sky, 'I have to get that tarp battened on.'

'All right. You do that while I get a meal started.' She smiled encouragingly. 'When you've finished, come in and we'll talk while I cook. We'll sort things out, you'll see!'

Despite Laura's unshakable optimism, as David worked on the roof he could find no answers to his problems. The same questions had been going round and round in his head all night. His mind was weary trying to make some sense of it all.

He'd walked out of his father's house eight years ago with little more than the clothes he stood up in, a few books that had belonged to his mother, and his precious guitar. He'd only left school a few months before and hadn't a clue what he wanted to do with his life. What he didn't want was to become the kind of man his father was. Not for him a life of betrayal and deception! He'd left what remained of his family, his friends and Polkerris. And never gone back. He'd picked fruit and hops, laboured in the fields, even worked in a foundry to pay for his horticultural training. What little free time he had was spent hiking the length and breadth of the country, searching for a place where he could belong. A few years later, when he was working for a large-scale co-operative of organic cereal growers, David came upon Riverside Mill.

It had stood empty since the thirties, and even then it must have been an austere, cheerless place to live. No electricity. No gas. No plumbing. Only cold water from a single tap. Bats had moved in, and rabbits, pigeons and a varied assortment of mice. The rafters were open to the sky, the precariously crooked stone chimneys crumbling . . . But David was convinced some day it could be a real home. And as for the land that came with it! At first, he couldn't believe his good luck. Uncultivated for over fifty years, the rich, dark earth was packed with vital nutrients and mineral salts. With growing excitement he did countless soil tests and discovered the land was perfect for a market garden producing organic fruit and vegetables.

Frantically, he'd scraped together the money to acquire the mill. Then for more than a year he had slept in a sleeping-bag on the floor beside the great quern-stones that long ago had been used for grinding a whole range of grains and grades. Rarely setting foot beyond the mill's boundaries, David had worked sixteen-hour days month after month after month. Every minute was worth it because by the end of summer he was starting to see some profits, and then he finally turned his attentions to the mill-house itself. He made it sound and weatherproof, swept the chimneys and rebuilt the stone fireplaces. He got it connected to all the modern amenities and began scouring auction sales for furniture.

He'd been rather self-consciously buying cushions at the Sandford Christmas Fayre the day he'd met Laura. Walking home across the snow-covered village green, David had met the first woman he'd ever wanted to share his life with . . .

However, Laura wasn't free. Oh, she wasn't married or engaged; she didn't even have a boyfriend. She was just devoted to her family. Caring for James and Becky and keeping house at Spryglass always came first with Laura.

While David admired her for that, and loved her for it, sometimes he couldn't help resenting it, too. He'd never tried to hide his feelings for her, yet she'd always kept him at arm's length. There always seemed to be a good reason for them not being together. For not making plans to marry. But after her father remarried and came ashore, when Laura had still turned down David's proposal in no uncertain terms . . . Well, he was beginning to doubt she loved him at all.

★　★　★

The mill-house felt chill and damp when Laura entered. The first thing she did was make a fire in the long living room. As soon as it began to crackle, the mill seemed brighter and cheerier. Slipping off her coat, she hesitated by the telephone. It was getting late, but she really couldn't just walk out and leave David. Quickly, she phoned Monk's Inn and explained to Mrs

Lancaster what had happened. Could she possibly go into work later? 'I'll make up the lost time, of course,' Laura concluded soberly.

'Don't be silly. Frank and I wouldn't hear of it,' Beattie Lancaster replied kindly. She and her husband had been Riverside's first customers, placing a large regular order for fruit and vegetables. The elderly couple had come to know David well, and liked him. 'It's not as though we're rushed off our feet here,' she went on. 'It sounds as if you're needed more where you are. This must be a terrible blow for David.'

Despite Mrs Lancaster's suggesting she take the whole afternoon off, Laura promised she'd be in later. As she hung up, she was reflecting that Monk's Inn was awfully quiet these days. Nothing like as busy as it usually was at this time of year.

In the kitchen, the ancient range David had never quite been able to afford to replace had long since gone out and was stone cold. Laura hurriedly cleaned and lit it, but nothing could be cooked until the contraption heated up. While she was waiting, Laura noticed the open books and invoices spread out over the let-down lid of the bureau. David had obviously spent the previous evening tackling Riverside's accounts. She felt a pang of remorse. Until their recent quarrel, she'd taken care of all the paperwork.

Sifting through the papers, Laura saw that everything was up to date. She did some calculations. David should be able to tick over until at least the middle of next month. By then, he should have received the money from his insurance claim. She began to leaf through the pigeonholes, searching for the relevant documents.

It was raining heavily again when David came in. When he saw the warmly welcoming kitchen, with its glowing range and the hearty breakfast waiting to be served, his face lit up. 'I really didn't want you to do this, Laura,' he said quietly, adding with a rueful smile, 'But I'm very grateful. Thank you.'

'It's only breakfast.' She returned his smile. 'Not a banquet!'

'Well, it looks good to me.' He ran a grimy hand through his wet, tangled hair. 'Have I time for a wash and shave?'

When David came back downstairs, clean and dry, Laura set the plates on the kitchen table. 'I've been looking over the paperwork,' she began gently. 'You're dreadfully underinsured.'

'Couldn't afford the premiums,' he answered simply, taking a sip of coffee from the big earthenware mug. 'I know I'm in trouble.'

'Ye-es,' admitted Laura slowly. She'd been racking her brains for a way to help Riverside survive. If she were in trouble, she'd turn to her family. But David . . . She knew so little about his past. Hadn't he mentioned his father was a Cornish fisherman? And something about two sisters older than him? Laura suspected that no matter how desperate his situation became, David would never seek help from them. 'What you need,' she went on thoughtfully, 'is a quick crop. Something that — that — '

'Grows fast, preferably underwater,' he supplied with a faint smile. 'And makes lots of money very, very quickly.'

Laura shrugged apologetically.

'No, you're absolutely right. That's exactly what I need.' He took more hot toast and buttered it. 'I don't have any ideas at the moment. All I do know is Riverside Mill is mine. I'll do everything in my power to save it.'

They were brave, determined words. And even if he didn't know how he was going to do it, Laura was glad to see David more like his usual, confident self.

'You're sure I can't drive you into the village?' he asked when Laura was ready to leave.

She shook her head, glancing out to the bright sky. 'There's no need; the rain's gone off.'

'Hmm, I must call in at Monk's Inn myself,' commented David dismally. Even in the brilliant sunlight, Riverside was an incredibly depressing sight. 'Tell the Lancasters I shan't be able to supply the inn's order.'

'They'll realise that,' Laura told him. 'But I can pass on a message if you like.'

'No. Beattie and Frank stuck by me through all the teething troubles when Riverside first opened. I want to have a word with them personally. I need to go over to McCobb's and see Lindsay, too,' he added as an afterthought. 'She's just put in a big order for the barn dance supper.' Lindsay McCobb's annual barn dance in aid of the local animal shelter had become a popular event in Sandford. People of all ages went along and thoroughly enjoyed themselves.

'Auntie Helen is organising the barbeque, and Gran and I'll be doing some baking.' Laura smiled. 'And this year, Becky is going to cook up a tray of her fudge whirls.'

'I'd buy a ticket just to get my share of those,' David said, grinning, as he walked her to the gate. 'Is Alison helping, too?'

'I've no idea,' answered Laura stiffly, her face set. 'I shouldn't think a country barn dance and supper would interest her very much.'

David glanced at her, and the vague doubts that had been nagging at the back of his mind came into focus. Would Laura have come back to him — wanted to marry him — if she wasn't finding life with her new step-mother so difficult?

At the gate, Laura half turned. David was studying her with a brooding expression in his dark eyes that she'd never seen before. That look stayed with her all afternoon as she checked the freshly laundered linen in her cubbyhole of an office at Monk's Inn. David hadn't kissed her goodbye. Usually he was eager to be with her, reluctant to let her leave. Yet today they'd parted without even a caress. Without David saying when he would see her again . . .

Laura methodically ticked off the items of linen on her list one by one, then folded each piece neatly into the basket, trying to ignore how cold her hands were and how she couldn't stop them trembling. She'd always felt utterly sure of David. Certain he loved and wanted her. It had never occurred to her that he'd be the one to end it all . . .

The jaunty ringing of the brass bell on the reception desk jarred Laura from the unhappiness of her thoughts. Hurrying out into the lobby, she found a deeply suntanned ebony-haired young man wandering about looking at the watercolours on the walls. He was wearing a loose-fitting summer shirt and jeans, and a motorcycle helmet dangled from one hand.

'May I help you?'

He turned and smiled at her, sauntering over to the desk.

''Evening! You have a room for me, I

believe? I'm not certain exactly how long I'll be staying.' He watched Laura reach for a registration card. 'You'd best book me in for a week, to begin with. My name's Shaun Pembridge.'

* * *

A few days later, James was waiting outside the village shop for Becky. Absently, he gazed at the window display of chocolates and sweets. That evening he was taking Charlotte into Liverpool to see *Hamlet* at the Playhouse. It was part of their school English syllabus, but this evening wouldn't be like their usual trips to the library. For a start, they were having a meal first in the theatre restaurant. James stared at his reflection in the shop window. It was more like a date. A proper date. Their first ever. What would Charlotte be expecting? he wondered. He'd never taken a girl to dinner at a restaurant before. James began to feel uneasy. Suppose he made a complete fool of himself?

'Becky, if you were a girl,' he began vaguely when his young sister finally emerged from the sweetie shop, 'would you like chocolates?'

'I *am* a girl, and I *do* like chocolates!' retorted Becky indignantly, adding impishly, 'I bet Charlotte does, too!'

James aimed a playful swipe at her.

'A great big box!' she laughed, and ducked. 'With a shiny bow!'

'I don't know about a great big box.' James looked at the prices in dismay. He'd needed to save hard just to afford the tickets and dinner. 'As for the bow . . . Can I borrow one of your hair ribbons?'

'Hurry up,' Becky urged impatiently. 'I want to show Laura my necklace.'

Becky's class had spent the afternoon cutting up egg boxes and turning them into flowers. Becky had strung her vividly painted flowers into a long necklace. As she rushed ahead of James into Monk's Inn, Laura was in the lobby pinning up a notice about

McCobb's barn dance.

'Laura, look!' cried Becky excitedly, holding out the necklace. 'Look what I made!'

'It's lovely!' Laura dropped to her knees so her face was near Becky's. 'It's the nicest necklace I've ever — '

'Becky made it for Alison,' cut in James hastily, his eyes meeting Laura's. 'She wanted to ask you if Alison will like it. I'm sure she will, aren't you?'

'Oh — yes. Of course she will,' Laura reassured her, grateful James had interrupted when he had. Becky had always given her the things she made at school. With a tinge of sadness, she realised another of the old ties had been broken. 'Alison will love it.' She walked out into the hot sunshine with Becky and James. 'You just wait and — '

'There's David!' shouted Becky suddenly, breaking away and running towards the churchyard. David had been earning extra money jobbing for the churchwarden.

'Watch the road, Becky!' called

James, returning David's wave of greeting and then resting a hand on Laura's arm as she turned to hurry back inside Monk's Inn. 'Hang on, Laura. Last night I heard Dad asking when you and David planned to get married.'

'I've already explained what with the storm damage at Riverside, we've postponed making any plans,' she responded warily. 'It's only sensible.'

'True — and Dad accepted it,' James continued carefully. 'But he doesn't know how things used to be between the two of you. David was like one of the family. At Spryglass every morning for breakfast, and most evenings for tea. Now he hardly ever comes to the house, and when he does, it's when he's fairly certain you won't be there.

'I've watched you with him at Riverside. Oh, you were working hard to help him clear up, but you scarcely spoke to one another. And just now, you didn't even wave to him!' He looked at his older sister with concern.

'What's wrong, Laura?'

'I don't want to talk about it,' she said miserably. 'I can't.'

The expression in Laura's eyes told its own story, and James touched her shoulder sympathetically. 'I'm really sorry,' he murmured, frowning as he searched for the right words. 'Laura, when Dad and I were helping rebuild the glass houses earlier today, he insisted David come round for tea tonight. I could see David didn't want to, but you know what Dad's like. He just wouldn't take no for an answer. David couldn't refuse without being rude.' He hesitated uncomfortably. 'I thought you should know.'

'I'll pop in at Gran's when I finish at Monk's,' Laura decided after a minute. 'I won't be home for tea.'

★ ★ ★

'Since you're eating at the theatre with Charlotte, it'll be just David, Becky and I for tea, then,' commented Alison later,

123

taking a huge jug of freshly squeezed orange juice and adding ice cubes. They were in the cool, airy kitchen and she was wearing the flower necklace Becky had given her. She'd accepted it with such pleasure that James had watched his little sister lose some of her shyness.

'Have you time for a glass of this?' Alison gestured with the jug.

'Yes, thanks. I don't have to get changed for ages yet. Where's Dad?'

'Out with your grandfather. Nancy's standing in for one of the other hospital visitors and Dan didn't want to spend such a gorgeous evening alone in the flat. He said he was off to collect coal — from the beach.' Alison shrugged, perplexed. 'Perhaps I misunderstood?'

'No, that'd be right,' replied James, taking the day's post from the dresser. 'Granddad reckons there's a coal seam under the river. After certain tides, a lot of coal does get washed up. I'm glad Dad's gone with him. Granddad really shouldn't be . . . ' His voice trailed off as he came to a long, slim envelope. It was postmarked Manchester. From the Royal Northern College of Music.

James stared at it. He'd nearly given up hope of getting a reply.

Alison glanced across at him. 'What's wrong?'

He didn't answer at first. Merely slit open the envelope, withdrawing a single sheet of headed paper and almost fearfully looking down at the few typewritten lines. James hadn't told anyone — not even Laura — that he'd applied for an audition. Wordlessly, he passed the letter to Alison.

'Oh, James! Congratulations!' she exclaimed, giving him a hug. 'This is marvellous!'

'It's only an audition.' He grinned. 'I may not be good enough to get a place.'

'Yes, you will,' she responded confidently. 'I've listened to your playing, James. You have great talent. It must be developed.'

'I wish Dad thought so.' James's face was suddenly grave. 'He has all kinds of plans for me, Alison! Getting back into the football team. Going to university. Having a career in professional sport. He'll hit the roof when I tell him about this!'

'Choose your moment. Then talk to him quietly,' suggested Alison. 'Since you've been working together at Riverside, Ken has realised you're no longer a child but a young man. A young man is expected to have ideas of his own, James. You may be surprised at his reaction.'

James remained unconvinced. His father wasn't given to changing his mind. 'I'll carry that,' he offered, folding the letter into his shirt pocket and taking the heavy tray from her hands. 'You won't say anything, will you?'

'Of course not. It's your news.' She smiled at him over her shoulder as he followed her outdoors. 'Thank you for sharing it with me.'

James was too preoccupied to join in the light-hearted conversation in Spryglass's sunny garden. Presently, he went up to change for his date with Charlotte. From the landing window, he spotted Laura coming towards the front gate. She was earlier than he'd expected but, of course, she wouldn't have got any answer at Gran's flat. Checking that he had both wallet and theatre tickets, James went back down-stairs and into the kitchen.

'Laura?'

She was standing absolutely still just inside the open door, looking out to the garden. James could see past her to where Alison was sitting on the lawn, laughing and chatting with Becky and David.

Slowly, Laura turned around. James was shocked to see her cheeks were wet with tears. He'd hardly ever seen Laura cry before.

'I've lost him, Jamie,' she murmured brokenly. 'And I want him back. I want him back so very much!'

James didn't know what to do or say. How could he comfort her? Finally, he just drew his sister away into the privacy of the living room. Then, putting his arms around her, he patted her shoulder, exactly as he would with Becky.

*   *   *

The clock in the village church was striking one, and the moon was washing Spryglass's garden with silvery light when James silently let himself into the house.

'And what time do you call *this* to come sneaking in?' demanded Ken, his voice uncharacteristically harsh. 'Where have you been until now, my lad?'

James tensed. In the shadows of the unlit kitchen, he hadn't noticed his father sitting at the table.

'I walked Charlotte home,' he answered evenly. He hadn't done anything wrong, and resented being made to feel as though he had. 'I did say I'd be back late, Dad.'

'Ah, I'm only having you on, Jimmy!' Ken grinned and raised a conciliatory hand. 'I don't remember much about being seventeen, but I *do* remember how a ten-minute walk with a lass can take three hours. And I wasn't waiting for you,' he continued, getting up and refilling his mug. 'I couldn't sleep and didn't want to disturb Alison by tossing and turning. Want one?' He held up the teapot.

'No, thanks.' James hesitated. Amazingly, he'd almost forgotten about having to tell his father of the music college audition. 'Er yes, OK, then.' Pulling back a chair, he sat down at the table. 'Dad, I want to talk to you.'

'Fire away,' Ken returned genially, setting down another mug and shoving the biscuit tin in James's direction. 'I'm in the mood for listening.'

James met his father's gaze steadily.

'Dad, after my A-levels are over I'm finished with school. I'm not going to Liverpool University like you want.' He took a deep breath. 'I want to have a career in music, Dad. Become a professional musician.'

# 5

'A man has to make his way in the real world, Jimmy,' Ken told his son practically. 'It's a hard place if you've no skills and no qualifications.'

'I *would* have qualifications, Dad,' replied James, with no trace of the silent, immature sullenness this kind of conversation had previously provoked. 'After three years I'd get my degree — Graduate of the Royal School of Music.'

'And then what?' Ken sounded unimpressed by the fancy-sounding name.

'Then it would be up to me to work hard enough to earn a living. Make a career for myself.'

'No,' his father declared. 'It just won't do.'

James didn't reply. He sat perfectly still, his eyes meeting Ken's. He'd been jubilant about getting that audition. No one had helped him. He'd done it completely on his own. Alison had been thrilled for him. *She'd* understood how important it was. But Dad hadn't even said well done!

Resentment flared. Dad had ignored his news. It was almost as if an RNCM audition meant nothing at all! Why did he always have to belittle everything James did? Just once, couldn't Dad be proud of him?

Ken was watching his son from across the table. James's face looked very young and earnest in the moon-light. Suddenly, Ken recalled something of what it was like to be seventeen, filled with enthusiasm and impossible dreams . . . Would it do any real harm to let the lad attend this high-falutin' audition? It might even do a bit of good. Help get this musical nonsense out of his system once and for all.

'All right, Jimmy. I'll tell you what we'll do,' he began evenly. 'I'll let you go to the audition on one condition. If you fail, that's it. Finished. The end of any talk of you being a musician. I want your word you'll buckle down at university and build a real, solid future for yourself.' Ken half smiled, still not fully convinced he was doing the right thing by consenting to the escapade. 'Understand?'

James's pulse quickened. Dad was still treating him like a child. Still not taking him seriously! His earlier elation hardened into an uncharacteristic arrogance. Ken was still waiting for his answer. 'OK.' James shrugged in a burst of bravado. 'It's a deal. You have my promise — but I won't need to honour it, Dad. I'm going to pass that audition with flying colours!'

Ken was so dumbfounded by James's self-confidence he didn't say another word as his son strode from the kitchen. With a shake of his head, Ken rubbed a hand across his face. He'd been surprised when Jimmy held his ground that way. The lad had always been so shy to speak up, preferring to fall into line rather than cause a row. Ken got up and took the mugs to the sink, admitting a grudging respect for the boy. At least he'd promised, and Jimmy never broke his promise.

'So here you are!'

Ken glanced around as Alison padded barefoot into the kitchen.

'I woke up and you weren't there!' She put her arms about his waist, resting her head sleepily against his shoulder blades. 'It's almost two o'clock. Whatever are you doing, darling?'

'You won't believe it.' He turned around, wrapping his arms about her. 'Jimmy's just told me he's — ' Ken broke off, watching her. 'You know already, don't you?'

She nodded. 'I was here when he opened the letter.'

'And you said nothing about it?' he retorted. 'Didn't you think I had a right to know?'

'James wanted to speak to you himself,' she answered calmly. 'I naturally felt obliged to respect his wishes.'

Ken sighed, nodding slowly as his initial annoyance ebbed. 'Aye, I suppose so.' He released her, wandering aimlessly across the kitchen to the window and staring across the shadowy garden to the distant moon-washed waves beyond. 'Maybe it's because I was away at sea so much, Alison. I haven't been a proper father to Jimmy. How can I make him see I only want what's best for him?'

Alison followed him, taking his hands into her own. 'James isn't a child, darling. He's a young man. An intelligent, extremely responsible young man. It's no longer a matter of what you think is best for him, but for him to make his own decisions.'

'It's not just this daft music idea. We don't see eye to eye about anything. We can't even talk to each other for what we're at odds! My only son's like a stranger to me,' he concluded despairingly. 'You seem to know him better than I do, and you've only been here five minutes.'

Ken's voice trailed to silence as he looked down at her. In the silvery light, Alison's face was as young and earnest as Jimmy's had been. And with a jolt of realisation, he suddenly knew why she and his son got along so well together. Instinctively, he tightened his arms around her. The difference in their ages had never mattered before; he'd hardly ever even thought about it. But suddenly Ken was conscious of every single one of the years that separated him from his wife. She slipped from his arms as, with a tell-tale clicking of claws, Smokey trotted curiously into the kitchen.

'Hello, boy!' She bent to scratch the dog's shaggy ears. 'It's not time for your walk yet!'

Ken watched her. Her smooth blue-black hair was tumbling loose about her shoulders, a stray strand falling across her forehead. He took a deep, steadying breath. How he loved her!

'Why *don't* we go for a walk?'

suggested Ken impulsively, reaching for her hand. 'The moon's up, the shore will be deserted, and it seems a mighty long time since I had you all to myself for a while. Sandford Beach may not be Silvermine Bay or Turtle Cove,' he added softly, 'but it's the best I can offer.'

'As long as I have you — ' Alison stood on tiptoe to kiss him before starting upstairs to dress. ' — I don't care where in the world we are!'

When they reached the shore she sprinted away ahead of him across the hard, flat sand to the water's edge. When Ken caught up with her, Alison was splashing barefoot in the shallows, holding her long Indian muslin skirt up clear of the softly rippling waves.

'Phew, I'm more out of condition than I thought!' Clutching his chest, he exaggerated being out of breath. 'I'll have to take up keep-fit like you!'

'That will be the day!' she returned dryly. 'I remember asking you to jog with me around the Tiger Balm

Garden. You went terribly quiet and disappeared behind the pages of a Chinese newspaper!'

'We-ll, I've seen lads pounding along, and it's not for me,' he replied. 'I played football when I was . . . ' He hesitated before finishing. ' . . . younger.'

'Since I left Hong Kong I've really missed my exercise classes,' commented Alison, slipping her arm through his. 'When James took me to the library I saw a notice about fitness classes starting next month in the village hall,' she went on. 'Helen and I have put down our names.'

'Helen?' echoed Ken in surprise. 'Well, if that's what you want, love, I've no objections. And I'm glad you're friendly with Helen. She's a fine woman.' He'd long held a deep affection for his mild-natured sister-in-law. 'For all her and Alex being well off, Helen doesn't look too happy just now.'

'She hasn't confided in me,' remarked Alison quietly. 'However, I think she and Alex are maybe having difficulties.'

'Aye, and Alex himself is the main one!' returned Ken scathingly. 'How did you talk Helen into this keep-fit lark? She's such a sensible down-to-earth sort. It's not her cup of tea at all.'

'Don't you be so hasty making assumptions! Helen is extremely keen, as it happens,' laughed Alison. 'We're both looking forward to the classes very much. To begin with, we're taking yoga and dance.'

'Dancing? Who'll be your partners, then?'

'Oh, Ken! It isn't that kind of dancing.'

'So it's that stuff I've seen on TV.' He grimaced. 'A crowd of you stand in a big room and jump up and down?'

'Don't mock!' she scolded lightly. 'It's tremendous fun — as well as being very good for you!'

'I suppose you think I should come too.' Ken ruefully patted his middle. 'I've put on weight since I came ashore.

If I get any fatter, I'll need new trousers.'

'You'll need a few new clothes before you start teaching at the college anyway. We can go shopping together.' Alison smiled, then put her arms about Ken's waist and gave him a hug. 'And you're not fat, darling. You're just cuddly!'

* * *

Laura nipped the faded flowers from the trailing fuchsia and, carrying the heavy basket carefully, headed for the front doors of Monk's Inn, quickly drawing back into the shadows of the porch as David Hale's van rumbled by. Watching from the side window, she saw David park further along the street. He carried several boxes of salad produce into the greengrocer's before continuing through the village and away towards Riverside Mill. It seemed strange he no longer stopped at Monk's for a chat.

She hung the flower basket on the cast-iron bracket outside the lead-paned doors. In the early morning sunlight, the flaking plaster of the inn's walls and the faded paintwork were more noticeable than ever. It was such a shame — and not Beattie and Frank Lancaster's fault — that Monk's Inn was becoming run-down and dilapidated. The elderly couple were working as hard as ever, but the hotel just wasn't doing so well anymore. Even now, in mid-summer, Mr Pembridge and the elderly Misses Forwood were the only guests. Laura returned indoors. It distressed her to see Monk's Inn so shabby. The old coaching inn was so much a part of the village — and of her childhood memories.

When Dad was away at sea, Mum had tried to make any family occasion a little special by bringing Laura and James to Monk's for a wonderful cream tea. The inn had been spick and span then, with everything silver and shining. To Laura's eyes, the Lancasters had already been terribly old. Beattie, small and round with lots of chins and voluminous print frocks, chattering and fussing that the children had all they wanted. Frank, tall and thin as a twig, quiet and serious and hardly ever getting a word in edgewise. Laura sighed, remembering. The Lancasters had been kind to her. They'd taken her on when she was barely sixteen, patiently teaching her about catering and running a busy little inn. Although Beattie and Frank had never changed, Monk's Inn certainly had!

Laura was back in her little office when Beattie Lancaster looked in. 'Frank and I will be off shortly. Mrs Middleton is seeing us at nine sharp.' Beattie fiddled with the white collar of her neat navy two-piece. 'Thanks for looking after things while we're in Liverpool. It's good of you to give up your day off.'

'I'm glad to help,' replied Laura quietly. She was very fond of the Lancasters, and had willingly agreed to help when the couple's accountant had asked them for a meeting. Beattie looked so agitated, Laura felt she had to say something. 'I'm — I'm sure everything will be all right, Mrs Lancaster.'

When the Lancasters returned from the meeting with their accountant, they went straight to their private sitting room. Both looked grave, and Beattie was watery-eyed. Laura waited ten minutes, then prepared a tray of tea and took it to them. The inn's books were spread out across the table in front of them. Beattie hastily pushed a damp handkerchief into her sleeve as Laura entered the cluttered, old-fashioned room.

'Sit down, dear,' she sniffed, exchanging a glance with Frank. 'You've been with us a long while. It's only fair you know what's happening.'

'Our meeting with Mrs Middleton was pretty grim,' Frank Lancaster began in his forthright fashion. 'We must make even more economies. We might even have to let some of the staff go.'

Laura stared in consternation. She'd realised things were bad, but —

'Your job's safe!' put in Beattie hastily. 'You're practically family. As long as Frank and I are at Monk's Inn, there'll be a job here for you.'

Despite the Lancasters' reassurances, Laura was shaken when she left the sitting room. She hurried into the lobby.

'Sorry!' Shaun Pembridge almost cannoned into her as she turned the corner. 'My fault entirely! I wasn't looking where I was going.'

'Neither was I,' conceded Laura with a polite smile.

'Actually, I'd like a word — ' Shaun broke off, bending slightly to look at her face. 'Are you all right? You look rather upset.'

'It's nothing, really.' She forced another polite smile. 'How may I help you, Mr Pembridge?'

'What? Oh, yes. I've got a slight

problem.' He set the gaily wrapped box he was carrying down onto the lobby desk. 'My elder sister lives up at Hesketh Bank. It's her daughter's birthday, and as a treat I usually take Pippa out. I've missed her last two birthdays because I was out working in Saudi, so I wanted this outing to be really good. I thought bouncy castles, clowns, jelly and cake . . . But Pippa was highly offended. Said she was too old for kid's stuff like that. She's mad on tennis right now. Wants to go to the ladies' singles final at the Wirral Tournament. She's even invited three of her pals along!'

'You want me to organise tickets?' Laura prompted absently, her thoughts still on the Lancasters' financial problems.

'Tickets are the least of my worries. It's the girls! One excitable nine-year-old is scary enough, but *four*! And Pippa's best pal, Donna, apparently gets car sick. I do realise I've got an awful nerve asking — ' 'He gazed at

144

Laura imploringly. ' — but would you come with us? Please?' he finished a shade desperately.

'It is my day off . . . ' Laura looked straight back at him, not sure what to do.

Shaun Pembridge was in his twenties. He seemed nice enough, always bright and breezy, with a smile for everyone. During the time he'd been staying at Monk's Inn, Laura had found him polite and likeable — but that was no measure of his ability to cope with four children! She considered his hopeful face and made up her mind all at once. 'Yes, I'll come.'

'Thank you!' He heaved an enormous sigh of relief. 'Thank you so much. You've saved my life! I haven't brought my car up from Staffordshire yet. I've been doing all my sightseeing by motorbike. Can you arrange a hire car for me?'

'No problem.' She was already leafing through the index of telephone numbers. 'I'll get on it right away.'

'Fantastic. And thanks again.' Shaun picked up his package and headed for the stairs, turning to smile across at her. 'Will twelve-thirty be all right for you?'

Laura nodded. 'Twelve-thirty will be fine.'

* * *

'Well, that was a huge success!' declared Shaun that evening, when the last of the little girls had been safely delivered home. He and Laura were just beginning the drive back to Sandford. 'Phew, what a day, eh?'

'We had a lovely time,' Laura chided mildly, smiling sidelong at him. 'The tennis was nail-biting — and so was the strawberry-and-champagne tea.'

He groaned. 'You mean all those gooey pink sundaes and the fizzy lemonade?'

'The girls thoroughly enjoyed it.'

'Yes, they did, didn't they?' he agreed with satisfaction. 'And Donna wasn't ill once. But why did she keep insisting she was about to be?'

'It's a horrible sensation for a child,' Laura replied sympathetically. 'My sister Becky is miserable when she goes anywhere in a car.'

Shaun glanced sidelong at her. 'I've seen you in the village with her. You're really good with kids,' he commented. 'I'm surprised you don't work with them. Teacher, nanny, something like that.'

'Actually, I would've liked to teach,' Laura confessed. 'Little ones, you know.'

'Why didn't you?'

'Oh, I wanted to stay at home.' She smiled. 'Be close to my family.'

'Ah, yes,' Shaun murmured. 'Mrs Lancaster mentioned you'd lost your mother when you were still very young.'

For a while Laura had almost forgotten about the problems at Monk's Inn. Now they came flooding back.

'Can't you tell me what's upsetting you, Laura?' he enquired after a moment. 'Something is, and it might help to share it.'

Laura gazed at him in dismay. Oh, how she longed to confide in someone! To talk out her fears. However, loyalty to the Lancasters held her back.

'Are you worried you may lose your job at the inn?' he ventured at length.

She glanced up at him sharply. 'Why do you ask that?'

'I've got eyes. The Lancasters are a nice old couple, but running the inn is becoming too much for them,' Shaun remarked matter-of-factly. 'It's sad, but it's a familiar story. *Are* you afraid you'll lose your job?' he persisted gently.

Laura hesitated before slowly nodding. 'Mr and Mrs Lancaster said I needn't worry, but . . . '

'But you can't help it?' he asked. 'Well, stop! Right now.'

They were only a mile or two from Sandford. Shaun slowed the car, turning off the open coast road and down on to the seafront. It was a sunny evening, and warm air was rolling in from the beach. Shaun switched off the car's engine and turned to Laura.

'I've been watching you. You can cope with anything without getting flustered. You're good — so you'll never be out of work,' declared Shaun emphatically. 'Trust me. I've stayed in dozens of hotels all over the world. I know what I'm talking about.'

She didn't reply, so after another minute or two Shaun started the engine and they were soon on the sand-dusted crescent approaching Spryglass. It was considerate of Shaun to try to cheer her up, Laura thought. But he didn't realise what with all the recent upheaval in her life, her job at Monk's Inn was all she had left to cling on to.

★   ★   ★

'Good luck, James!' Becky dropped her schoolbag and reached up to put her arms about her brother's neck as he sat at the piano in the dining room. 'I hope you pass!'

'So do I.' James smiled, but he looked pale and anxious.

For the past week, his first thought on waking up had been the audition. Then all through every day there had been moments of stomach-churning nervousness. And last night, he'd scarcely slept at all.

'Here's my lucky shell.' Becky gravely opened her hand to show him a pinkish-orange buckie shell she'd found on the shore three summers ago. 'You can take it with you.'

'I will.' He accepted the token and placed it on top of the piano next to his composition notebook. 'Thank you.'

'Don't forget it!' cautioned Becky, scooping up her bag.

'I won't!' James ruffled her curls. 'Have a good day at school.'

As Becky went out into the hall, Ken turned into the gate from the shore. Jogging up the cracked stone path, he stamped the sand from his trainers before coming up into the vestibule. 'Be right with you, Becks.' He hurriedly pulled tracksuit bottoms on over his shorts. 'You get your bike out. I want a word with Jimmy.'

James held his breath, wondering what was coming. Since the night he'd told him about it, his father hadn't mentioned the audition once. There had been none of the hassles James had anticipated. He'd come to the conclusion this was Alison's doing. She had a quiet manner of smoothing things over.

'If I had my way, you wouldn't be going to Manchester today, Jimmy, but . . . ' Ken gave a shrug, extending his hand. 'All the best, son.'

James accepted his father's hand gladly. This was probably the most important day of his life. Whatever happened, it would shape his whole future. To take with him his father's good wishes was more than James had dared hope for.

'Can I borrow your bike again?' Ken queried as an afterthought.

'Sure.' James approved of his father's new interest in exercise and keeping fit.

It made sense to take care of your body, especially when you got to Dad's age. 'If you like,' he suggested tentatively, not looking at Ken, 'maybe I could come running with you some morning?'

'That'd be great!' Ken grinned buoyantly. 'I'm already doing more than two miles. I'll soon give you a run for your money!'

After Ken and Becky had gone, James went back to practising his composition. He had little experience of composing, but playing a piece of his own was part — probably a vital part — of the audition. He was determined to be note-perfect and was several bars into the soaring, romantic music when suddenly James realised he was no longer alone, and stopped playing.

'Sorry. I didn't intend to distract you.'

'You're not.' James half-turned to face Alison as she perched on the arm of the sofa. 'Tell me, honestly, do you think it sounds like Rachmaninov?'

'A little,' she answered frankly, then

smiled. 'What's so wrong with sounding like Rachmaninov?'

'You know what I mean.' He returned her smile, but his eyes were solemn. 'The composition is supposed to be my own, original work. I didn't copy or borrow from anyone — yet now I play it back . . . ' James spread his hands despondently. 'It sounds exactly like a poor copy! As if I'm trying to cheat or something.'

'Every artist is influenced — and inspired — by those who have gone before,' Alison told him gently. 'Shall I leave you alone to go on practising?'

He grinned ruefully, shaking his head. 'If it's not right by now, it never will be!'

'Music is more than simply technique — it's an expression of emotion.' Alison rose and came to stand at James's side. 'Before you go in to play, try to feel the mood of your music *inside* yourself. The rest will follow naturally.'

'Is that a promise?' he asked wryly.

'You bet!' she laughed.

James laughed, too. Alison was the only person in the family who had a real passion for music. She understood how much playing and writing meant to him. Just as Mum had understood . . . His eyes rested on the framed picture of Mum and Dad on their wedding day. When Alison had arrived at Spryglass, Becky had hidden the picture away and it had accidentally been broken. But Granddad had fixed it as good as new, and Alison insisted it went back in pride of place on top of the piano. The piano Mum had bought second-hand for James's eighth birthday.

'Your mum would be tremendously proud of you today,' murmured Alison, as though reading his thoughts. 'I know I am.'

James gave her an appreciative glance. 'It's a weird feeling, now it's here at last. It's everything I want. Imagine being able to spend all day, every day, just studying and working and playing music!' he declared enthu-siastically. '*If* I get in . . . '

'Concentrate on your music,' Alison advised. 'Put everything else from your mind.'

'Easier said than done!' he responded doubtfully.

Alison returned his smile sympathetically. She'd been astounded when Ken told her of the ultimatum he'd given James. In the middle of taking his A-levels, he had already been under immense pressure to succeed. Didn't Ken realise the additional stress his rigid attitude was causing? Although Alison had voiced her opinions passionately, Ken remained adamant. He was utterly convinced what he was doing was in James's best interests. Alison had had to be content with supporting and encouraging her stepson, ensuring he received peace and quiet and space to study and prepare. The grandfather clock in the hall struck the quarter.

'I'd better go.' James slowly lowered the lid of the piano over the yellowed keys. Going through to the hall, he took his jacket and violin case from the table at the foot of the stairs.

Alison followed him to the front door. 'What time's your train?'

'Not for nearly an hour. I'm meeting Charlotte and walking her to the school bus first.'

'You're sure you have enough money? For lunch and — Oh, wait!' She darted back indoors, returning in a few seconds. 'Becky's lucky shell!'

'I mustn't forget that!' James smiled, slipping it carefully into his pocket. 'Thanks, Alison.' He hesitated only a fraction before stooping to kiss her cheek. 'For everything. You've been a real friend!'

'You — you're very welcome!' she faltered, touched and surprised by his gesture of affection. 'Good luck, James!'

\* \* \*

When the almost-empty train pulled into Sandford station that evening, James was relieved there was no one there to meet him. He felt miserable and disappointed, not ready to face a barrage of questions. Especially not ready to face his father. James wandered aimlessly into the village, unwilling to go home. Finding himself outside Monk's Inn, he realised Laura would still be there working.

'James!' She looked up from the desk as he entered the lobby. 'How — ?'

The question faded on her lips as she saw her brother's expression. With a twinge of guilt, Laura was suddenly aware she'd been so wrapped up in her own troubles, she hadn't spared any time to talk to James. She hadn't given a thought to helping him through any problems he might be having.

'I was about to have a cup of tea,' she began quietly. 'Let's go into my office, shall we?'

As Laura plugged in the electric kettle and popped teabags into the mugs, she purposely didn't press James for explanations.

'I blew it, Laura.' he said eventually. 'It was my one chance — and I blew it.'

Her heart sank. She was standing with her back to James, so she didn't have to look at him. And she managed to keep her voice even when she replied. 'Do you know that for certain?'

'No — the official decision comes by post. But I'm sure.'

James slumped into a chair. The sleeplessness of the previous night and the day's emotions were fast catching up on him. His eyes felt gritty and tired, and he kneaded them with the heels of his hands.

'If you haven't actually had a decision yet, then there's still hope,' Laura encouraged. 'Isn't there?'

James shook his head, and sighed heavily. 'When I was sitting waiting to be called, I was so nervous I couldn't stop my hands shaking,' he began with some embarrassment. 'Yet, once I started to play, it was just as Alison said it would be. Somehow, I wasn't nervous anymore. I even began to think everything was going pretty well. The questions. The interview. All of it, really.'

'That doesn't sound so terrible,' ventured Laura. 'You're not the world's most confident person, James. Perhaps you're being overly pessimistic?'

'If only!' he returned fiercely, suddenly furious at himself. 'I played my composition. When I'd finished, one of the board looked up from his papers and said I'd obviously been heavily influenced by Rachmaninov. It was the way he said it, Laura! That was when I knew I'd failed.'

'I'm so sorry,' she whispered, reaching to touch his cheek to comfort him.

James shrugged defeatedly, saying nothing more. Laura sat silently, watching his expressive face. There was something else, something James wasn't telling her. He drank his tea, and at length got up to leave.

'I'll hang around, if you like,' he offered. 'Walk you home.'

'Thanks, but I won't be ready for ages yet,' she answered. 'You go on home — you look all in.'

James stopped, his hand on the door. 'I made Dad a promise,' he said without turning around to look at her. 'I agreed if I didn't get a place, I'd give up music.'

'Oh, no!' Laura knew full well what that would cost James. 'Whyever did you agree to such a thing?'

'You know what Dad's like. He was pushing and pushing — I just had to do . . . say . . . something to prove . . . ' James broke off abruptly, pausing before continuing with painful candour. 'No. It wasn't Dad's fault. It was mine. I'm to blame. No one else. It just happened. I promised. Even as I was saying the words, I was already regretting it. But I couldn't take them back.'

Brother and sister's eyes met. Neither one spoke, but each was aware exactly what the other was thinking.

'If you won't say it, Laura,' began James harshly, 'then I might as well. We both know Dad will keep me to my promise!'

160

# 6

Although Laura enjoyed her job at Monk's Inn, she'd never liked working on Sundays. Sunday was a family day at Spryglass. Church with James and Becky — and Dad, too, when he'd been home on leave. Then Gran and Granddad would come over after the service . . . Laura and David would savour the only day of the week they could spend together.

Sundays were different now. Laura lingered at the inn for as long as she could, before wandering out into the hot sunshine. She crossed to the green and sat down, paying little attention to the cricket match being played.

'Laura!'

Shaun Pembridge dropped down onto the grass beside her. He was wearing whites, and his suntanned face was flushed.

'I spotted you watching while I was playing. That's probably why I was bowled out.' He grinned at her, then lay on his back in the grass. 'Distracted by a pretty girl!'

Laura laughed. It was impossible to take Shaun — or his compliments — too seriously!

'You really should do that more often,' he observed, running a hand through his black hair as he turned his head to look up at her. 'It suits you. Why do you always look so sad and lonely, Laura?'

'I don't!' she returned defensively, embarrassed he should make such a personal remark. 'Do I?'

'You do. Especially when you think there's no one around to notice,' he replied gently, pausing. 'Will you come out with me this evening, Laura? Dancing, perhaps?' Shaun's smile was back, his eyes twinkling at her. 'You do *like* to dance, don't you?'

'Ye-es, I suppose so,' she faltered. David had been her only boyfriend; she wasn't accustomed to being asked out on dates. Besides, she didn't feel ready to begin seeing somebody else. 'Thanks, Shaun, but I can't,' she answered finally.

'Why not?' he challenged mildly, propping himself on one elbow to study her better. Laura didn't know how to respond, so said nothing. 'We enjoyed ourselves that afternoon, with my niece and her friends, didn't we? Or was I mistaken?'

'Yes — That is, no. You weren't. I *did* enjoy it,' Laura flustered, wishing Shaun would stop staring at her that way. It was making her feel uncomfortable. 'But that afternoon was different.'

'How?' he persisted amiably. 'Because the little girls were there to chaperone?'

Laura felt the colour rising to her cheeks. She realised Shaun was only teasing but, unwittingly, he'd touched upon the very reason. The prospect of being alone with him, of being close to someone other than David, made her nervous.

'Forgive me! I shouldn't have said that!' Shaun touched her hand apologetically. 'I'm too pushy — and I know it!' he added humbly. 'Won't you at least have tea with me? I've heard the cricket teas at Monk's Inn are nothing short of incredible.'

'That's true!' She relaxed, responding to his warm smile. 'Monk's is famous for its cricket teas.'

'You'll come with me, then?' He caught hold of her fingers as she began to rise.

Laura drew free and shook her head. 'I can't, Shaun. My family's waiting for me.'

She let herself into Spryglass and went through to the empty kitchen. Everyone was in the garden. Sunday tea was enjoyed outdoors now, if the weather was fine.

Alison had unearthed some ancient garden furniture from the cobwebbed clutter of the old house's cellars. Granddad had lovingly restored the wood and she and Becky had made a tablecloth and napkins. Although Ken had declared the fabric's leafy pattern of blues and greens far too fancy for the garden, Alison had been undaunted and gone on to make matching cushions for the chairs.

Despite making fun of his wife's efforts, Laura could see, from the window where she stood a moment, the pride in her father's face as he watched Alison and Becky setting the table. The striking glass tableware was another of Alison's recent buys.

During tea, Nancy observed that almost everything they were eating was home-grown by David at Riverside Mill, or by Dan on his new allotment.

'Aye, it's my first harvest from the plot. Not too bad, is it?' said the elderly man, beaming. 'There'll be plenty of fruit ripe for picking later. That'll come in handy for the barn dance jams and pies.'

The end-of-summer fête and dance at McCobb's barn was to raise funds for the local animal shelter and was eagerly awaited by everyone in Sandford. Laura and Nancy always baked for the homemade stall and the open-air supper.

'Becky's joining in this year!' said Laura, smiling. 'Her cherry cookies and fudge whirls will be a sell-out!'

'I would like to help, too,' offered Alison. 'If I may?'

'It's thoughtful of you,' Laura replied quickly. 'But Gran and I have everything organised.'

'Oh, I understand,' murmured Alison, glancing along the table. 'More tea, anyone?'

'Yes, please!' replied Dan cheerfully. 'I'm playing the spoons at the barn dance, you know. Now *there's* something you could do, Alison!' he went on, with a sly look to James. 'Make fancy shirts for James and David — the Singing Cowboys!'

Dan grinned broadly, relishing the circle of astonished faces.

'Now you've started,' laughed Alison, 'you have to finish!'

'Nay, it's James's story!'

'I was hoping to keep it quiet.' James shrugged sheepishly. 'David and I were working at Riverside, and Mrs Almond came by selling tickets for the barn dance. When David invited her in, she spotted his guitar. Apparently, not all the music for the dance was arranged . . . and one thing sort of led to another.'

'It sounds fun. I'll be delighted to make the shirts, James,' said Alison, smiling. 'I'll do a few sketches, and you and David can choose the design you like best.'

'Can I help you?' asked Becky in a small voice. 'Like I did with the tablecloth?'

'I'm depending on you,' replied Alison seriously, looking around at everyone. 'Becky made these napkins, you know. She did all the sewing herself.'

'That's my clever wee girl!' Ken said, beaming, and giving Becky's shoulders a hug as they left the table and drifted down the sloping garden to the shade of the trees. 'What about you, Laura? You used to be pretty good at sewing. Are you making some fancy outfit for the dance?'

'I'm not going,' Laura answered clearly. She'd decided upon that weeks ago. 'I'll be helping at the fête during the afternoon, but in the evening I'll stay at home with Becky.'

'I'm not a baby, Laura!' protested Becky indignantly. 'Besides, *I'm* going to the barn dance, too!'

'We'll have a nice time at the fête,' Laura said gently. 'But you know you can't stay up to go to the dance.'

'Alison said I could!' Becky insisted, turning to her step-mother as she came from the house carrying her sketch pad and colours. 'I can, can't I?'

'Can what?' enquired Alison, sitting next to Ken on the swing.

'Go to the barn dance!'

'Of course, Becky.' she replied, unaware of Laura's disapproving glare. 'We're all going.' Then Alison sensed the sudden tension, and glanced around the gathering. 'Aren't we?'

'It's far too late for Becky,' Laura retorted crisply. 'The dance never ends until after midnight.'

'Surely one late night won't hurt?' countered Alison mildly, conscious of Becky's beseeching eyes and unwilling to go back on her promise.

Ken looked on uncomfortably. He realised Laura was looking to him for support. He'd never questioned her decisions over Becky before. And Alison deliberately *wasn't* looking at him. But he knew she was waiting for his answer as keenly as Becky and Laura.

'I want to go, Daddy!' pleaded Becky, gazing up at him. 'I can, can't I?'

'We'll *all* go,' he announced firmly, and Becky threw her arms around him in delight. 'It'll be a late night, that's true, but it is the school holidays,' went on Ken appeasingly. 'And McCobb's barn dance is a family affair, Laura.'

When Granddad persuaded James to

fetch his violin and play his cowboy tunes, Laura slipped away up to her room. She'd been mother to Becky for so long . . . It was hard to let go.

She'd been upstairs only a few minutes when James knocked at the door. 'A visitor for you — that Shaun what's-his-name, from Monk's Inn.' James hurriedly looked in from the landing. He was carrying his violin and two dessert spoons. 'I've put him in the sitting room.'

Laura went straight down. As Shaun rose to greet her, he proffered a small bouquet of apricot carnations and white rosebuds together with a large box of chocolates.

'Peace offering,' he said simply. 'I'm sorry if I offended you earlier. Won't you give me another chance? Have dinner with me tonight? Please?'

Laura wavered. For all his brashness, she was discovering Shaun Pembridge was awfully easy to like.

★ ★ ★

170

'When you asked if I enjoyed sailing, I didn't guess you had *this* in mind!' Laura exclaimed. She and Shaun were standing on the deck of the illuminated paddle-steamer which cruised the river each evening during summertime.

'You haven't been aboard before?' he enquired. 'Good. I'm glad! And the food's excellent!'

Liverpool and New Brighton were pincushions of light in the *Empress*'s wake, the open water ahead silver-grey in the glow of the rising moon.

'I've a confession to make,' Shaun began softly. 'At least, I think I have.'

'Mmm?' Laura was so eagerly drinking in all about her, she wasn't really listening.

'Did you know I'm related to the Lancasters? Beattie is my great aunt.'

He had Laura's attention now. 'I sometimes wondered why you were staying at Monk's Inn! It never seemed quite your sort of place.'

'Oh, I don't know about that. It's quiet and peaceful — just what I

171

needed. I'd had a pretty serious accident. Needed somewhere to recuperate.' Shaun hadn't confided many details about the accident to the Lancasters, and the kindly couple hadn't pried. Before Laura could enquire further, he rushed on. 'Aunt Beattie must have been surprised to get my letter! She and my father don't get along. I hadn't seen the Lancasters for years. Don't misunderstand me, my family is marvellous. Dad and Mother have always backed me up — even when I dropped out of university to go off to Spain.' Shaun laughed, shaking his head at the colourful memories. 'That was a *real* wing-and-a-prayer operation — but I loved every minute!

'I'm a pilot, Laura. Helicopters. Small planes. Gliders. It's my profession — and my passion.' His slim features were animated, his dark eyes alight with enthusiasm. 'I'd rather fly than do anything else.'

'Then it was a flying — ' Laura broke off in consternation at her tactlessness.

'Yes, it was a flying accident,' he put in brightly, easing her discomfort. 'I mentioned I'd been working in Saudi for several years? I was a pilot for a small air-charter company. My plane went down. It wasn't as bad as it sounds, really,' added Shaun quickly, silencing Laura's instinctive concern. 'I was lucky. I'll be flying again in no time. Just need a spot of R and R. I hadn't had a holiday in years, so . . . ' He shrugged, taking Laura's arm as they went from the paddle-steamer's deck into the softly lit restaurant. 'Here I am!'

\* \* \*

Alison tiptoed from the bedroom, not wishing to disturb Ken. Since starting his new teaching job, he hadn't been sleeping well.

Once downstairs, she discovered she wasn't the first to be up and about. Still wearing her nightie, Becky was sitting in the garden with her elbows on her knees.

'You're up early,' whispered Alison, sinking cross-legged on to the parched yellow grass beside Becky.

'I had to give my birds some water,' answered Becky simply. 'They get very thirsty in hot weather. They need baths, too. To keep their feathers nice.'

'Do you know something, Becky?' remarked Alison, gazing around the walled garden with its wild grasses and vivid splashes of cornflowers and poppies. 'This is the very first garden I've ever had. In fact, Spryglass is the very first *house* I've ever lived in!'

'I want to make a pond,' Becky said after a minute. 'I've been thinking about it for ages. I've tried asking Daddy, but he wasn't listening. Do *you* think we could make a pond?'

'I don't see why not,' said Alison, smiling.

Taking Becky's hand, they went indoors. Alison glanced back at the garden with a sigh of contentment. 'A pond will be beautiful . . . '

'Why didn't you wake me?' demanded Ken in exasperation a morning or two later, striding into the kitchen already shaved and dressed.

'Because you need some sleep,' returned Alison calmly. 'Besides, you aren't late. There's plenty of time before your train.'

'I want to finish grading these papers!' he called through from the sitting room. His briefcase lay open on a chair, the paperwork he'd brought home spread across the low table.

'Shall I bring your breakfast in here?' Alison followed him into the comfortably furnished room.

'Won't have time!' He shook his head impatiently.

'Daddy, look, I've made you toast!' Becky raced in, precariously clutching a plate. 'I put marmalade on and — '

'Becky! Look out, can't you?' Ken warned sharply, snatching an open text-book from the table. 'You're dripping

175

butter everywhere!'

She froze, wide-eyed in horror.

'Becks — I'm sorry!' He pulled her onto his lap, smiling ruefully and giving her a cuddle. 'I didn't mean to bite your head off. Is this toast really for me? And you made it all by yourself?'

Reassured, Becky chatted while Ken ate, but Alison was aware of the way he was repeatedly glancing at his wristwatch. Sensing his mounting agitation, she gently interrupted. 'Becky, why don't you wrap a slice of the seed cake you made so Daddy can take it for his lunch?'

When the little girl had scurried off to the kitchen, Alison closed the sitting room door quietly. 'Ken, what's wrong?' she murmured. 'If you have problems, I want to share them.'

'There aren't any problems,' he answered without glancing up from the page he was reading.

Alison expelled a resigned breath. She was learning Ken was a man who didn't care to speak of his emotions and worries, but she was his wife. Surely he could confide in her?

'Ken, each evening you disappear into this room with your work. You hardly sleep at all. You're tense and distant with me, you snap at the children. Don't shut me out, darling. Please tell me what's wrong.'

He glanced at her briefly, gathering the papers together as he did so. 'Don't fuss. There's nothing for you to worry your head about.' Ken hurriedly kissed her forehead as he marched out through the front door. 'See you tonight.'

'Why is Daddy grumpy all the time?' Becky asked out of the blue later that day. She and Alison were in the village shopping for buttons for the party dress they were making. 'He never used to be cross all the time.'

'He isn't cross, Becky,' replied Alison sadly. 'He's just working hard trying to do well at his new job, and he's very tired.'

'Oh.' Becky sighed. 'I wish we could

do something nice to cheer him up.'

They left the haberdasher's, and Alison paused to look in the window of the shoe shop. 'School starts again soon. You'll need new shoes,' she remarked. 'You're growing so quickly, I expect you'll need lots of other new things, too.'

'I don't want to go back to school,' murmured Becky, turning away from the window. 'I don't want to go back — ever! I want the holidays to go on for always!'

Alison gave her a cheerful hug. 'There's still the barn dance to look forward to. And your new dress.' She unlocked the car, opening the rear door for Becky. 'And speaking of dresses, do you think we'll be able to help Auntie Helen . . . ?'

⋆   ⋆   ⋆

'You've done wonders, Alison!' Helen Fairbrass exclaimed, relieved that the cocktail dress which had been unflatteringly tight now fitted smoothly. 'It's an important business dinner, and Alex wanted me to buy something new. But it seemed such a waste of money, when I've a wardrobe full of clothes I hardly ever wear.' She grimaced, patting her full hips. 'I hadn't realised I'd put on a few inches, though!

'Can you stay for coffee and a natter?' she went on, slipping out of the dress and into slacks and an over-shirt. 'Milk and biscuits for you, Becky? Oh, that reminds me — I got a leaflet from the library that'll interest you. It's in the magazine rack in the lounge.'

'This is a beautiful house.' Alison admired the bungalow's modern, spacious fitted kitchen as her sister-in-law made freshly ground coffee.

'When we were first married, Alex and I dreamed of living in Ingle Green,' replied Helen wistfully. 'It took us twenty-five years to get here. But sometimes, I think we were happier in our little house in Sandford. We were a proper family then.

'Now, Ashley and Diane are grown

up, and Alex doesn't — Oh, just listen to me!' She smiled self-consciously. 'I miss being close to Mum and Dad, and Laura and the children, that's all.' Helen picked up the tray of coffee. 'Let's see if Becky's left us any biscuits.'

They went through to the lounge. Becky lay on her stomach, nibbling a custard cream and gazing at a colourful leaflet.

'You're very absorbed,' said Alison, smiling. 'What are you reading about?'

Becky glanced around quickly. 'Birds.'

'What does it say?' Alison bent to peek over her shoulder.

'It . . . It's . . . ' the little girl faltered uncertainly.

'There's a slide show at the nature reserve,' Helen supplied, pouring the coffee into delicate little cups. 'I thought Becky might like to go.'

★  ★  ★

'This looks serious!' James came into the kitchen in search of a snack and found Alison sitting at the scrubbed table surrounded by cookery books. 'I didn't realise we had any cookery books!'

'That's because Laura's such a good cook she never needs to use them,' laughed Alison, going on more seriously. 'It was something Becky said recently that gave me the idea. Ken has been so — so — '

'Uptight? Irritable? Argumentative? Unreason — '

'Yes, yes, all right!' she interrupted wryly. 'Embarking upon a new career is extremely stressful, James, and your father is under a great deal of pressure at the college just now. I thought perhaps a special dinner might help him unwind. Get the weekend off to a relaxing start.'

'Sounds good. Dad would never let on, but my guess is that he's finding teaching a lot tougher than he expected.' James helped himself to cold pie. 'I promised to take Becky to the slide show at the nature reserve next Friday, but we can just as easily go this evening. Laura's working, so it'll give you and Dad some time alone together . . . '

* * *

It had been another long week, and Ken was mightily relieved it was over at last. He attempted to work on the crowded, noisy train, but finally gave up in exasperation. Even after reading the same paragraph several times, his brain just wasn't taking in the information concerning assessment criteria. What was the matter with him? He'd been an engineer for most of his adult life. He knew his subject backwards. So why was he finding all this so darned difficult? Putting away his books, he snapped shut the clasp of his briefcase and exhaled a despondent breath.

Teaching was fine for those cut out for it, but he missed real engineering. Suppose he couldn't make a go of this job at the college? Ken closed his eyes wearily as the packed train trundled northwards. He just wanted to be home, finish up this paperwork, and then do absolutely nothing for the next couple of days.

'You're early!' Alison greeted him with obvious pleasure, standing on tiptoe to kiss his lips. 'What a wonderful surprise. I'm cooking something special, but I'm afraid it won't be ready for a while yet.'

'That's fine. I've papers to sort out.' Ken held her for a moment.

'I really want us to have this evening, darling,' she whispered. 'Together.'

'Just give me an hour.' He turned and went into the sitting room with his briefcase. 'Then I'm all yours.'

It was rather more than an hour, however, when Ken finally did emerge. Alison brought the meal through to the dining room and lit the candles. After they'd eaten, she curled up next to Ken on the sofa in the big bay window.

'Becky started digging the hole for her pond today,' murmured Alison, and even though her face was in shadow, Ken knew she was smiling. 'David's getting her some water plants, and the liner.'

'Just as long as it doesn't cost too much!' laughed Ken quietly. 'Becky's like you — she gets carried away. If we're not careful, we'll have a lake out there!'

'Enthusiasm's an admirable quality.' Alison kissed him, savouring their closeness. 'Oh, I'm so glad it's Friday, darling! This week has seemed endless!'

'Don't I know it,' replied Ken with feeling. 'And I've still got a mountain of college stuff to wade through.'

'You're bringing so much work home, you really ought to have a study where you can be undisturbed. And after the school holidays are over, could we make a start at redecorating? The girls' bedroom badly needs doing. So does the kitchen, but a study for you to work is the priority. The sitting room's not at all suitable. You need better light. A proper desk, too, so you don't have to juggle your papers — '

'Steady on!' he put in with some amusement. 'I'd like a fancy study, and to decorate the house from stem to stern! But an old place like this needs constant attention — I never realised just how much until I came ashore. We could do with central heating, and the window frames really need renewing, but I've taken a big drop in salary and I don't want to take on any big expenses for a fair while yet. Sorry, love. Your plans will have to wait.'

'Not necessarily.' She stroked his cheek. 'We can afford it.'

Alison saw his jaw set stubbornly. 'You mean *you* can afford it!' Ken snapped, moving from her arms. 'I've always provided for my own family, Alison. I'm not about to start depending on my wife's money at my age.'

'Don't be so Victorian!' she exclaimed incredulously. 'I can't believe it! We're married, Ken. It's *our* money.'

'It's yours. From the sale of your

shop. I'll not touch a penny of it,' he said tersely, turning to her. 'And you're not to, either. Not for a study, not for the girls' bedroom, or the kitchen — Not for anything. Do I make myself plain, Alison?'

'How dare you!' Alison glared at him, her dark eyes glittering with anger. 'You're making me feel like an outsider! This is my family now! Spryglass is my home! You're being stubborn and unreasonable. And *selfish* — '

'That's enough! I've made up my mind!' With that, Ken got up and left the room.

Alison sat alone in the candlelight. She was trembling, her anger spent. The evening which started so hopefully had ended in their first row. At length, she blew out the candles and cleared the dishes. She regretted losing her temper — but Ken simply didn't understand how very deeply he'd hurt her.

⋆ ⋆ ⋆

'How does it look, James?' Charlotte Green knelt on top of the hay bales in McCobb's barn, considering the bunting she'd tacked along the rafter. He paused from measuring timber for the platform where he and David would be singing.

'Good.'

'*Good?*' Charlotte hurled a handful of hay at him, sliding down the bales to his side. 'Is *good* really the best you can do?'

'It looks terrific.' He put his arms about her, brushing wisps of hay from her chequered shirt. 'So do you.'

Charlotte caught his hands, holding them in hers. 'That letter from the music college will arrive sooner or later,' she began practically. 'Brooding and being miserable won't change whatever it says.'

'It's not *that* I'm bothered about,' answered James truthfully. 'I came to terms with having failed my audition ages ago.'

Charlotte was about to protest that

187

he didn't actually know he'd failed, but saved her breath. James was really, really talented — but he had so little self-confidence! 'Start believing in yourself,' she said instead. 'Don't let your dad order you about. It's your life — stand up to him!'

'You don't know him like I do,' James retorted drily. 'Anyhow, it's not so straightforward as that. You know why.'

'You don't have to stay at home,' she suggested only half seriously, curling her fingers into his hair and tickling the nape of his neck, trying to make him smile. 'You could run away. I'd come with you!'

'No, you wouldn't.' James gave a rueful laugh. 'Although it is tempting! Not running away — that'd just be cowardly — but leaving home. I'm eighteen. My A-level grades were good. I could leave Sandford. Get a job.' He frowned. 'But even that would mean breaking my promise to Dad.'

'James, for goodness' sake!' cried Charlotte in exasperation. 'Just tell him you're not going to keep that stupid agreement. Why should you give up your music and go to Liverpool University to study some boring old subject you loathe?'

'I gave Dad my word, Charlotte!' returned James in despair. Nonetheless, the prospect of breaking it appealed to him hugely. How was he ever going to *keep* a promise like that? And yet, keep it he must. There just wasn't any way out. James felt trapped, like he was being torn apart inside. Whatever was he going to do?

★　★　★

David Hale came up from the shore and looked into the garden, where Alison was cutting roses. 'Is James about?'

'I heard music from his room a while ago.' She smiled. 'Go on up.'

A few seconds later, David came downstairs again. 'James isn't there.' He grinned. 'Guess I'll have to mosey along and catch up with my pardner later!'

That evening, when Becky was digging her pond and Ken was working, Alison started hand-sewing multicoloured sequins and glass beads on to the fringed yokes and shoulders of the shirts she was making for the boys. At dusk, she called Becky indoors and put her to bed. James still wasn't back. A couple of hours later, when Laura came home from Monk's Inn, Alison asked if James had mentioned going out somewhere.

Laura shook her head. 'He's probably with Charlotte,' she suggested. 'Or at McCobb's barn?'

'Would you like something to eat?' asked Alison absently, her thoughts with James.

'No, thanks.' Stifling a yawn, Laura started upstairs. 'All I want is a bath and bed!'

Alison hovered in the hall, looking at the rod of light shining from beneath the door of the sitting room. Ken was still engrossed in his college work.

Should she disturb him, to tell him she was beginning to worry about James? Alison decided not to. It wasn't terribly late, and James was eighteen and very sensible. But she still couldn't shake off her anxieties and settle to her sewing. Throwing a sweater around her shoulders, she went to the garden shed. James's bicycle was missing.

Back inside, she discovered his house keys on the hall table. Then, for no reason she could explain, Alison checked the fridge and the pantry. Wherever he'd gone, James had taken food with him. She didn't delay another second before rushing in to Ken and pouring out her fears.

'I'm sure you're fretting over nothing,' he said calmly. 'Jimmy is often out later than this. He's probably with his pals and lost track of time. Lads his age do that sort of thing. You're surely not imagining he's run off?'

Ken had intended this remark lightly, however Alison took it absolutely seriously. 'James is far too considerate to do such a thing. But he's troubled and unhappy — and he's been gone hours and hours. Anything could have happened to him!'

As their eyes met, Ken caught Alison's fear. Her urgency. She hadn't said it straight out, but she was blaming him. Blaming him for being too hard on his son. Ken's throat was suddenly tight, but before he could even draw a breath, Alison was out in the hall and making for the front door.

'I'm taking the car to drive around and look for him.'

'Alison, I'll go!' He strode after her, grabbing his coat from the rack. 'You can't go roaming — '

The telephone shrilled as Ken was on the doorstep.

'Dad?'

'Jimmy!' Ken's tone was unintentionally sharp. 'Are you all right?'

'Yes, I — '

'Wait a minute.' Ken clunked down the phone, running to the open doorway and shouting above the roar of the starting engine. 'Alison! It's Jimmy — he's OK!'

'I went for a ride to get my head together,' explained James over the crackly line when Ken picked up the receiver again. 'I went farther than I realised. Then I got a puncture miles from anywhere. I couldn't fix it, so I had to walk for hours before I even came to a phone box.'

'Have you any idea what time it is?' Ken rubbed the palm of his hand roughly over his forehead. 'Where exactly are you, Jimmy?'

'Somewhere near Rufford Old Hall.'

'Rufford? That's miles away! Of all the irresponsible — '

'I'm sorry if you were worried, Dad,' chipped in James apologetically.

'I wasn't — ' Ken broke off as he heard Alison coming back into the hall. Sensing her standing at his side, he reached for her, pulling her close. He was grateful for the warmth of her against him. Grateful Jimmy was safe. 'I was worried, Jimmy . . . and scared,' murmured Ken, his voice uncharacter-istically soft. 'We both were.'

He hesitated, bending to touch his lips to Alison's raised face. Her eyes were glistening with tears.

*　*　*

'It was great seeing the car coming towards me the other night,' James confessed as he and Ken jogged along the hard sand fringing the pine woods. 'I was about ready to sleep under a hedge.'

'Would've served you right,' Ken got out breathlessly. 'I was all for leaving you stranded — but Alison insisted we go and fetch you home.'

They reached the lifeboat station and turned around for home.

'I did plenty of thinking while I was out that day, Dad.' He slowed his stride to keep pace with Ken. 'I'm getting in touch with Liverpool University. It isn't what I wanted to do,' he added honestly. 'But I'll do my best to make a go of it. I can still play and compose in my spare time.'

'I've been thinking, too,' admitted Ken. 'I could've been a bit more understanding. Not pushed you quite so hard. I've never doubted you'd keep your word to me, and I know it'll be tough for you to give up your dreams.' He paused to rest. 'But you're doing the right thing. You've a good brain. Work hard at university, and you'll have a secure future.'

'What about your future, Dad?' began James, doing stretching exercises while he waited for Ken. 'Will you go on teaching?'

'Providing they don't sack me,' his father returned wryly. 'The funny thing is, I'm actually starting to enjoy working with the students. It's the paperwork and endless staff meetings, inspections and moderations I can't abide.'

Ken jogged onwards, glancing back to James. 'Get a move on,' he called. 'I'm ready for my breakfast even if you're not.'

Becky had been up with the lark, and was already wearing her new party dress when James and then Ken burst into the kitchen.

'We raced from the shore,' puffed Ken, clutching the sink. 'I let the lad win.'

'Naturally.' Alison pushed a glass of orange juice into his hands.

'Wow! Who's a pretty girl!' exclaimed James, as Becky appeared from the pantry, carefully carrying the fudge whirls and cherry cookies she'd baked. 'Have you got a date for the barn dance tonight, Becky? Or is your big brother in with a chance?'

Becky's reply was drowned out by Smokey's barking. Dog and child raced to the front door to retrieve the post.

'One for Laura and one for you, James.'

James's smile faded. Unceremoniously, he tore open the envelope.

'I'm in!' he murmured disbelievingly, reading the letter from the Royal Northern College of Music over again to make absolutely certain. He looked to Alison. To Ken and Becky's expectant faces. Everyone was suddenly very quiet. 'They've offered me a place.' His own face broke into an astonished beam. 'I'm going to music college!'

The kitchen erupted into voices and questions and barking. Becky flung her arms about James's waist and Alison hugged him hard. Ken hesitated for only a second before thumping his son's shoulder.

'Well done, Jimmy. I'm proud of you.'

Presently, James went upstairs to shower and change for his milk round. He met Laura on the landing. She was on her way to work, too.

'Becky's just told me your news!' she exclaimed, kissing his cheek. 'I'm so happy for you, Jamie!'

'Thanks. Oh, this is for you.' He handed Laura her letter. 'Who's it from?'

'Shaun.' She slipped it unopened into her pocket.

'Shaun Pembridge?' echoed James in

surprise. 'You see him every day at Monk's Inn.'

'He's been in Staffordshire visiting his family,' she explained, checking her handbag. 'But he'll be back in time for the barn dance.'

'Surely you're not starting to go out with him, Laura?' asked James abruptly. 'What about David?'

'David was the one who ended our relationship, not me.' Her quiet voice was dangerously close to anger. 'I'm free to see whoever I choose.' She turned away from him, running lightly down the narrow staircase. 'And it's none of your business!'

 

\*   \*   \*

 

It had been the happiest day of James's life. Getting his place at music college and playing at the barn dance. Charlotte, and the whole family, pleased and proud of him ... James was reliving every wonderful, incredible moment of it as he ambled through the village after walking Charlotte home. Approaching the Jessups' flat, he saw their lights were still on. James smiled. Granddad had been a big hit with his spoons, and Gran won a prize for guessing the weight of a cake. He rang the bell, then had to wait a while for an answer.

'James! Come on in!' Nancy was tying the cord of her dressing gown. 'Sorry to keep you standing on the doorstep. I was getting ready for bed! Dan mustn't have heard the bell,' she went on as she led the way indoors. 'He's making cocoa — ' Nancy broke off, her hand flying to her throat as she pushed open the kitchen door. 'Dan!'

James moved quickly past her and fell to his knees on the linoleum. Dan lay pale and still. Taking his grandfather's wrist, James fumbled for a pulse-beat . . .

# 7

Granddad's hand was icy cold. Clumsy with urgency, James desperately tried to find a pulse. If there was one, he couldn't feel it.

'Is he . . . ?' Gran's voice sounded awfully quiet and calm and ordinary as she stood beside James, her hand lightly upon his shoulder.

'I don't know!' James almost cried, fighting down the fear and panic that were boiling up inside. 'I don't think he's breathing!' he blurted, the words tumbling over each other. 'I daren't — '

'He *has* stopped breathing!' Nancy bent stiffly to touch her husband. 'Do it, James — you must!'

Every split second was vital. James had never felt so scared or helpless or clumsy or slow as he heaved at his grandfather's inert body, turning him onto his back. 'Call an ambulance, Gran — quick!'

He bent Dan's head full back . . . Then, with thumb and forefinger, pinched his nose closed. James's own chest was so tight he could scarcely take the deep breath necessary as he lowered his face to Dan's. Exhaling. Inhaling. Counting. He had to give these first four breaths very fast . . .

James had taken classes with the St John's years ago. Ken had insisted he learned first aid before he'd take him out sailing. Now James forced his agitated brain to remember, praying he was doing it right. Third breath. Watching Granddad's chest rise and fall. Fourth breath . . . If after this one there was no pulse . . .

'Got it!' he yelled at the top of his voice. Granddad's pulse was weak, but it was there! James's face was scarlet, and hot tears of relief and gratitude flooded his eyes. But he continued breathing steadily into Dan's lungs, timing himself by the natural rise and fall of his grandfather's chest.

'Oh . . . Thank heavens!' James heard Gran's slippered feet coming behind him into the kitchen. Her hand touched his hair. 'The a-ambulance is on its way.' Nancy could hardly speak. 'Oh, Jamie — if you hadn't been here . . . '

James darted a sidelong glance up at her. The look in her eyes was the saddest thing he'd ever seen. He longed to reach out and comfort her, but he couldn't. All he could do was try to keep the slender thread of life between himself and Granddad. Silently, he willed the old man to hang on until help arrived.

'Put all the lights on, Gran,' murmured James between breaths. 'And open the front door, so they'll know which flat to come to.'

Nancy patted his shoulder again, and went into each of the small rooms, switching on lights. Opening the front door, she wedged it back with the pottery dog doorstop that Dan had brought home from a jumble sale when their daughters were little. She went into the kitchen again and saw the two cocoa mugs where Dan had put them ready on the drainer. It wasn't even five minutes since he'd been making their bedtime drinks.

'I — I'd better get dressed,' she mumbled.

'I'm OK here,' answered James, not looking up. 'You get ready.'

Nancy went deliberately into the bedroom, opening the wardrobe and taking her skirt from the hanger. Dan's jacket hung there, too. She let her hand stroke the warm roughness of its sleeve. Was this it? Was she going to lose him tonight? He'd been ill before. But this time was different. This time, it had happened so suddenly and without warning.

As Nancy stepped into her skirt, she caught sight of Dan's slippers at his side of the old-fashioned bed. His pyjamas were folded neatly under his pillow, and the counterpane drawn back ready for him.

She wasn't weeping, but she realised her face was wet with tears. As she was putting on her shoes, blue, brilliant beams of light swept the walls of the room.

Swift footsteps in the hall. The loud voices of strangers. James's shout of relief.

The bedroom door burst open, and suddenly everything was happening in an unreal blur of noise and speed and activity.

★　★　★

James had been waiting for the opportunity to find a pay phone and call Dad and Alison, but he didn't want to leave Gran on her own just yet. They were sitting in the quietness of a waiting area just along the corridor from the intensive care unit, where Granddad had been rushed by the ambulance woman and waiting nurses.

What were they doing in there? Why didn't somebody come and tell them what was happening? At least let them know how Granddad was getting on?

'They're doing their best,' murmured Gran, as though she'd been reading his thoughts. 'Just like you did.' James felt her small hand closing around his. 'Bless you, Jamie.'

He returned her smile, turning her hand so he was holding it firmly. 'He's going to be OK, Gran.' James pretended a conviction he couldn't really feel. 'He is!'

Nancy patted his arm. 'I want to talk to you while we've a minute,' she began quietly. 'Tomorrow — today, rather — is Sunday. You'll be playing in church — '

'I can't!' he broke in. 'Not — not after — I *couldn't*!'

'If you're thinking it wouldn't be fitting to find joy and solace in your music today, then you're wrong,' replied Nancy earnestly. 'You know how much Granddad loves to hear you play, especially in church. You have to play as you always do.'

James stared at her disconsolately. He wanted to stay here with her and Granddad, not go off playing his violin. Not even in church.

'We've all — you and Laura, and the rest of us — got to do everything as usual,' his grandmother continued. 'Granddad wouldn't want us to sit around with long faces feeling miserable.' Nancy paused. 'Whatever happens, the family goes on.' She smiled gently at him. 'Do you understand me, Jamie?'

He nodded vigorously, too choked up to speak. He should be comforting her, trying to make her feel better. Yet here was Gran, thinking only of him and Laura and the others. Just as she and Granddad had always done.

'All right,' he said unsteadily. 'Will you be coming to church?'

'No. I'll stay here with Granddad,' she answered. 'Maybe I'll pop down to the hospital chapel later on.'

James gave her a hug and realised that, despite the warmth of the summer night and her thick, double-knit cardigan, Gran was cold. And her face was pinched and greyish-looking. Why hadn't he noticed that before? Annoyed with himself, James got up and took off his jacket, wrapping it round Nancy's shoulders.

'There's a machine over there,' he said. 'I'll get you some tea. They've got biscuits and snacks, too. Would you like anything?'

'Just tea.' She smiled up at him.

James crossed to the vending machine, slotting in the coins. His reflection stared back at him from the machine's mirrored panel. He was still wearing the brightly sequined cowboy shirt. The barn dance, all the fun and laughter. It seemed so far away! When the family had been so happy. Granddad singing along, joking, full of life and smiling . . . Now the whole world was torn apart. Just like it was when they'd lost Mum.

He took the strong tea to Nancy, wrapping the scalding-hot plastic cup in his handkerchief before giving it to her.

'Army tea!' she declared, taking a small sip. 'That's what Granddad would call this!'

'So strong you could dye your boots with it,' finished James with a wan smile. 'Gran, will you be OK while I find a phone and call home?'

The telephone at Spryglass seemed to ring for ever before finally someone answered. 'Hello?' the sleepy voice was followed by a yawn. 'Who's there?'

'Becky?' His mind was racing ahead of itself. 'What's wrong? Why are you up?'

'I'm not up.' She yawned again. 'The phone woke me.'

'That's all right then,' he sighed. 'Will you fetch Dad — or Alison?'

There was silence for a moment.

'They're asleep.'

'I expect they are, but would you wake them?'

'Why?'

'Becky, just go and wake them up!'

'What are you shouting for?'

208

'I'm not — !' began James in exasperation, then lowered his voice and tried to sound cheerful. 'I'm not shouting at you, but I will — unless you get your little legs upstairs quick-smart and wake Dad and Alison!'

He heard Becky's muffled giggle and the clunk of the phone banging down on the hall table. Then the thump-thump of her feet racing up the stairs. It was Dad who came down to the phone. James hastily explained.

'I'll come straight away,' said Ken tersely. 'Oh, Jimmy! Does Helen know?'

'Auntie Helen — I'd forgotten all about her!' exclaimed James, crest-fallen. 'As soon as I put down the phone, I'll call her.'

'No, hang on a minute. Let me think.' Ken rubbed a hand across his face. Helen was devoted to her father, and if Dan was as bad as he sounded . . . 'No, don't call her. Alex is still away at some toy show or other so, unless Ashley or Diane are home for the weekend, Helen will be on her own. I don't want her hearing bad news like this over the phone, then driving all the way to the hospital,' he concluded as Alison came silently downstairs, her arm around Becky's shoulders. 'I'll go over to Ingle Green, and we'll come in together.' Ken paused, adding as an afterthought, 'Is Laura there with you, Jimmy?'

'No. Isn't she home yet?' James was surprised. He'd noticed Laura leaving the dance with Shaun Pembridge, but that had been hours before the end. 'She doesn't usually stay out this late.'

'True — but as I keep reminding myself, Laura's a grown woman with a life of her own. And this Shaun seems a decent enough lad,' remarked Ken with a resigned sigh. 'Give our love to Gran, Jimmy. Tell her we'll get there as soon as we can.'

\* \* \*

After leaving the dance, Shaun and Laura had driven out to Beacon Point.

210

There, the dunes were so high, she felt she could reach out and touch the tops of the tall, ragged pines that fringed the beach below.

The tide was far out, but rivulets and pools gleamed like saltwater pearls touched by the full moon. As she and Shaun watched, it slowly rose into the star-scattered velvet of the night sky. The first luminous streaks of dawn were appearing now. Not across the water, where the hills and valleys of north Wales were still deep shadows of darkness, but inland, far away, beyond the trees and roofs and steeples.

Laura had never stayed out so late before. With a pang of guilt, she realised she'd never even thought of suggesting Shaun should take her home. She heard his slow, contented sigh as his hand moved tenderly across her shoulder, drawing her even closer against him. She'd never expected to feel this way with anybody except David. It was strangely disturbing to discover just how much she wanted to stay in Shaun's arms.

He stroked her hair, delighted to be away from the crowd at the dance. And pleased that Laura so obviously enjoyed being alone with him. For the first time in his gypsy life, Shaun was being forced to consider settling down. All his adult life, he'd roamed wherever fancy and opportunity beckoned. A casbah soothsayer had once told him he led a charmed life. He'd been inclined to agree with the canny old fake, until the day his luck ran out and he was forced to crash-land out in the desert. Off course, and miles from where he ought to have been, it was thirty-six hours before he'd been located and dragged from the tangled wreckage. And by then —

Shaun bent to kiss Laura's forehead, closing his eyes against the memories. He hadn't told her much. Hadn't told anyone in Sandford, in fact. He couldn't bear it if people — particularly Laura — were to start pitying him or treating him as some sort of invalid. Shaun supposed that was the main reason he'd come to Sandford in the first place. To recuperate away from his family and friends. They'd meant well, but . . .

Laura moved slightly in his arms, and he held her closer. She'd already become incredibly special to him. When he arrived in Sandford, Shaun had never expected fortune to turn in his favour once more. But it had. He'd met Laura. She was so warm and sweet. Although it was in his nature to be impetuous, for once in his life, Shaun had had sense enough not to rush. He didn't want to frighten her off. She wasn't like other girls he'd known. Laura was reserved, wary of being hurt. Shaun had heard local gossip about her broken relationship with David Hale, and he'd taken pains to win her confidence and, hopefully, gain her trust. He opened his eyes, gazing down at her face in the cool, blue light of morning. She was lovely. That sundress with the scallopy bits on the straps looked great and it was typically modest. So like Laura . . .

'Laura, I want us to go somewhere together,' he said impulsively, all of his wise, cautious intentions swept away on a sudden rush of emotion. 'Will you come with me?'

She turned around in his arms, raising her face to his, and he resisted the urge to kiss her. 'Oh, Shaun,' she murmured. 'I can't!'

'Why not?' he asked quietly.

'Well, there's my job, for one thing,' she replied practically, avoiding his searching gaze. 'I can't take time off when I feel like it.'

'Oh, my great aunt and uncle think the world of you,' persisted Shaun impatiently. 'Surely you could talk them into giving you a few days' holiday?' He broke off, tilting her chin with his hand so she was looking directly at him, and went on gently. 'But Monk's Inn isn't really the reason, is it?'

Laura slowly shook her head. 'It isn't

that I don't care for you,' she answered guilelessly. 'I do. Very much. It's only that we haven't known each other for long and — '

'Shh, it's OK. Don't look so worried!' Shaun pulled her tight against him, shaken by the jolt of excitement rushing through him. 'Patience isn't one of my virtues. I probably don't even have any virtues,' he murmured thickly. 'But I do understand. Honestly, I do.'

Laura could only whisper his name as he moved closer. Shaun was only the second man ever to really kiss her, and she felt breathless and overwhelmed by the strength of emotion flowing between them. She didn't want the moment to end. Shaun was leaving Laura in no doubt that he was feeling exactly as she did, but eventually he moved gently away from her.

'I — I suppose I'd better take you home,' he mumbled at last, unwillingly releasing her from his embrace. 'Or I'll never want to take you home again!'

Shaun drove slowly, but still reached

Spryglass all too soon. They said a lingering, reluctant goodbye, and Laura watched until his car disappeared from sight along the sand-dusted crescent. Then she went quietly into the silent house.

It was Sunday and still early. Laura slipped off her shoes and ran lightly up the stairs, opening the door into the attic bedroom noiselessly so as not to awaken Becky. Then she stopped. The covers of Becky's bed were rumpled, but her sister wasn't there. Had she woken up and slipped out to the garden to feed her birds? Laura started downstairs again. Passing James's room, she glanced through the wide-open door. His bed obviously hadn't been slept in. What on earth was going on? Where was everybody — ?

'Laura!'

She half-turned to see Alison emerging barefoot onto the landing. Looking past her into the room, Laura could see Becky curled up in the big double bed, sleeping soundly. But Dad wasn't there.

'What's happened?' she began, her alarmed voice sounding loud in the quietude of the old house.

Alison raised a finger to her lips, partially closing the bedroom door so as not to disturb Becky. 'I'm sorry — I must have fallen asleep,' she whispered. 'I intended waiting up for you. Your grandfather's been taken ill,' she explained gently, her hand reaching out to touch the younger woman's arm. 'Ken and James have been at the hospital all night.'

⋆　⋆　⋆

James had warned her not to get a fright when she saw Granddad, but seeing him later that morning, lying so white and still, connected up to all those tubes and wires and machines and monitors, terrified Laura. She sat rigid at his bedside, trying not to let Gran and Auntie Helen see how afraid and upset she truly was.

During the anxious days ahead,

Laura, like the rest of the family, tried to carry on as usual, but wherever she was, whatever she was doing, a corner of her thoughts and all of her heart remained in that quiet little hospital room. And never more so than on a warm, sunny September afternoon like this one. A blackberrying afternoon, Granddad would've called it. He loved ambling along the country lanes with his grandchildren, spinning his tall tales and picking ripe berries for Gran to make into his favourite jam.

Gran had been the one to suggest the outing. So Laura and James had collected Becky from school, and now they were strolling along together in the golden, mellow sunshine while their young sister dawdled, sampling as many berries as she collected, and spotting and naming the hedgerow butterflies and birds.

'All the doctors ever seem to say is that he's 'very poorly, but stable',' commented James despondently. 'What's that supposed to mean?'

Laura sighed. She understood James's anxiety only too well. The whole family were desperate for hopeful news.

'When Granddad opens his eyes, and we hold his hand, do you think he really knows we're there?' went on James unhappily.

'I'm sure he does!' she exclaimed with conviction. Granddad was drifting in and out of deep sleep. Whenever he stirred, there was someone there, so he'd hear a comforting voice, see a familiar face.

'I'm not keen on leaving for college, you know,' commented James at length, when they were taking a short cut through the pinewoods towards the allotments. 'Not with Granddad the way he is.'

'Gran will have something to say if you *don't* go!' Laura said with a smile, pausing while Becky set out blackberries on a tree stump for the bright-eyed squirrels watching from high in the pines. 'And Granddad will, too, when he gets better. You know how pleased and proud he was when you passed your audition and got a place.'

'Do you truly think — ' began James, but Laura interrupted him.

'There's David! What's he doing at Granddad's allotment?' she exclaimed sharply, as the neat plots of flowers, fruit and vegetables came into sight through the thinning trees.

James shrugged. 'We've both been looking after it.'

Laura wheeled to face him suspiciously. 'Did you know David would be here?'

'Don't be silly,' he returned shortly. 'It was *your* idea to come and gather some of Granddad's favourite flowers to take in to him. And besides, there'd be no point in trying to get you together with David, would there? You've made it perfectly plain you don't care about him anymore.'

'That's a dreadful thing to say,' retorted Laura, more hurt than annoyed. 'I *do* care about David. I always shall!'

'You certainly haven't shown it lately,' countered James bluntly. 'David doesn't have any family of his own — none he's close to, at any rate. And you know how much Granddad means to him. He's as scared and worried as the rest of us, yet you haven't once been out to Riverside, or even phoned him,' James continued scathingly. 'Just because you're going out with Shaun Pembridge isn't any excuse to treat David so . . . *heartlessly!*'

Laura stared, shocked by her mild-mannered brother's angry outburst. Had she really been so insensitive and selfish? Her honest, inward answer filled Laura with remorse and left her unable to reply.

'For all his smooth talk and flashy ways, Shaun Pembridge doesn't have any genuine feelings for you,' James finished emphatically. 'If he did, he wouldn't have left you alone and taken off to London just when you needed him most.'

'Shaun *had* to go to London,'

retaliated Laura defensively. 'It was something to do with his work. I don't know what exactly — '

James shook his head impatiently. 'Why can't you see him for what he really is?' he demanded. 'All Shaun cares about is Shaun! He'll let you down!'

'Stop it, James!' she warned, her temper rising. 'You don't know what you're talking about. You don't even know Shaun!'

James glared at her, his gentle eyes blazing. 'Do *you*?' he challenged.

\* \* \*

The autumn afternoons were drawing in quite early now. It was already dusk, but Alison and Becky were still busily tidying the back garden.

'I love sweeping leaves! Granddad made me this witch's broom 'specially,' Becky explained, pausing red-cheeked and breathless with the child-sized besom clutched in both hands. 'Should we leave some leaves for Daddy to sweep?'

'Oh, he'd like that!' laughed Alison, loading the barrow. 'Becky, what are you doing down there?' Becky had disappeared head first into a deep drift of leaves under the hedges.

'Looking for hedgehogs,' she replied solemnly. 'They fall asleep in places like this. James told me to make sure there aren't any there before we put the leaves in the compost basket.'

'I see. Well, if you find a hedgehog, do you want to give it some bread and milk?'

'Oh, no — that's bad for them!' Becky got up and straightened her woolly hat. 'Dog food's better. And James said if I see a hedgehog walking around in the daytime, that means he's not well and needs help.' She chewed the inside of her cheek thoughtfully. 'James used to tell me lots of things. I miss him now he's gone away to Manchester.'

'I do, too,' said Alison with a smile,

tugging at the bobble on Becky's hat. 'However, according to his letters, James is enjoying college tremendously and he's working very hard.' She turned at the sound of a motorcycle approaching the front of the house. 'That must be Shaun bringing Laura home. I hadn't realised it was that time already.' Quickly emptying the barrow, she hurried indoors. 'I haven't even thought about a meal for us all yet!'

When Alison reached the kitchen, however, she sensed the last thing on Laura's mind was food. 'What gorgeous flowers!' she exclaimed. 'From Shaun?'

Laura nodded happily, the faintest blush coming to her cheeks. 'He left them on my desk this morning.'

'Oh my, if only Ken were so romantic,' Alison laughed gently. 'I can't remember when he last gave me flowers. Or Belgian chocolates!'

'I don't think Dad's the flowers and chocs type, somehow,' said Laura with a self-conscious smile. They both laughed this time, and Alison fetched the fresh vegetables from the pantry.

'Alison,' began Laura uncertainly, when they were scrubbing the carrots, 'I'd like to ask David to dinner.'

'That's a good idea,' she replied evenly, concealing her surprise. Up until now, Laura had gone to considerable lengths to avoid David Hale. 'How about Thursday?'

'No, not then. Shaun is having to go to London again,' explained Laura awkwardly. 'If David comes to dinner then, it'll seem ... Well, that while Shaun's away I'm — '

'I understand,' responded Alison tactfully. 'So when are you inviting David?'

'I'm not!' Laura stared at her in consternation. 'That is, I thought ... Would *you* ask him, Alison?'

'I believe the invitation would mean a great deal more to David,' she replied in a measured tone, 'if it came from you. He's feeling very down at the moment. Worried about Dan, of course, but there's more to it than that. The casual gardening work David's done throughout the summer has come to an end now. He's having to rely entirely on Riverside's market garden for his livelihood. The winter months will be extremely difficult.'

'You've seen him?' enquired Laura casually. 'Spoken to him about such things?'

'Oh, yes. He brings me things from Dan's allotment. Also, I've been out to Riverside Mill on several occasions.'

'And David has confided in you?' Laura's eyes remained lowered, but her voice was unexpectedly sharp.

'We've talked, yes.' Alison frowned thoughtfully. 'Remember, I've also struggled to make a small business survive. I can understand what he's going through. If you ask him to dinner with the family, I know David would be very pleased.'

Laura didn't comment. She finished chopping the carrots, dried her hands, and went to set the table.

\* \* \*

Ken had already gone up to bed, but Alison stayed up to finish hemming the curtains she was making for the Jessups. When she finally climbed the stairs, she left the light in the porch on and the front door unbolted. Laura wasn't home yet from her date with Shaun.

Quietly, Alison went up to the girls' bedroom to check on Becky. She stopped at the door, surprised to hear muffled sobbing. 'Becky . . . ?' Light from the landing fell across the bed. Becky lay hunched under the covers. 'What is it, sweetheart?' Alison sat on the edge of the bed, her hands gentle upon Becky's trembling shoulders. A full minute went by before the little girl wriggled around so she was looking at her.

'Don't tell anybody I was crying,' she sniffed, scrubbing her eyes with the backs of her hands. 'I'm too big to cry now. Daddy said so.'

'Then he's wrong!' Alison mopped up the tears on the child's face with her handkerchief. 'No one is ever too big to cry. And that includes your daddy. Why don't you tell me why you're upset?' she prompted, wrapping her arms about Becky and drawing her comfortingly close.

The little girl struggled with her thoughts for a long moment. 'We had to stand up in class and read,' she muttered at last. 'I made a mess of it, and everybody laughed at me!'

Fresh tears came. Alison held Becky tightly, swallowing the lump in her own throat. What could she say? What could she do to help? If only she had Laura's intuitive way with children, her years of experience . . .

'Becky, when we first got the car, you used to feel sick, didn't you?' began Alison tentatively. 'So we took short trips together, just you and I, and now you don't feel so poorly anymore, do you?'

'No.' Becky's blue eyes were never leaving Alison's face.

'So we could practise reading together,' she went on, acutely conscious of Becky's trusting gaze. 'Then that would soon turn out all right, too.'

'It won't!' Becky shook her head miserably. 'Reading's different from going in the car. The others can all read and I can't! They're cleverer than me.'

'That's simply not true!' exclaimed Alison. 'People are clever at different things. Laura's a wonderful cook, but when I made fairy cakes, they were so hard Granddad wanted to go bowling with them!' She was relieved to see the glimmer of a smile lighting up Becky's face as she remembered that day. 'Maybe some of the children in your class do know more about reading than you,' continued Alison, her confidence building. 'But you know far more about other things.'

'What things?' queried Becky doubtfully.

'Well . . . hedgehogs,' returned Alison. 'I'm sure most of the boys and girls in your class don't know where they sleep or what they eat, or how to spot a hedgehog in need of help.'

Becky sighed heavily and rested her head against Alison, thinking things through. 'Do you really think we could do reading?' she asked after a while. 'Like we did going in the car?'

'I'm positive,' Alison declared, deciding she and Ken must make an appointment with Becky's teacher as soon as possible. And have a word with the children's librarian in the village, too.

'Can it be our secret?'

'If you wish.' Alison smiled down at her. 'Do you think you can go to sleep now?'

Becky nodded, but didn't move from Alison's arms. 'Will you stay? Just a bit longer?'

'For as long as you want me to.' Alison plumped up her pillows and tucked in the covers as Becky snuggled down. 'Close your eyes, now.' Alison bent to kiss Becky's forehead. 'Your dreams are waiting for you . . . '

★ ★ ★

Nancy's telephone call from the hospital came just as Alison and Becky arrived home from school. Seconds later, they were driving back into the village.

At Monk's Inn, Becky raced from the car, through the lobby and into Laura's office. 'Granddad's better!' she shouted, flinging herself at her big sister. 'Granddad's better!'

Laura's astonished eyes met Alison's above the child's head. 'Dan's being transferred to an ordinary ward!' explained Alison in delight.

Laura took a deep, thankful breath. She realised there was still a long way to go before Granddad would be well again but, at last, the worst was over. Suddenly she felt weak at the knees, and sank down into her chair.

'Alison said we could go to see Granddad tonight,' Becky told her sister excitedly.

'I hoped we might all visit the hospital together,' Alison ventured. She wanted Laura's approval for what would surely be a tremendously emotional family gathering. 'What do you think?'

'It's a wonderful idea,' responded Laura with genuine pleasure. 'Granddad will be pleased as punch to see the whole family at his bedside — except for Jamie, that is. What a pity he won't be here with us.'

'I can drive into Manchester and bring him back for the evening,' began Alison eagerly. 'He doesn't know about Dan yet. Nor do Ken and David. I'll telephone them when we get home.'

'Why not phone from here?' Laura suggested, getting up from her desk and beaming from Alison to Becky. 'And while Alison's busy doing that, why don't we go in to the kitchen and choose the best cake we can find to take home for tea?'

A few minutes later, Becky was gazing at the chilled glass shelves of gateaux, pavlovas and cheesecakes, spoilt for choice. 'Granddad likes chocolate cake best,' she said at last, pointing to an enormous Black Forest gateau. 'Can we have that one? And take a big piece to Granddad?'

'You can have any one you want,' Laura laughed, cuddling her young sister. 'But I don't think Granddad is quite up to eating — '

She spun around as the outer door was pulled open, banging back loudly against the catch. 'Shaun!' She was thrilled to see him. 'I didn't expect you back.'

'I didn't expect to be back,' he returned tersely, shoving a hand through his hair as he strode across the inn's spotless kitchen. 'I need to talk to you.'

'I'm at work,' began Laura in protest, then her heart lurched as she saw the distress in his eyes. 'I'll be finished in about twenty minutes,' she went on more gently. 'We can talk then.'

'This won't wait.' He grasped her wrist urgently. 'It's important, Laura. I must see you. Alone. *Now!*'

# 8

Shaun impatiently paced the floor of his room at Monk's Inn. He hadn't drawn the heavy curtains, nor switched on the lamp. He hadn't even noticed that the wintry evening was rapidly filling the room with cold blackness. What was keeping Laura? It was almost ten minutes since he'd left her in the kitchen. How long did it take to give a child back to its mother and explain to the Lancasters she'd be away from her office for a while?

Why couldn't Laura have just come with him when he'd asked? Didn't she realise how much he needed her right now? Shaun threw himself down on the seat by the window and stared out despairingly at the village shops with their illuminated windows. A second later, he was on his feet again.

Pacing. Pacing. Where *was* Laura?

Shaun bit his lip. All those months of treatment, physio, counselling . . . He'd gone through it all for nothing!

There was a quiet tap at the door. Laura came in carrying a tray of coffee and sandwiches. 'I thought you'd want something to — ' she began softly, setting down the tray. 'Why are you in the dark? And it's freezing in here! I'll close the curtains and — '

'Leave the blasted curtains!' He caught her in his arms and held her fiercely. His voice was muffled and indistinct as he bent to kiss her.

'Shaun, what's happened?' she whispered fearfully.

He pulled away from her. Too agitated, too distraught to be still. 'What I told you about my accident,' Shaun began at last. 'It was all true — but selective. It wasn't exactly the harmless little prang I implied. It was serious.' He sighed, meeting her eyes. 'Pretty near fatal, in fact. I was hospitalised overseas, then they flew me back to the UK for further surgery and treatment.'

'You were badly hurt?' she cried in alarm. 'But you said — '

He sank down on to the window seat and gazed up at her. 'When the doctors told me the chances of my ever flying again were remote, I refused to believe them,' he answered simply. 'I came to Sandford determined to prove them wrong. Nearly did it, too!'

The sadness of his smile tore at Laura's heart. Impulsively, she put her arms around him, allowing herself to be drawn down onto his lap, her cheek caressing his tousled hair.

'You're sweet, Laura.' Shaun expelled a slow breath, snuggling her to him. 'I never wanted to have to tell you, but I've been going to London to see just about every consultant, specialist and clinic in the book.' He smiled bleakly. 'I came to the end of my list this afternoon. They've all said the same thing: I'm recovered. Healthy again. As fit as I'll ever be — but no more flying.' There was no smile now to conceal the naked bitterness behind the words. 'I can do anything — except the one and only thing in the world I *want* to!'

'Oh, Shaun,' breathed Laura brokenly. She could only begin to guess at the anguish he'd been going through these past months. His almost frantic participation in physically demanding sports suddenly took on a new, poignant significance. 'I'm so terribly sorry — '

He jerked away from her. Even in the twilight, Laura was shocked at the coldness in his dark eyes.

'*Sorry?*' he echoed curtly, turning to stare at her. 'I don't want your pity!'

'I — didn't mean — ' she cried desperately. 'I just — well, I know how much being a pilot means to you and — '

'Flying is all I lived for,' he returned savagely. 'Now I'll never be able to do it again!' There was a charged, tense silence.

'You've had a dreadful disappointment,' Laura ventured at last. 'But you're alive and well. Life has many — '

'Don't tell me to count my blessings!' he cut in warningly.

'That's exactly what I'm asking you to do,' Laura murmured gently. 'It's all any of us can do when we're in trouble. That, and practical things to help.' She moved quietly around the room, closing the curtains, switching on the lamps and the log-fire, so that warmth and light replaced the chill darkness. 'This coffee's cold.' Laura gave him a small smile. 'And you look the same. I'll send up a fresh pot and some supper on a tray. This time, don't waste it!'

'You're not going back to work?' he exclaimed in disbelief.

'I have to,' she replied mildly. 'Since the Lancasters let the full-time staff go, there's only Ruby and me. We've got a golden anniversary dinner party booked in this evening and — '

'There's always *something* with you, Laura!' snapped Shaun vehemently. 'If it's not your family, it's your job. Never once do I come first in your priorities!'

'It isn't that way at all!' protested

Laura, touching his face. 'You mean far more to me than you realise. But I do have responsibilities, people who depend upon me. I can't let them down.'

'I'll see you when you finish work, then,' he said, still annoyed.

'No, I can't,' she replied apologetically. 'My family and I are going to the hospital. Granddad came out of intensive care today.'

'OK.' Shaun gave a brief, grudging nod of resignation as Laura took the tray and left his room.

* * *

Dan Jessup was still poorly, and a young nurse had warned Laura and the others that he tired easily. He looked very pale, propped up in the narrow white bed, but he seemed comfortable and relaxed, smiling at his family as they told him all their news.

'Seems I've plenty to catch up on!'

'I'll send Hilda Almond in to see

you.' Ken grinned artfully. 'She'll soon bring you up to speed on village gossip.'

'Nay, nay.' Dan gave him a baleful glance. 'I'm not ready for *that!*'

'That's quite enough, the pair of you!' interrupted Nancy disapprovingly. 'Hilda's a good neighbourly woman.'

'Granddad always says she's a right battleaxe,' Becky piped up innocently.

Nancy pursed her lips, but everyone else laughed.

Laura was seated between Alison and Auntie Helen, while David and James were at the far side of Granddad's bed, facing her. She caught herself watching David as he spoke about Granddad's allotment. Laura hadn't yet found the right moment to invite him to dinner. It was such an ordinary, friendly thing to do, so why couldn't she simply ask him straight out?

'Afraid I'll have to throw you out, folks.' The young nurse popped her head around the door. 'It's nearly time for the cocoa round.'

Dan and Nancy exchanged a quick

glance. Nancy blinked hard.

'There, there, Nanny,' whispered Dan as she stooped to kiss him goodnight. 'We'll have none of that. I'll be home again before you know it and getting under your feet like always . . .'

David closed the door soundlessly as Laura and the others went ahead of him into the corridor. He turned to the nurse as she moved towards Dan. 'Could you give them another minute or two alone, please?' he asked quietly.

She glanced through the glass-paned door at Nancy and Dan, and nodded up at David cheerfully. 'Oh, I don't suppose a bit longer will hurt, do you?'

'Are you sure you won't come back to Spryglass with us, Helen?' pressed Alison while they were waiting outside for Nancy.

'We-ell, I ought to get home,' her sister-in-law hesitated. She was reluctant to spend yet another long evening alone in the bungalow while Alex was working late at his factory in town. Helen hadn't minded the dark winter nights so much when Ashley and Diane were living at home, but now . . . 'Yes!' she decided suddenly. The prospect of the rambling, friendly old house filled with family and activity was wonderfully appealing. 'Why not? Thanks, Alison.'

'Great,' said Alison with a smile. She'd become very fond of Helen and understood how very lonely the older woman was feeling just now. 'How about you, David? You'll come back with us?'

'Best not. I've a stack of bills waiting for me at the mill.' He grimaced good-naturedly. 'I have to figure out a way to pay them on time.'

When Nancy joined them, the family started across to the car park. 'I — I'm not coming home just yet,' murmured Laura self-consciously as Ken began organising who was travelling in which car.

'You're surely never working again tonight, are you?' he exclaimed, then felt Alison's elbow in his ribs. 'Er, oh.

Right. Well, the rest of us will get off, then.'

Laura waved Auntie Helen and Dad's cars away, hesitating a moment before calling David's name as he climbed up into his van.

'I've been meaning to ask if — ' she began, vexed at her uneasiness and breaking off as a horn hooted three times, and Shaun's gleaming maroon car swept through the double gates. 'Sorry — I have to go!' flustered Laura.

'Me, too!' David started up the van's noisy old engine, leaning out from the window to be heard. 'Night, Laura.'

As the ramshackle van moved off, Shaun's car glided to a halt alongside her.

'Wasn't that your ex-boyfriend?'

'Mmm,' Laura said, nodding, and watching the van's red tail-lights disappearing into the night. 'He came to see Granddad. We were just talking,' she added.

'Well, *don't*!' Shaun returned, a flash

of his usual humour appearing. 'I'm a jealous guy!'

Laura laughed. She was still laughing when Shaun caught her to him and kissed her until they were both breathless. 'I want to get away from here — have some fun again. Come with me, Laura!' he whispered urgently, taking her face into both his hands. Kissing her again and again. 'Pack a bag and we'll just go. Right now.'

'We can't,' protested Laura, her senses spinning. '*I* can't! Nobody can simply disappear at the drop of a hat. It's not — '

'Sensible? Practical?' demanded Shaun sarcastically, his handsome face set.

'No,' she answered firmly. 'It isn't. It won't change anything, either.'

'I need you — and I want you with me!' he returned sharply, no longer able to contain the anger and frustration within him. 'Do you care for me or not, Laura?' Shaun gripped her shoulders. 'Make up your mind! Please — say you'll come with me!'

Slowly, sorrowfully, Laura shook her head. With all her heart, she wanted to be with Shaun. But she knew going away together now would be the most terrible mistake.

*   *   *

The evening Ken set off for a week-long college field trip, Alison put Becky to bed and slipped the storybook they were reading under the pillow. The little girl's reading was progressing well, and everyone was delighted by her new-found enthusiasm for books.

After kissing Becky goodnight again, Alison went downstairs to press the gingham jam pot covers they'd made together. Spryglass had never been so large and empty. The grandfather clock in the hall seemed to tick louder than ever as she smoothed the iron over Becky's neat cross-stitching.

This was foolish!

Ken had been gone only a few hours. How could she be pining for him already? Alison mended one of his shirts, then measured the sofa for new loose covers. She kept herself deliberately busy until it was time to go to bed. Once there, however, she lay wide awake. Alone for the first night since her marriage. Turning on her side, she rested her face against Ken's pillow. Where was he? What was he doing? Was he thinking of her? Missing her . . . ? Eventually, Alison drifted into sleep.

It was raining heavily next morning. Laura came downstairs shortly after Alison. The two women hardly spoke. It wasn't because they'd fallen out. In fact, Alison was delighted at how well she was getting on with Ken's eldest daughter. However, they still weren't sufficiently close for Laura to feel able to confide in her. Alison could easily guess the reason for her step-daughter's recent moodiness — Shaun Pembridge.

Although the couple were still seeing each other, Laura no longer radiated the sparkle of a young woman falling in love. Perhaps that wasn't a bad thing,

Alison had decided. She liked Shaun, but the better she began to know him, the more convinced she became he was the wrong sort of man for a sensitive, rather naïve girl like Laura.

Laura was in the hall fetching her raincoat when Becky squeezed by, still in her nightie and slippers, and padded into the kitchen.

'Becky! Why aren't you dressed yet?' Alison smiled at her from the stove. 'We'll be late for school if you don't hurry!'

'I don't feel well.'

Alison knelt down and took both of Becky's hands. They were ice-cold and clammy, and her little face was drained of its usually rosy colour. 'You're awfully cold, sweetheart. Come over beside the fire,' she suggested gently. 'Perhaps you'll feel better after you've eaten your breakfast.'

'Don't want it,' she murmured forlornly.

'Becky, where does it hurt?' Laura asked kindly but firmly. She'd come into the kitchen, and now touched her sister's forehead and looked into her face. 'Where don't you feel well?'

Becky looked away from Laura and chewed the inside of her cheek. 'All over.'

'Away you go and eat your breakfast,' Laura said with a sympathetic smile, giving her a hug. 'Then get ready for school.'

'I don't want to go to school!' Becky tugged away from her and darted across the kitchen to Alison. 'I feel sick. I want to stay at home!'

'Suppose I take you to school today?' suggested Laura brightly. 'Once you get there, you'll be all right. I promise.'

'I want to stay *here!*' Becky sobbed, her blue eyes huge.

Alison felt the child's cold little hand slipping into hers. While she was relieved Becky wasn't actually ill, she certainly was genuinely distressed. She looked so small and alone and unhappy standing there.

'Becky, go upstairs and get dressed.

Then we'll have breakfast together.' Even as she spoke, Alison was unsure she was acting wisely. 'You can stay at home for today.'

The little girl didn't need any second bidding.

'Why did you do that?' demanded Laura shortly as Becky darted up the stairs. 'You know full well there's nothing wrong with her!'

'Something is troubling her,' Alison answered carefully. 'She's upset about school. I don't know why — but I want to find out.'

'For heaven's sake, Alison! All children go through phases when they don't want to go to school! I know I did. And James, too. Becky's a shy little girl. She learns slowly and sometimes she gets teased.' Laura was trying to make Alison understand. 'But letting her stay away from school so she falls further behind the rest of the class isn't helping her. It'll only make life more difficult for her. Surely even you can see that?'

'I'm keeping Becky at home today,' replied Alison steadily. 'Because this is where she wants to be. Very badly.'

Laura shook her head in vexation. 'You should have backed me up, not encouraged her,' she snapped, buttoning her raincoat. 'If Dad were here, he'd agree with me!'

'Ken *isn't* here!' Alison returned crisply. 'While I may not be Becky's mother, I regard her as my daughter. And I shall do whatever I believe to be in her best interests.'

Laura drew a quick, sharp breath. 'As you say, you're responsible for Becky now.' She tied the belt of her raincoat tightly and picked up her bag from the dresser. 'But you're wrong to let her miss school, Alison. Very wrong indeed!'

\* \* \*

'Becky won't tell me what's wrong, Dan,' Alison said anxiously later that morning while Becky was temporarily out of hearing. 'I shouldn't have kept her from school — Laura was right. I should have listened to her.'

'Hmm, happen you were both a bit right. And a bit wrong,' replied Dan mildly. 'Would you like me to try to find out what's bothering Becky?'

'I'd be very grateful if you could. I don't know where to start to help her — ' She broke off. Becky was coming into the hospital dayroom where Dan now spent much of his time.

'Hello, sweetheart,' Alison began, getting up from the chair next to Dan's. 'I'm just slipping along to — to — '

'To the hospital shop,' chipped in Dan helpfully, craning his neck to peep into the small basket Becky was carrying. 'What have you got there, Becky?'

'It's for you!' she said, beaming, and swishing away a tea towel to reveal a dumpy glass jar topped with an embroidered lid cover.

'My favourite jam, eh?' chuckled Dan, taking the jar and holding it up to the light. 'Looks smashing — and all this fancy sewing, too! You know what I'm going to do with it?'

Becky shook her head.

'Stand it on my bedside table, so I can look at it. Then, the very first morning I'm home, Gran and me'll have your blackberry jam for breakfast.'

'Will you be coming home soon?' Becky clambered onto his knees.

'I hope so — hospital food's not a patch on Gran's cooking.' He lowered his voice. 'The rice pudding looks like something you'd stick wallpaper on with!'

'It's like that at school,' laughed Becky.

'Why didn't you want to go today?' Dan asked amiably.

'I've been picked to read a poem in the Christmas play,' she answered matter-of-factly, folding the tea towel neatly. 'We were going into the hall to practise today. Mr Carruthers told me I'd have to stand up on the stage and read out of a book.' Becky hesitated, looking away and fiddling with the corner of the tea towel.

'And?' Dan prompted, giving her a gentle nudge.

'I was scared, Granddad.'

'It sounds pretty scary,' Dan agreed. 'But you've always got your nose in a book these days. I thought you liked reading now?'

'I do! But reading out loud with everyone listening is different,' Becky explained seriously. 'I'm awful slow at it. I have to keep stopping at the big words, and everyone starts to laugh.'

Dan nodded, his arm about her shoulders. 'Why didn't you tell Alison? She's worried about you, you know.'

'I can't tell her!' exclaimed Becky in dismay. 'When I told her about reading before, it made her awful sad, Granddad. I can't tell her about this now, I just can't!'

'Phew — tricky, isn't it?' remarked Dan, scratching his chin thoughtfully. 'You know those cassette tapes I've been getting since I've been in here?'

Becky nodded. He'd let her put on

the big headphones and listen to bits of the audio stories.

'Well, I've got an idea . . . '

* * *

'So how's it coming along?' Helen asked cheerfully when she and Alison were shopping in the village. Alison had just stocked up on scarlet and holly-green crêpe paper, packets of sticky glitter and gold doilies.

'Marvellously! It's tremendous fun,' she responded enthusiastically. Along with several other parents, she and Ken had volunteered to help make costumes and scenery for Becky's school play.

'The girls are delighted to be fairies and sugar plums — however, the boys aren't too keen to be dressed up as candy canes and pumpkins!'

'I can imagine the difficulties,' Helen laughed as they turned into the haberdasher's before going on to meet Ken and Becky at the library. 'Oh, I do envy you, Alison. I loved it when Ashley and Diane were little and we did things together.'

'It is fun,' agreed Alison warmly. 'Especially watching Becky enjoying herself. She was awfully nervous at first, utterly convinced she'd never be able to read aloud in front of an audience. But Dan's idea of her speaking into his cassette recorder, and then playing it back so she could actually hear herself reading, gave her the confidence she lacked.'

'I wondered what Dad was up to!' exclaimed Helen with a smile. 'I asked — but he wouldn't say a word.'

'Becky probably swore him to secrecy,' Alison replied, selecting several rolls of shiny ribbon and moving along to the trays of buttons. 'She likes secrets. What do you think, Helen?' She held several glittering, crystal-effect buttons on her palm. 'Sparkly enough for a snowman?'

'Definitely. But isn't it about time you began thinking of this sort of thing?' She jokingly indicated a display of fine super-soft white yarn. 'It would knit up into a beautiful layette.'

'I'm sure it would,' laughed Alison, choosing the glass buttons. 'But when we married, Ken and I agreed not to have a family.'

'Ah, I see,' Helen said, nodding. She could understand her brother-in-law's decision not to have more children at his age. However, she'd watched Alison and Becky together — had seen the tenderness in Alison's eyes whenever she spoke of the child — and Helen couldn't help wondering how much longer her new sister-in-law would be content to abide by that decision.

\* \* \*

Laura sat before the dressing-table mirror teasing a comb through her damp hair. It had been a bitterly cold, dreary day and she'd been glad to leave Monk's Inn and come home. She hadn't seen Shaun since yesterday. He'd driven off after supper last night, so Mrs Lancaster explained. He hadn't said where he was going, nor when he'd be back. And he hadn't left any message for Laura. She sighed, putting down the comb and staring despondently at her reflection in the mirror.

Shaun had been depressed these past weeks. Laura had tried to be with him as much as she could, tried to help him . . . She understood the reasons for his caustic moods and made allowances for them. What she couldn't understand was his coolness. Was he still hurt by her refusal to go away with him? They'd never spoken about it again, but . . .

Laura rose abruptly and putting on her jeans and sweater, wrapped a towel into a turban around her hair. She curled up onto the bed, pulling the list of the inn's regular guests and a notepad towards her. Anxiously, she tried to concentrate on composing a letter that would go out to each name on her list. Business at Monk's Inn was worse than ever. And it had been Laura's suggestion that people who stayed there regularly should be offered a winter discount.

Despite Frank and Beattie Lancasters' fierce determination Monk's Inn would never close its doors, Laura kept the inn's books and knew only too well a successful Christmas and New Year period was crucial. She slowly wrote an opening paragraph on the notepad, only to cross it out and start over again. It was no use! Laura tossed her pen down in frustration. She just couldn't concentrate. Her mind was filled with unsettling thoughts about Shaun.

In so many ways, he was still a complete mystery to her. His attitudes, the things he did . . . She'd never in her whole life met anyone quite like him. Sometimes she felt she hardly even knew him. Then there were those days when she didn't see him — days that felt endless, and unbearably empty.

Feeling suddenly chilled, Laura went downstairs to the warm, brightly lit living room. She sat beside the fire, toasting her toes on the hearth as Dad,

Becky and Alison hurried back and forth putting on warm coats and scarves. They were taking the ferry across the water to Wallasey, having tea out and then going on to the cinema.

'Won't you come with us, Laura?' invited Alison amiably. It seemed so unkind that she, Ken and Becky were going out for a nice evening, leaving Laura all alone at home. And rather sad, too.

'Aye — come on, Laura,' urged Ken with a broad grin. '*Snow White* used to be your favourite.'

'It still is,' Laura returned with a smile. 'But I've some work to finish — and the rota of who's doing what at the village bonfire display. I'd almost forgotten about that,' she added in consternation. Usually, Nancy and Hilda Almond attended to the organisation of the November the Fifth festivities. However, this year, Laura had offered to stand in for Gran. 'You go and have a super time,' she went on, turning to Becky, who was struggling into her boots. 'When you come home, you can tell me all about it.'

'All right,' Becky agreed readily. 'I'll bring you a choc ice!'

'It might be a bit drippy by the time you get it here,' laughed Laura. 'A bag of popcorn would go down very nicely, though.'

'Popcorn it is, then.' Ken shepherded Alison and Becky out of the kitchen ahead of him.

Laura watched them go with mixed feelings. It was wonderful to see Dad and Becky so happy. They and Alison were very much a close-knit little family now. Although neither Dad — nor Alison, Laura admitted fairly — ever excluded her intentionally, she did feel increasingly left on the outside of the family. Especially with James away at college. Perhaps Laura's wistfulness showed on her face, because Ken paused in the doorway and glanced back at her. 'Still time to change your mind?'

Laura smiled, shaking her head

decisively. 'I really have got things to do, Dad!'

She'd hardly taken up her pad and pen to have another try at writing the letter, when there was an impatient thud on the front door's heavy brass knocker.

Before they'd exchanged a word, Shaun exuberantly kissed Laura's lips, spontaneously banishing the weeks of coolness and distance between the couple. She responded instinctively, their re-established intimacy both pleasurable and wonderfully reassuring.

'I met your family at the corner. Your father said you needed cheering up, and you'd be pleased to see me.' Shaun looked down, studying her with twinkling eyes. Laura was vexed to feel herself blushing to the roots of her hair. Why ever did Dad say such things? 'Are you pleased to see me?' persisted Shaun mischievously, brushing her flushed cheek with his lips. 'Are you?'

'As if you need to ask,' she owned up shyly.

'Don't be embarrassed.' His voice was suddenly tender. 'It's the same for me. When I'm away from you, all I can think about is this . . . The moment when I'll get back to you. Take you in my arms again.

'It was thinking about you that turned today around for me,' he continued at length, still holding her close as they moved into the fire-lit sitting room. 'You know I've received the insurance and compensation for my accident? Well, I had to go to London to tie up a last few loose ends. It was ghastly, Laura. Like a funeral. Everything that's been going on in my head these last weeks just crowded in on me.

'From having a career I loved, a life I loved — suddenly I had nothing! No present. No future. No hope left . . . ' Shaun's voice trailed off and he shrugged, shamefaced. 'What I was doing — what I've *been* doing for ages — is wallowing in self-pity. Then I came up from the Tube at Covent Garden and there was a street flower-seller near the opera house. I wasn't even looking, but I saw this.' From his jacket pocket, Shaun withdrew a rosebud and offered it to Laura.

'Oh, Shaun,' she murmured, touched by the simple gift. The flower was rather faded and crushed, but the biggest bouquet in the world couldn't have meant more to her at that moment.

'I don't know how you've put up with me recently,' he said quietly. 'I saw those flowers and started thinking about you. And for the first time since the accident, instead of looking back, I began looking ahead. The past is over. It's time for me to move on.'

'You're not going away?' breathed Laura, her eyes revealing all she was feeling. 'Leaving Sandford?'

'How could I, when you're here?' asked Shaun softly. 'No, I'm staying, Laura.' He stood away from her, smiling, his hands resting upon her waist. 'I'm going to buy Monk's Inn.'

'Buy Monk's?' she echoed in astonishment. Shaun had always been rather critical of the little inn with its homely atmosphere.

'It's very run-down at the moment, of course, but that's only because it has become far too much for Frank and Beattie to cope with. There's no denying Monk's Inn has charm and character, though. And plenty of potential,' commented Shaun shrewdly. 'About four years ago, an old friend from university bought a sixteenth-century tavern not far from Stratford-upon-Avon. It was virtually in ruins when Miles got his hands on it, but he's restored it and now it's the most gorgeous, romantic little country hotel you've ever set eyes on. I'd like to take you there sometime soon, Laura,' he added cautiously, recalling her previous rejections. 'Would you come with me?'

'Yes,' she answered quietly, her earlier reservations dispelled. 'Yes, I think I would, Shaun.'

'Super!' For once, he was almost lost for words. 'Great!' He smiled at her in delight, recovering quickly. 'I'll get on to Miles and make some arrangements. You're going to love the Hearts of Oak, Laura! It's a quite *enchanting* place. And I use that description deliberately. It's got exactly the sort of look and atmosphere I want Monk's Inn to have. I may not know as much about Shakespeare and antiques as Miles Weaver, but what's he's done with the Hearts, I can do with Monk's Inn!'

'I don't doubt it for a second,' Laura said, beaming, her eyes shining. Shaun wasn't going to leave the village as she'd always believed he one day would. He was staying! Staying, and taking over Monk's Inn! 'What do Mr and Mrs Lancaster think of it all?' she asked suddenly. It was difficult to imagine Monk's without the elderly couple. 'I bet they were nearly as surprised as me, and thrilled the old place is to stay in the family.'

'They don't actually know yet.' Shaun grimaced. 'I wanted to tell you first.'

'Oh!'

'Exactly.' He sighed soberly. 'Monk's is rapidly going downhill, but I'm not sure Frank and Beattie will be keen to sell. What do you think?'

'I don't know. It isn't for me to say, anyhow.' Laura was very conscious of her loyalty to the elderly couple. 'The Lancasters are more than my employers, Shaun. They're friends. It doesn't feel right to even be discussing them this way. All I can really tell you is what you already know. The inn has been their home for years and they love it.'

'I was afraid you'd say something like that,' conceded Shaun soberly. 'Although I'm related to them, you know both of them far better than I do. They respect and value your judgement, too. If you dropped a few comments about the wisdom of selling up before the place deteriorates any further, I'm sure they'd listen and take note. Then when I approach them with my offer, they'll already be softened up — '

Laura stared at him in total disbelief.

'Shaun! That's deceitful!' she exclaimed, shocked he'd even suggest such a thing. Hurt and disappointed he'd asked her to be party to it. 'Worse, it's despicable and dishonest!'

'It's business, Laura,' he countered reasonably.

'It certainly isn't the way Mr and Mrs Lancaster do business,' she returned crisply. 'They're straightforward and honest. If you want to buy Monk's Inn, go and speak to them openly.'

'What are you making such an unholy fuss about? All I'm asking you to do is help me out a little,' began Shaun tersely. 'Just a word here and there. It could make all the difference! I really *want* Monk's Inn!' He caught both her hands urgently. 'And I thought you'd want what I want!'

Laura snatched her hands free, her heart pounding. 'I do — but not like this! You're not being fair, Shaun!' she cried passionately, her eyes smarting with hot tears. 'I can't do as you ask! I *won't* do it. Not even for you!'

# 9

'Laura — calm down!' exclaimed Shaun in amazement. 'There's no need to make such big deal about it!'

She gazed at him. Despite the warmth of the cosy room, her hands were cold and she was shivering. Suddenly, Laura felt she didn't truly know Shaun at all.

'Am I really asking so much of you?' he persisted persuasively. 'Business is business. If you and I are — '

'*No!*'

There was determination in Laura's quiet voice. She heard Shaun's sharp intake of breath as he half-turned from her to stare into the fire. When he faced her again, he gave a conciliatory smile. 'Why don't we just agree to differ for the time being?' he suggested mildly. 'All I ask is that you don't mention my plans to anyone, until I find the right moment to talk to the Lancasters. Will you at least do that for me?'

Laura knew they'd been on the brink of having a real row. As she felt the tension ebbing, she returned Shaun's smile.

'When I want something badly, I want it *now*. Often I push too hard,' Shaun told her frankly, moving towards her and gently taking her hands. 'It's a problem, and I admit it. But whatever our differences, I don't want to quarrel over them.'

'Neither do I,' replied Laura softly.

'I don't want to lose you,' he murmured, kissing Laura's fingertips before slowly drawing her into his arms. 'And I don't want to waste this romantic fire-light either . . . '

\* \* \*

'Thanks for holding the fort, dear,' Beattie Lancaster said, bustling into the hotel and putting down her shopping bags.

It was Laura's Saturday off — and the day of the Sandford Christmas Fayre — but she'd popped into Monk's Inn for a few hours to put up the decorations.

'Oh, it's all looking lovely and festive!' went on Beattie, admiring Laura's handiwork. 'Have you organised the tree yet?'

Laura shook her head, folding up the step-ladder. 'I've tried ringing the nursery, but there's no reply.'

'Good!' exclaimed Beattie surprisingly, taking off her hat and coat. 'Because I've just met your gran and Becky in the post office. Becky was telling me you're getting your Christmas tree from Riverside Mill. I didn't even know David had pine trees out there! Anyhow, since he does, I think we should get our tree from him, too.' She smiled ruefully. 'This hasn't been much of a year for Monk's or Riverside. But, hopefully, things are starting to improve a bit now for David and — thanks to all your hard work here for us, Laura — perhaps we'll have a bright New Year ahead, too.'

Laura forced a smile she didn't feel. It was awful, working for Mr and Mrs Lancaster and sharing their hopes and plans for the inn's future, yet all the while knowing Shaun intended to take it over. He obviously had still not found the right moment to talk to the couple.

The disturbing situation was still uppermost in Laura's mind when she left the inn and crossed the green to the village hall. Becky was going to help her with the hand-knit stall at the Fayre, and soon both sisters were busily arranging woolly socks, hats, gloves and tea cosies. It wasn't until Laura spotted David's van drawing up outside the hall that she recalled something Beattie Lancaster had said.

'Becky, why did you tell Mrs Lancaster we were getting our Christmas tree from Riverside?'

'Because we are! And soon, too.' Becky's sharp eyes had glimpsed David entering the hall, his arms filled with trays of plants and flowering bulbs. She stood on tiptoe and waved enthusiastically. 'David! Over here!'

He peered over the topmost tray and grinned broadly. Setting down the plants, he crossed the hall towards their stall.

'Hello, David,' said Laura, adding needlessly, 'I see you're doing the plant stall.'

'First time I've been in charge of a stall,' he replied amiably. 'To be honest, I fancied doing the cakes and candies, but Mrs Almond said I looked far too lean and hungry to be trusted with eatables, so here I am with the poinsettia, hyacinth pots and Christmas roses!' David gave a resigned shrug and considered Becky's display of tea cosies. 'Very impressive! Will you help me set out my stall later?'

The little girl nodded readily. 'Is it still all right for us to have that Christmas tree I picked out? The bushy one down by the stile?'

'Of course — providing you put it

back after Twelfth Night!' He laughed.

Laura remembered the tree now! Late last spring, she and David had been picnicking at the edge of the small wood skirting one of Riverside Mill's boundaries. Becky and Smokey had gone off exploring and discovered several pines growing amongst the thicket of sprawling sycamore. Trust Becky to remember David had promised she could have the tree at Christmas time! Laura recalled something else, too, with a curious mixture of sadness and regret. It was upon the afternoon of the Sandford Christmas Fayre when she and David had first met . . .

She glanced at him now, chattering and laughing with Becky. That snowy day seemed a lifetime ago! So much had happened. So much had changed.

' . . . We can dig the tree up whenever you're ready, Becky,' David was saying.

'There's an afternoon when Daddy doesn't have to give any lessons, so he's taking Alison Christmas shopping in town,' replied Becky, her forehead creased into concentration. 'I think it's next week — so Laura and me will fetch the tree then.'

'Steady on!' Laura chipped in. 'Next week is awfully early. We usually leave the tree until a few days before Christmas.'

'This year's different. Alison hasn't had a proper Christmas before,' Becky answered seriously. 'Daddy wants it to be extra-special for her. He said he'll keep her out of the way in town, while we get the tree for a big surprise. Daddy and me only planned it last night, when we were reading our story,' she went on. 'We couldn't tell you about it then because you were out with Shaun.'

'Oh.' Laura lowered her eyes, fussing with the fringes of a blue scarf. 'Well, that's what we'll do then.'

'Just let me know when you're coming.' David smiled easily. 'I'll have my spade ready and waiting!'

'Granddad usually comes with us to

choose our tree,' murmured Becky, raising sad eyes to David's face. 'I wish he could be home for Christmas.'

'Not much fun being ill, is it?' he replied gently, dropping to his knees so his face was level with hers.

'No. But Granddad said he's better now and they should let him out,' explained Becky solemnly. 'He said the food's tougher than old boots and he misses his allotment.'

'Mmm, but there's not much growing at this time of year,' commented David thoughtfully. 'Although I've some special plants on my stall that Granddad could grow — even in hospital.'

'How?' Becky was puzzled.

'Some grow in stones. Or air, even. And there are flowers whose roots grow down into a vase of water.' He winked at Becky, then glanced sidelong up at Laura. 'If your boss can spare you for ten minutes, I'll show them to you.'

'Away you go, then,' said Laura, nodding and smiling at Becky's hopeful face. 'But hurry back if we get a sudden rush of customers!'

David straightened up, extending his hand towards the child.

'Are the flowers magic, David?' she asked, slipping her small hand into his.

'Oh, even better than magic!'

Laura watched them walking away across the brightly decorated village hall, and wondered if David was remembering another Christmas Fayre and that snowy afternoon when they'd met. Somehow, she hoped he was.

\* \* \*

It was a raw, bleak morning when Laura and Becky walked Smokey over to Riverside Mill for the Christmas tree. Becky did some of the digging, and David took an instant photograph of her to give to Granddad. Laura was aware it was Becky's happy presence that was making the day so carefree and enjoyable with none of the awkwardness she had anticipated. David took them back to Spryglass in his van, and the three carried the tree indoors. Smokey excitedly raced around their ankles, barking and grabbing at the prickly branches with his mouth.

'Are you sure the tree will be OK in the hall?' David queried, glancing back at the tall, bushy pine.

'It's only until Dad and Alison get home,' replied Laura. 'Becky wants them to see it as soon as they open the front door.'

'She's really thrilled about it all, isn't she?' said David affectionately.

'Christmas means more to her than ever this year.' Laura smiled, showing him out. 'Dad being here, and Alison. The whole family will be together.'

David started down the steps, and Laura followed him.

'Would you like to come for dinner tonight?' she asked tentatively. 'We'll be decorating the tree afterwards. We'd all like you to join us.'

'You're sure?' his eyes met hers levelly.

'I've been intending — wanting — to

ask you for ages,' she confided uneasily. 'I never wanted you to stay away from the family because . . . Well, because of what happened between you and me. Please come tonight, David — If you'd like to, that is, of course.'

'I'd like to very much. Thank you.'

As they reached the gate, Shaun's car drew up alongside. He parked, but didn't get out.

'I'll get the meal started straight away,' Laura was saying thoughtfully. 'If we eat a bit earlier than usual, Becky won't be too tired for doing the tree.'

'That's a good idea,' agreed David, glancing at his watch and crossing towards his van. 'See you in about an hour, then?'

When the van pulled away, Shaun immediately strode from his car and glared at Laura from beyond the weathered gate. 'What's going on?' he demanded. 'I call round to see you — and find you asking your ex-boyfriend to dinner!'

'For heaven's sake, Shaun!' exclaimed

278

Laura shortly, hurrying back up to the path to the house. 'Don't be ridiculous!'

'Oh, so I'm expected to like your inviting — '

She stopped in mid-stride, turning around on the steps to face him. 'David is a family friend, coming to a family dinner. If you disapprove of that, well, I'm sorry, but I think you're being selfish and totally unreasonable and — '

'All right! All right! I give up!' Shaun grinned at her, holding up both hands. 'I was out of line. I apologise.'

'So you should.' She was unable to prevent herself smiling at him. 'Shall we stay out here in the freezing cold, or would you like to come in?'

'I would, but I can't. I'm on my way to Liverpool on business,' he replied. 'But I do want to take you out this evening.'

Laura shook her head ruefully. 'We're decorating the tree.'

'Ah!' remarked Shaun wryly, slipping his arms about her waist. 'Well, when you've finished with the eggnog and fairy lights, call me.' He paused, relishing the moment. 'The Lancasters have decided to sell Monk's Inn. I want to go out tonight so we can drink a toast to the future — *our* future!'

★ ★ ★

James was enjoying college. He was studying hard, developing both as a musician and composer. However, this first semester hadn't been all work! James was sharing a house in Manchester with nine other students and, apart from the occasional squabble, they had a lot of fun together and he'd already made several firm friends. Packing the last of his clothes into a suitcase, James glanced around his shoe-box of a room to make sure he hadn't forgotten anything. College was terrific, but he was looking forward to going home for Christmas.

'Ah, you're still here!' William Bayldon stuck his head around the door and walked in, flopping down on the bed.

'It's not too late to change your mind about coming skiing with us?'

'Uh-uh,' James said, grinning. 'I've never even been on a pair of skis!'

'Nor have I!' William returned, his round face creasing into a beam. 'But is that going to stop me? I'll be down those hills like the abominable snowman! Is this it?' he went on, his attention distracted by the pages of neat manuscript stacked on James's bedside table. 'The score you've been writing for your local church?'

'Yes.' James paused from his packing. William was in his final year and, despite all his clowning and larks, was a very fine musician. James respected him, and valued his judgement. 'Reverend Whitfield asked me to write a piece for the Christmas services. There'll be traditional carols too, of course. We've got the organ, five children playing recorder, an acoustic guitar, and me with my violin.'

James waited almost fearfully while William read the music. Good friend that he was, if he considered the work without merit, he would tell James so.

'What do you think, Will?'

'It's very simple. And all the more effective for that,' he observed at last. 'It's good, James. I like it. The treble solo is quite moving. Demanding, though.'

'Yes, but Nicholas has a terrific voice.'

'How old is he?'

'Fourteen-ish, I suppose,' said James with a shrug.

'Is he the only boy in the choir good enough to sing this?'

James nodded. William sucked air through his teeth. 'Then you'd better be prepared, just in case!'

'In case of what?' asked James in alarm.

'In case his voice breaks!' laughed William, getting up and bringing the score to James. 'Why not rework it a bit? Choose the best choirgirl and make your solo a duet — boy and girl together? Then, if the worst happens, she can sing alone and you've still got the heart of your piece.'

The two mulled over the score, improving and polishing, until it was time for James to leave for his train to Liverpool.

'Have a great vacation!' William bellowed down the landing as James waved goodbye. 'And good luck with your Christmas music!'

A few days later, and following William's advice to the letter, James was feeling quietly pleased. The rehearsals at Sandford village church were progressing far better than he'd dared hope. Young Wendy, the best of the girl choristers, had a warm, expressive voice and she sang very well with Nicholas. Even more than that, James realised the piece sounded far richer and was greatly improved by having two voices. Despite the inevitable butterflies and cold dread that something ghastly would go wrong at the last minute, James was beginning to really look forward to hearing his music performed before the whole congregation at Christmastide.

He was softly whistling the tune to himself as he sat in his bedroom at Spryglass, wrapping Becky's present. He'd arranged to go over to Riverside Mill later on. There'd been an unexpected rush of pre-Christmas orders for vegetables and salad produce and David was working flat out to fill them. He simply couldn't afford to turn business away so, whenever James wasn't at church rehearsing, he was helping at Riverside. He glanced from his window. Sleet — again! He and David would be frozen stiff and drenched — again! But not even that prospect could dampen James's high spirits today. He'd had a letter from Charlotte and —

Becky and Smokey were galloping up the stairs and along the landing. James hurriedly stuffed her half-wrapped present into his wardrobe. He was slamming the door shut when Becky burst into the room.

'The mince pies are ready,' she began, staring at him suspiciously. 'What are you doing?'

'Nothing.'

'You were wrapping something up.'

'I wasn't!'

But Becky had already spotted the sticky tape and ribbon on James's bed. Her inquisitive gaze swept the room. 'You were! I heard the paper rustling!'

'No, honestly . . . I — I was reading a magazine.'

'You weren't! It's in the wardrobe, isn't it?' She darted forward. James got there before her, jammed his shoulder blades against the wardrobe door and held it shut.

'OK, your present is in my wardrobe,' he admitted. 'But I want you to promise you won't look.'

She lowered her eyes, chewing the inside of her cheek.

'Well?'

'I promise,' she agreed reluctantly, as James bustled her out on to the landing and down to the kitchen.

'Your pies are great, Becky!' he declared when they were sitting at the table. 'Haven't broken my teeth on the pastry or anything!'

'Your baking is smashing, Becky,' put in Alison, smiling across the table to James. 'Ignore your elder brother; he's in love! What did Charlotte have to say in her letter?' she added. 'Or oughtn't I to ask?'

'That's OK,' he replied cheerfully, unable to keep from smiling at the mere thought of Charlotte Green. 'Charlotte's coming on the nineteenth. I can't wait to see her again.'

'Weren't you able to visit during term-time?'

'Early on, I made it down to her university a couple of times, but once I got my weekend job at the supermarket . . . ' He exhaled, shrugging. 'We haven't seen each other for nearly two months. And lately Charlotte hasn't written much. Too busy studying, I suppose. You know how ambitious she is.'

'Studying medicine is hard work. Charlotte is determined to do well,' reasoned Alison sympathetically. 'So, what are your plans for your reunion?'

'I've got it all thought out,' said James, beaming. 'Dinner at the restaurant where we went on our first date, then across the water to see *La Bohème*.'

'Oh, James, that's perfect!' exclaimed Alison enthusiastically. The vivid opera set in Paris on a snowy Christmas Eve was one of her favourites. 'Have you seen it before?'

James shook his head. 'I know some of the melodies, but I've never actually seen an opera.'

'You'll love it — so will Charlotte.'

'Is that what we're going to see?' Becky asked.

'No, we're going to see *A Christmas Carol*. That's a ghost story. And it's a play — like the one you're putting on at school,' Alison explained, getting up to fetch more mince pies. '*La Bohème* is an opera. The characters sing instead of talking. It's a tragic and beautiful love story.'

Becky gave it some thought. 'I'm glad we're seeing the ghost one instead.'

'Well, that's put Puccini in his place!' James laughed, ruffling Becky's curls as he rose from the table.

'James, please don't be offended,' Alison began quietly. 'However, I was an impoverished student once myself. Opera tickets and restaurants are terribly expensive, so — '

'I understand what you're trying to say, and I'm not offended.' James came over to her chair and, putting an arm about her shoulders, bent to kiss her smooth cheek. 'It's thoughtful of you, and I really do appreciate it, but I've saved a fair bit from my supermarket wages, so I'm OK for money.'

'If you're sure,' she returned, going with him out into the hall. 'But remember, you have only to ask.'

James nodded, zipping up his waterproof jacket and considering her affectionately. What a kind and lovely woman Alison was. And what a lucky man Dad was to have married her.

'Can I come with you?' Becky was tugging at his sleeve. 'I want to help, too!'

'You can't today. David and I will be out in the fields. We have to dig or cut the veg, and then weigh it and pack it into sacks ready to be sold,' James answered. 'You can come tomorrow, and work in the greenhouse packing the salad things into boxes.'

'Here, these are for you.' Becky held out a small parcel. 'Mince pies for your tea break. There's some for David, too.'

'Oh, thanks!' He bent and gave her a hug. 'That reminds me — I've something else to give to David.'

James went back to the hall table and picked up an envelope the postie had left at Spryglass earlier that morning. David's van was just juddering to a halt outside, and James turned up his collar against the icy sleet as he opened the front door and sprinted down the path.

'Mince pies from Becky!' he said with

a grin, diving into the shelter of the van. 'And an envelope from the postie. Ted said he was rushed off his feet this morning and wasn't about to add another half hour to his round just to deliver a Christmas card to you all the way out at Riverside Mill.'

'That's our Ted, all right,' laughed David, tearing open the envelope. 'Just brimming over with seasonal goodwill. Oh, this is from Martin Tregarth. We were friends when we were boys. Haven't set eyes on each other for years, but we keep in touch — sort of.' David wedged the card into the dashboard and moved off along the crescent. 'Martin's father was coxswain on the local lifeboat. Most Sundays, we'd be down at the harbour helping to swab the decks and polish the brass. We thought we were grand, I can tell you!' he laughed. 'Martin's a lifeboatman in Polkerris himself now.'

'Are you going back to Cornwall for the holidays?' James enquired amiably, and was startled at the sudden grimness

290

which darkened David's face.

'I left when I was sixteen,' he retorted brusquely. 'I've never been back. There's nothing there for me now.'

'Sorry,' James said, perplexed. 'I assumed you had family there. I didn't mean to pry.'

David sighed heavily, offering James an apologetic smile. 'You're not. It's . . . oh, it's just that you think you've got the past buried then, suddenly, it's back. Haunting you all over again.'

David stared intently at the curving, slush-covered road ahead. James could no longer see his expression.

'My mother was ill for years, but she never complained,' David said at length. 'She was the gentlest woman, yet strong, too. Much stronger than I could ever be. Barbara and Joyce, my sisters, are a lot older than me. They looked after Mum and me and the house. Cared for my father.' He spoke the last word contemptuously. 'Joshua Hale is a fisherman. Has his own boat. The catches were usually good, but we always seemed so poor. Barbara and Joyce had to scrimp and save. There was never money enough for little pleasures or comforts that might have made Mother happier.'

David paused, battling with the memories. James became increasingly uncomfortable, as though he were eavesdropping on his friend's most personal thoughts.

'I was nearly sixteen when she died,' murmured David, turning onto the rough track that led to Riverside Mill. 'Soon after, I was reading one of her favourite books. Amongst the pages was a letter from my aunt. It was obviously a reply to something Mother had written to her. I shouldn't have read it. I should have burned it straight away. But I did read it.' His voice was unusually hard, cold with fury as he recalled that fateful day. 'Joshua Hale was deceiving my mother. She knew yet she loved him still. And forgave him. But I couldn't forgive him, James,' stated David bitterly. 'I'll never be able to forget the pain and unhappiness he must have caused her.'

★ ★ ★

Alison finished sewing the small, shiny wooden toggles onto the rose-pink duffel jacket she was making for Becky. She was only able to work on it when the child was at school, so she'd brought it into the dining room to listen while James was practising carols. How swiftly the mood had changed! Alison's gaze wandered from her sewing to James's violin, lying forgotten upon the cushion of the fireside chair where he'd left it when the telephone rang.

She heard the click of the front gate and Ken's key in the door. Quick footsteps came downstairs, and there was a brief exchange of voices out in the hall, then the front door closed with a dull bang.

'What's got into Jimmy?' queried Ken, coming into the dining room and taking off his coat.

'Charlotte phoned,' Alison sighed sadly. 'She isn't coming home for Christmas. She's decided to go somewhere with friends from university.'

Ken raised an eyebrow. 'Left it pretty late to tell him, didn't she?' he commented. 'Hasn't he made all kinds of plans?'

'I imagine that's the last thing on his mind right now,' responded Alison regretfully. 'She didn't exactly say so, but James is convinced she's met somebody else.'

'Poor Jimmy!' Ken exhaled a slow breath. 'He was keen on her, wasn't he?'

Alison was watching James's solitary figure down on the desolate shore, his head and shoulders hunched against the keen offshore wind as he walked along the water's edge. 'Talk to him, darling,' she urged, turning from the window.

'*Me* talk to him?' echoed Ken in consternation. 'I wouldn't know what to say.' He saw she was about to protest and rushed on. 'I mean it, Alison. I could no more talk to Jimmy or Laura about — well, love and things, than fly to the moon. I'm just no good with fancy words.'

'Words don't need to be fancy, Ken.' She hugged him. 'Merely from the heart. Now — what are you going to wear for Becky's play? If it needs ironing, I'll do it now.'

'Ah! I was about to get to that,' began Ken ruefully. 'The brass have unexpectedly called a staff meeting and — '

'No!' Alison cried in dismay, realising what was coming. 'Becky's worked so hard and she's looking forward to it so very much. You *have* to be there, Ken!'

'It's not as simple as that,' he replied shortly. 'The head of department sent a memo round making it clear he expected everyone to attend this meeting. It's obviously important.'

'More important than your daughter's first school play?' demanded Alison crossly. Becky's struggle to overcome her reading difficulties, to conquer her shyness and actually take part in the play, had been because she wanted to please Ken and make him proud of her. The thought of the little girl's disappointment, if Ken wasn't there, made Alison furious. 'Don't you realise how much it means to Becky?'

'Of course, I do!' Ken retorted, his own temper fraying. 'Don't you think it means a lot to me, too? I'll get away as soon as I can, but if I'm not home by quarter to, don't wait.' Scraping back his chair, he snatched up his briefcase. 'You and Becky just go off to the school without me!'

And that was what they had to do. Alison had cheerfully explained that Ken would be a little late, but Becky had been subdued on the way to school. When they were about to part, she looked up at Alison trustingly. 'Daddy will come, won't he?'

Impulsively, Alison responded by doing a thing she had sworn never to do. She made Becky a promise she wasn't certain would be kept.

Reassured, Becky went off to change into her costume. Alison joined the other parents in the school hall, becoming increasingly anxious as the time slipped away and Ken didn't come. She was trying to work out how to explain to Becky when the head teacher began a speech of welcome.

'Got away as quick as I could, love,' murmured Ken, slipping into the seat beside Alison just as the play began. 'Sorry I'm late.'

'You're here,' she whispered gratefully, squeezing his hand. 'And that's all that matters.'

★　★　★

Becky and Ken came in at the rear gate after visiting Dan. Becky ran up to the house, but Ken hung back at the shed, where James was splitting dried-out driftwood for the fire. Ken couldn't help admiring the way Jimmy had handled that business with Charlotte Green. He hadn't moped about, he'd kept cheerful and got on with his work. Ken was proud of him. He cleared his throat.

'If it gets any colder, Alison and Becky'll get their snow!'

'Wouldn't be surprised,' James agreed, blowing on his hands before swinging the axe once more.

'Where is Alison anyway? I haven't seen her for hours.'

'Where she always is lately,' James said, grinning. 'Kitchen!'

'She's fretting herself into a state over the Christmas cooking and wanting the house just so.' Ken frowned slightly. 'I expected Laura to be doing more to help out.'

'She is working full-time now, Dad. With the Lancasters packing up, she's practically running Monk's Inn single-handed,' commented James, adding scathingly, 'I expect Shaun Pembridge is delegating a lot of the re-organisation to her, too.'

'Hmm, aye, I suppose you're right,' Ken conceded absently. 'Anyhow, that's not what I wanted to talk to you about. What are you doing about tonight? The opera, and that?'

James bent to retrieve the scattered wood. 'I'm not going.'

'That's an awful waste, Jimmy. I reckon you should go,' went on Ken awkwardly. 'The break will do you good and besides, you really enjoy all that sort of stuff.'

James shook his head, stacking the kindling.

'Actually, I thought you might do me a wee favour,' persisted Ken, trying again. 'Alison has hardly set foot out of the house in weeks. A trip to the opera would be a nice treat for her.'

'Yes, you're right,' James agreed readily. 'You're more than welcome to the tickets, Dad. They're good seats and —'

'No! That's not what I had in mind. I can't abide opera! Alison dragged me along to one in Hong Kong and, believe me, once was enough. No, what I was thinking,' he concluded, 'was that you could invite Alison to go with you.'

James's shy invitation surprised Alison and delighted her, too. She suspected Ken had had a hand in it somewhere but she agreed absolutely that it would have been a shame if James had missed the opportunity to see his first opera on stage. She dressed warmly in boots, cream trousers and a matching polo-necked jumper and went down to the dining room. The rest of the family were gathered around the hearth toasting crumpets.

'You look really great!' James exclaimed, colouring and adding self-consciously, 'I mean, you always do, but — '

'Thank you — and don't say another word!' She smiled, bending to kiss Ken and Becky goodbye. 'The compliment is already perfect.'

'I'll fetch your coat. *And* a scarf,' said Ken with a grin. 'You'll need them, crossing the river on a night like this.'

'Oh, I shan't feel the cold,' Alison replied happily. 'I'm wearing the beautifully warm mittens Becky knitted for me.'

'Granny showed me how.' Becky was pleased. 'I'm making a pair for Laura next.'

'Crossing on the ferry will be choppy,' Ken remarked, going with them to the front door. 'But I'm glad you're not taking the car. The roads'll be like glass later, if this wind freezes. Have a nice time,' he added cheerfully. 'Sooner you than me. Imagine spending three hours listening to folk howling at each other in a foreign language!'

★　★　★

Ken had been right about the ferry crossing being turbulent. A bone-chilling wind was whipping the river into spumy furrows, pitching the ageing vessel like a toy boat, deluging her decks with icy saltwater. Alison and James were forced to take shelter below

301

in the saloon for the trip across to the Wirral side. Their homeward journey, however, could not have been a greater contrast. The sea was completely calm.

'There's hardly a breath of wind now!' Alison exclaimed, as they climbed the open, metal-runged steps to the ferry's topmost deck. 'And it's almost warm, isn't it?'

'It's a lot warmer than inside that hall,' laughed James.

'You're right,' Alison agreed genially. 'I'm certain it wasn't only the soprano's tiny hands which were frozen!'

'She ought to have had a pair of Becky's mittens,' said James with a grin.

'Oh, but it was splendid, James,' remarked Alison with a contented sigh. 'The singing, the orchestra, costumes, sets . . . The whole production was simply breathtaking. How can it be that music which is sad and touching, leaves one feeling immensely joyful and inspired?'

'I don't know.' He shrugged. 'But it happens.'

In companionable silence, they watched from the rail while the ferry began its slow, swerving course across the river.

'Look, it's snowed over in Liverpool!' Alison pointed as the white-covered roofs of the city slid into view. 'Becky will be so pleased.'

In fact, there were several patches of deep snow, and the temperature was still dropping steadily out at Sandford. The lanes were slippery, and it was past midnight before Alison and James got home.

'Becky and Smokey have already been playing in the snow,' observed James in a low voice. 'Look at their footprints!'

Alison laughed, slithering up the path to the porch. Ken had left the downstairs light on, and the old house looked warm and welcoming. While James searched for his keys, Alison stared out across the garden. Then he paused, his gaze travelling with hers to the snowy shore, eerily beautiful in the hazy moonlight. It looked particularly poignant and beautiful.

Losing Charlotte hurt him very much. James had felt empty and pretty worthless these past days. So for him, this evening with Alison — not just dinner and the opera, but talking to her, just being with her — was like emerging from darkness into sunshine.

'Thanks for coming tonight,' he said earnestly as she turned to face him. 'It was wonderful, really special.'

'I had a lovely time, too.'

He bent to kiss Alison's cold cheek affectionately. But in that split second, James's heart lurched, and his lips tenderly sought the warm softness of her mouth. He pulled back abruptly, breathing hard, his horrified eyes meeting hers.

'I — I'm sorry,' he stammered thickly, shocked by what he had done. 'I wouldn't hurt you for the world!'

'Oh, James . . . ' she murmured, sensitive to the young man's distress and vulnerability, anxious she shouldn't add to his embarrassment or wound his fragile pride. Gently, Alison touched his flushed cheek, searching for the right words.

Neither she nor James noticed light spilling upon them through the open front door. Or Ken, standing watching them from the hall.

# 10

'So — you're back at last!' Ken said, beaming, as he drew Alison and James into Spryglass's holly-garlanded hall. 'I was about to send Smokey out with a barrel of brandy to search for the pair of you!'

'We *are* late — but we've had the most marvellous evening,' said Alison with a smile, her concerned eyes meeting James's for an instant before she looked again at Ken. 'You shouldn't have waited up, darling. But it's lovely that you did.'

'Oh, it's not just me,' he laughed, helping her off with her scarf and kissing her under the mistletoe at the same time. 'Becky woke up, saw the snow and was too excited to go back to sleep. I was out in the back garden helping her build snow-gnomes round the pond until half an hour ago! And

Laura's not long home from Monk's Inn. They're both cooking up a late-night supper for us all in the kitchen. How about you, Jimmy?' went on Ken amiably, as Becky emerged from the kitchen and raced down the hall to greet Alison. 'What did you make of your first opera, then?'

'Great,' mumbled James, turning to hang up his coat. He felt too ashamed — too guilty — to look his father in the eye.

How could he have kissed Alison like that? It seemed unbelievable. Those fleeting, disturbing moments on the porch were remote. Unreal. Like something which had never happened . . . But it *had* happened! James rubbed a hand across his forehead. He'd never felt more wretched in his entire life. And what about Alison? What must she be feeling? What must she think of him now? James stole a glance at her. She was listening to Becky, laughing as the little girl took her hand, wanting to hurry and show

Alison the snow-gnomes.

James watched miserably as they disappeared through the kitchen out into the garden. He liked Alison very much . . . Cared for her . . . and they'd shared a special kind of companionship. But now . . . In one stupid, irresponsible, childish moment, he'd ruined it all! He was vaguely aware of his father speaking, but James wasn't really listening. All he could think about was Alison. Talking to her. Apologising. Finding a way . . .

Ken's words suddenly penetrated. He had opened the sitting room door and was giving James a cheerful push. 'Away you go in.' He grinned broadly. 'And say hello to your visitor!'

James blundered into the comfortable room with its glowing fire and lamplight. Even before the door clicked shut behind his father, the dishevelled young woman who'd been sitting in the armchair was on her feet, rushing towards him and flinging herself into his arms.

'Charlotte!' He stared down at her blankly. 'What are you doing here?'

She was the last person James wanted to see right now. And he was too preoccupied to be aware of the displeasure in his voice. Charlotte froze, took a step back away from him.

'I wondered what sort of welcome you would give me, James,' she commented unsteadily. 'But I certainly didn't expect this!'

He walked to the window without looking at her. The heavy curtains were open and the reflected lights of the tree made smudges of red, blue, gold and green on the freshly fallen snow. 'What are you doing here?' repeated James, standing with his back to her. 'Shouldn't you be on your way to Norfolk tonight?'

'I was.' There was a slight tremor in Charlotte's usually assured voice. James turned to look at her, and she shrugged. 'On the way to Norfolk, that is. When we stopped at the services, I hitched a lift to Liverpool instead.'

'That was a stupid thing to do!' exploded James in disbelief. 'Anything might have happened!'

'You imagine I'd thumb a ride if I wasn't desperate?' she retorted, her eyes bright. 'I came to you because I believed I could rely on you! I thought you'd help me and wouldn't ask questions. But all you're doing is blaming me!'

'Charlotte — '

'Leave me alone!' She shook off the hand he'd laid on her shoulder and bent to retrieve the suitcase beside the chair. 'If I'd wanted to be lectured, I'd have gone home to my parents!'

'You're not going anywhere tonight,' he said evenly. James had finally gained a grip on his own composure and deliberately stood in front of the door, to prevent Charlotte leaving. 'You'd better stay here.'

Surprisingly, she offered no resistance when James took the suitcase from her and set it down. All the fight and indignation seemed to have drained from her. 'Thanks, James.' She spoke almost meekly, moving nearer but not touching him.

James gazed down into her white face, for the first time really looking at her. Charlotte wasn't the kind of girl who cried, but James realised that now tears were not so far away. He reached for her, and Charlotte came willingly, leaning against him, drawing comfort from his closeness. 'What is it?' he murmured thickly, his thoughts — his sudden fears — crowding in. 'What's happened, Charlotte?'

She didn't speak, but James felt her clinging to him, her fingernails digging into his shoulders. 'It's all right,' he soothed, stroking her hair. 'You're safe now. I'm here . . . '

Another hour passed before he felt able to leave her. Charlotte had said little, but he'd read between the lines. An end-of-term party, everyone splitting up afterwards and going their separate ways. The offer of a ride to Norfolk with a fellow medical student . . .

James went into the kitchen, assuming the family would all have gone to bed. He stopped abruptly when he saw Alison sitting at the fireside, the rose-pink duffel jacket she was making for Becky spread out across her lap. He'd wanted to see her, talk to her, but now he felt too ashamed, too embarrassed . . . She glanced up from her sewing and smiled at him.

'Since Becky has broken up from school, I haven't been able to finish this without her seeing it.' Alison got up, putting the work aside. 'And Christmas isn't so far off now.'

'No,' James agreed uneasily.

'Laura and Becky made supper,' said Alison, going across to the oven. 'I've kept yours and Charlotte's warm. Would you like to take in a tray?'

'Yes, thanks. I was going to fix some coffee and something to eat . . . ' He was hovering beside the table. 'I've told Charlotte she can stay here tonight. Is that all right?'

'Of course. Aren't her parents expecting her home?'

He shook his head. 'She's supposed to be in Norfolk. Spending the holidays with university friends. But something . . . went wrong,' James finished lamely.

'I see.' Alison tactfully didn't ask for any details.

'Alison — about what happened earlier,' he blurted out, unable to bear their going on as though nothing was wrong between them. 'Saying I'm sorry doesn't put it right, but — '

'James, you and I are friends!' Alison spoke very softly, coming to him and resting her hands upon his shoulders. When he summoned the courage to meet her eyes, James saw they were solemn, but without reproach. 'When friendships are tested, they can become stronger,' she continued earnestly. 'I very much want ours to do that.'

'So do I.' He nodded gravely. 'More than anything.'

'Then I'll leave you to your supper and say goodnight.'

Gently, but purposefully, she touched James's face. Everything was all right. James understood, and stooped to kiss her cheek.

'Goodnight.' He returned her smile gratefully, but still felt awful about what had occurred.

'You must think only of Charlotte.' Alison had paused at the doorway. 'She's welcome to stay here as long as she wishes.'

'When she phoned to say she wasn't coming home for Christmas, perhaps I was wrong,' James ventured slowly. 'She never actually said she wanted to break up. So maybe . . . Well, she has come back to me, hasn't she?'

'Yes, she has. And there will be plenty of time for you to talk later,' said Alison with a smile. 'For tonight, just have your supper and then try to get some rest. Charlotte must be exhausted, and you have to get up early to help David at Riverside.'

\* \* \*

Charlotte was still sleeping when James left quietly a little after five thirty next morning, setting off through the snow-bound woods and across the ribbon of frozen river to David's market garden. She was seldom far from his thoughts as he worked that whole day long, and again and again James caught himself looking forward to seeing Charlotte again when he got home to Spryglass later that evening.

The day seemed longer than usual to him, and when the weak winter sun finally paled into dusk, James left David cutting lettuce in the greenhouse and trudged across the yard to wash and change before going into the village. He'd arranged to run through the carol service with the organ and recorders before the choir arrived at the church for a rehearsal proper. James was concentrating so hard on the music, he didn't notice Charlotte entering the church. He was delighted when he glanced up and saw her standing there watching him. The instant the organist called a break to go over a hitch with the recorders, James set down his violin and hurried across the nave to her.

'Hi! This is a nice surprise.' His warm smile froze as he saw the suitcase at her feet.

'I'm catching the next train,' she said quietly, adding hurriedly before James could speak, 'I'm going to Norfolk.'

'Why?' he almost whispered, clasping her hands tightly. 'I thought you'd be here for Christmas. That we'd be together!'

'I'd planned to go to Norfolk with friends,' she said soberly. 'I don't intend to let what happened spoil my plans.'

'But won't . . . *he* be there, too?' persisted James. 'At this house-party place?'

Charlotte's chin jutted obstinately. 'Yes. And when I see him again, I'll tell him exactly what I think of him!' She'd regained her usual confidence and self-assurance. 'It would be feeble to let someone like him ruin my Christmas. You must see that, James!'

He was too disappointed, too hurt, to see anything much. Except the hopelessness of trying to change Charlotte's mind when she was so determined. 'At least I can see you safely on to the train,' he said simply.

'You'll miss your rehearsal,' Charlotte replied, going on more softly, 'besides, I'd rather you didn't come to see me off. It would be better if we said goodbye here.' She gave him a hug, kissed him, and was gone.

James wandered out onto the church steps, watching as Charlotte walked briskly towards the railway station. This time, it was goodbye. He had no doubts about that.

\* \* \*

On Christmas morning, Alison crept downstairs long before anyone — even Becky — stirred. The sky beyond the frost-spangled windows was still dark as she worked quietly in the kitchen, meticulously following her previously

317

prepared list. To everyone's delight, Dan had been discharged from hospital just two days earlier. Although he was still very much an invalid, he and Nancy were to come back to Spryglass after church and spend the day. Helen and Alex were popping in at teatime.

'Are you winning?'

Ken's voice came close to her ear. Alison jumped. She hadn't heard him coming in. 'Don't do that!' she laughed softly. 'Especially when my hands are full of trifle ingredients!'

'Hmm, looks pretty good, too.' Ken unrepentantly stole a flaked almond. 'How's the Christmas countdown going along? Everything ticked off that should be?' He indicated the festive timetable pinned up on the cork memo board.

'Don't tease! That schedule is vital. Without it, nothing would be right,' admonished Alison mildly. 'Until a few months ago, I'd little idea what a traditional Christmas was. Now I'm trying to arrange one for a dozen people! And they all know more about it than I do!'

'Look, love, if I've told you once,' said Ken patiently, pausing from setting the fire to look up at her, 'there's nothing to get yourself in a state about. It's only family, after all.'

'You're hopeless,' she returned in exasperation. 'Don't you see? It's precisely because it *is* for our family that I'm anxious all goes well and everyone enjoys themselves.'

'What I want — ' He rose, going across the kitchen to put his arms about her. ' — is for *you* to enjoy it! It's our first Christmas, something extra-special. I don't want you spending the day fretting — ' Ken broke off, hearing the almighty thumping of small feet and paws from the upper reaches of the previously silent old house. 'Brace yourself, love,' he warned. 'Here comes our own Christmas fairy!'

Seconds later, Becky charged into the kitchen wearing the rose-pink duffel jacket over her nightie. Smokey skidded around the doorway after her. 'Merry Christmas, everybody! I woke up and saw my coat at the end of my bed,' she cried breathlessly, racing into Alison's arms. 'Did you make it for me?'

'Yes,' laughed Alison, cuddling the little girl close. 'And Daddy helped!'

'I tied all the knots,' Ken said with a grin, holding Becky at arm's length to get a better look at the coat with its shiny wooden toggles and check-lined quilted hood. 'You look great, Becky!'

'I woke Laura up to show her,' said Becky proudly. 'Then I went to show James, but he was still asleep.'

'Bet he isn't now,' said Ken drily, watching Becky as she disappeared into the pantry to fetch the container of bird food.

'There's sponge left over from the trifle, and a bag of pastry crumbs on the shelf, Becky,' called Alison, smoothing a white cloth edged with embroidered December roses over the table. 'And after you were asleep last night, David left some bruised apples.'

'I've got them!' Becky emerged with her arms full. 'I'll cut some up. I wish David was coming today. It won't be the same without him.'

'Perhaps he'll look in this evening,' suggested Alison. She and Ken had asked David to spend Christmas at Spryglass, but he'd already accepted Lindsay McCobb's invitation to dinner at the farm.

'David's been helping out at Lindsay's animal shelter a lot lately, hasn't he?' observed Ken casually.

'McCobb's Farm is a large place,' replied Alison, placing the breakfast dishes to warm. 'And with only Lindsay and her brother and aunt to run it, and care for over a hundred rescued animals, there's always a great deal of work needing to be done.'

'Ah, but apparently there's far more to it than work,' grinned Ken mischievously. 'By all accounts, David and Lindsay get along very well. Not that I'm one to listen to gossip! But when I was collecting Dan's prescription, Mrs

Almond happened to mention that, in her opinion, wedding bells are in the air between those two.'

'Oh, no. That's not right, Daddy,' commented Becky wisely, making for the garden. 'Lindsay's going to marry Mr Davenport, the vet. And David's going to marry Laura!'

'Um, thanks for sorting that out for me, Becks,' said Ken, straight-faced, winking at Alison and taking her hand as they followed Becky out into the cold, clear air.

The sun hadn't quite risen, but its glow was colouring the sky orange, and spilling vivid light onto the shallow water of Becky's pond. While she filled the water bowls and scattered food, Alison and Ken strolled contentedly down the winding garden path. The coarse grass was crunchy beneath their feet, all the snow having melted except for a few patches in cold, dark corners.

'These eight months we've been married have been the best time of my whole life,' Ken said unexpectedly.

Despite being so busy with all the seasonal fuss, his wife had been unusually reflective and absorbed of late. He didn't understand why. 'I've been thinking about you, though,' he went on quietly. 'You gave up your career, your father, all your friends, and even your country to marry me. Are you happy, Alison?'

He asked the question hesitantly, however Alison's response was spontaneous. 'Darling — I've never been happier!' she exclaimed, astonished, yet touched, that Ken had needed to ask. 'I have never experienced so much love, or joy, as I've had from you and Becky and the family.'

Ken hugged her to him as they turned again to the house. Becky ran on ahead, glimpsing James through the kitchen window.

'James! James! Look at my new coat!' she shouted, taking the worn stone steps in a single leap and racing indoors. 'Mummy made it for me!'

'That — that's the first time Becky

has — ' Alison could say no more as her eyes filled with tears.

'It may be the first time she's said the words.' Ken drew Alison into his arms, knowing how much this moment meant to his young wife. 'But believe me, it's not the first time Becky has thought of you that way. She took you to her heart a long time ago.'

'Oh, Ken.' She held tightly on to him, gazing up into his face, her eyes shining with happiness. 'Wouldn't it be wonderful for us to have another child?'

'Steady on!' He chuckled gently. 'Don't get all misty and sentimental on me — Christmas has that effect on folk, you know.'

'It's more than Christmas. More than Becky calling me her mother,' Alison continued earnestly. 'Gradually — without my even realising it in the beginning — I've been thinking more and more about a baby . . . '

'We talked this all through before we got married, love,' Ken reminded her, not unkindly. 'And we agreed — '

'Everything was different then,' interrupted Alison, willing him to understand. 'My world was different. *I* was different. I didn't feel as I do now.'

Ken sighed heavily, not wanting to upset her, today of all days. How could he tell her he was as adamantly against the notion of starting another family now as when they'd first discussed it?

'If we had a baby, I'd be practically drawing my pension before the poor lad was a teenager,' he reasoned, frowning. 'Even if I was fifteen years younger, taking on the responsibility of another child would be foolhardy right now. If the rumours about cutbacks and job losses at the college are right . . . Well, I was last in, so I'll be first to go. And if that happens, we'll be lucky to hang on to Spryglass.' Ken couldn't disguise his anguish as he looked from Alison's wistful face to the tall, old house with its deep green woodwork and warm, cream-washed stone walls.

* * *

Although Alison didn't mention the subject again to Ken, she found herself thinking more and more often about a baby of her own. More than once she was tempted to confide in Laura, sure that the younger woman would understand. But they had little chance to talk these days. Although Monk's Inn was now closed to the public, Laura worked late most evenings, translating Shaun Pembridge's exuberant ideas and ambitious schemes into plans more suitable for a small country hotel.

'You look tired,' Alison said sympathetically, fetching Laura a cup of tea as she sat at the kitchen table sorting through a sheaf of plumbing quotations.

'I am a bit,' said Laura with a smile, sipping the hot tea gratefully. 'It's quite sad, being on my own at Monk's now Mr and Mrs Lancaster have moved out. I'll be glad when Shaun comes back.'

'With the Lancasters gone,' laughed Alison, setting down a plate of home-baked biscuits, 'your boyfriend will soon become your employer, too.'

'I hadn't thought of it that way before,' commented Laura. The notion unsettled her a little. Sensing Alison watching her, she gave a confident laugh. 'I'm positive Shaun and I won't have any problem working together, though.'

'It must be a thrilling project, with all the restoration,' observed Alison conversationally. 'Demanding, too. I'm rather surprised Shaun decided to go away on a holiday at this time.'

'He wanted a few weeks in the sun, that's all. Lots of folk go abroad during the winter,' returned Laura defensively. 'I'm perfectly capable of managing Monk's Inn, you know.'

'I didn't mean to suggest otherwise,' apologised Alison, sitting down across the table from Laura. 'I only meant I was surprised at Shaun's leaving you alone.'

Laura bridled again, misconstruing Alison's words and taking her remark personally. 'As a matter of fact, Shaun *didn't* want us to be parted,' she snapped truthfully. 'He asked me to go to Cairo with him.'

Alison stirred her tea and frowned. Shaun Pembridge was undeniably a handsome, sophisticated young man with a tremendous amount of charm. It was easy to understand how any girl would fall for him, especially one as guileless and trusting as Laura. Alison could only hope her step-daughter wasn't going to be hurt.

'You're sensible to be cautious,' she began affectionately. 'It's sometimes better to take things slowly. I imagine some of Shaun's ideas are rather different to yours.'

To Alison's horror, Laura rounded on her furiously, her cheeks burning. 'First James tries to interfere in my life, and now you! Well, you're wrong about Shaun! All of you!' cried Laura, her voice trembling. 'He loves me. And as soon as things at Monk's Inn settle down, we're going to go away together!'

* * *

Shaun returned from Cairo looking tanned and fit and relaxed. He was in the best of moods as Laura gave him a guided tour of Monk's Inn. The old hotel was now emptied of furniture and fittings and stripped back to its original walls, beams and stone-flagged floors.

'I'm wondering about changing the name,' remarked Shaun as their feet echoed on the bare wooden staircase. 'Something more oldey-worldey, more attractive than Monk's Inn.'

'I think Monk's Inn *is* attractive.' Laura responded. 'It's certainly linked to the past, Shaun. In medieval times, there was a monastery here in Sandford, and the original building on this site was an almshouse, run by monks. After the monastery was destroyed, the almshouse became a coaching inn, then a mail-stop. Of course, over the years, it's been rebuilt and enlarged.'

Shaun was watching her, a smile broadening his face. 'I'm impressed! I go away for five weeks, and when I get back, not only has my manageress got all the renovations organised, she's also turned herself into a local historian! You haven't missed me at all, have you?'

'Yes, I have!' she laughed, manoeuvring clear of his outstretched arms as she made a space for the telephone and trays on the lobby's makeshift desk. 'And you're only fishing for compliments, anyhow.'

'True,' he admitted. 'Seriously, though. How did you find out all that monastery stuff?'

'From Granddad. And the library. I was interested. I've also been contacting antique dealers for you to get period-style furniture and what not. I needed to know a little about what I was talking about.'

'You're blossoming, Laura!' Shaun gazed at her appreciatively. 'You really are — and it's beautiful for me to watch.'

Laura knew she was blushing. Quietly, she bowed her head to the bundle of applications which had been received in answer to her ad in the local paper for kitchen and housekeeping staff. 'I'm only doing my job,' she murmured.

'And you're enjoying it, aren't you?'

'Very much.' Laura raised her face, and although her cheeks were still pink, her eyes were serious when she looked across at him. 'I never liked to be away from Spryglass and the family. Becky's always longed for a mother . . . and now, well, Alison is a terrific one . . . so Becky doesn't need me anymore,' she finished with a self-conscious smile. 'And a whole lot of other things suddenly seem to be happening. All sorts of exciting prospects for the future that I'd never dreamed would be possible.'

'Feels good, doesn't it?' said Shaun with a grin, drawing her close to him with a contented sigh. 'Mmm, feels really good . . . I was miserable and lonely in Cairo,' he murmured, resting his head against Laura's shoulder and kissing her neck. 'I'm not going away without you ever again. Next time, you're coming with me — and I won't listen to any arguments!'

'I won't offer any,' whispered Laura, raising her face to his.

Shaun gave a groan of pure frustration as Laura moved from his arms to answer the telephone. He listened with growing impatience to the conversation. 'Laura,' he said in a low voice, coming to her side, 'put the call on hold!'

Perplexed, Laura did as she was told. 'It's Forrester's,' she began to explain. 'There's been a delay in getting that special panelling. The firm who'd agreed to supply it has — '

'I don't want Roy Forrester's excuses,' cut in Shaun tersely. 'I want that panelling! We have a schedule to keep! If one stage isn't completed on time, the next can't be and the whole job grinds to a halt!'

'I think you're overreacting,' protested Laura mildly. 'It isn't Forrester's fault if — '

'That won't get the work done,'

retorted Shaun, indicating she continue the telephone conversation. 'Now, have another go and push him! *Insist*, Laura!'

Laura stared at him. They'd occasionally disagreed before, but he'd never spoken to her like this!

'It's not my way to bully folk!' she murmured steadfastly. 'Being unreasonable doesn't solve problems — '

'Give me the phone! I'll attend to it this time.' Shaun took the receiver, holding Laura's hand a moment longer. 'If you're going to manage a successful business, you'll have to learn to do things like this. And the sooner the better!'

Shaken, she left the lobby and went into her own office. It was just the same as it had been in the Lancasters' days, with Laura's desk and filing cabinets and her personal belongings. Although she shut the door, and concentrated hard on the order for new soft-furnishing fabrics, Laura could still hear Shaun's voice. He sounded arrogant and bad-tempered. She leaned her elbows on the desk, pressing her fingertips to her eyes. Laura understood Shaun's wanting Monk's Inn to be perfect. His whole future was tied up with the hotel's success. Although he looked so well and healthy at the moment, she mustn't forget the terrible accident and how badly he'd been injured. He must still be adjusting, coming to terms with having to rebuild his life . . .

'Ah — here you are.' Shaun strode into her office with a satisfied smile. 'That's that. The panelling will arrive on time.'

'Good,' Laura replied sombrely. 'But did you really have to be — '

'Yes, I did! But I'm sorry I was sharp with you.' He came around and sat on the corner of her desk, obviously still pleased with the outcome of his conversation with Roy Forrester. 'One of the reasons I love you is because you're so warm and gentle.' He tilted Laura's chin, raising her face so he could kiss her mouth. 'Nevertheless, there are going to be occasions when you'll have to be tough.' He kissed her again and got to his feet. 'Oh, and I want you to contact your ex-boyfriend.' Shaun laughed at Laura's surprised expression. 'There'll be lots of odd jobs needing to be done and, according to the churchwarden and several others, David Hale works hard. And he'll come cheaply. No doubt he'll jump at the chance of some work.'

Laura sensed David's reluctance when she telephoned him; however he called in to her office at Monk's Inn later that same afternoon.

'These are always the leanest months of the year. Orders have slowed to a trickle,' replied David frankly, in response to Laura's concerned enquiry about how things were going at Riverside Mill. 'This weather isn't helping — it's holding back the planting. As for the other plans I had for Riverside, well, I haven't the money now. But you're busy; I mustn't keep you.' He changed the subject briskly, draining his coffee cup and getting to his feet. 'Thanks for the offer of work, Laura. I'll take it — and be glad of it.'

* * *

From the very first day, there was a wary hostility between David and Shaun. On far too many occasions Laura saw David swallowing his pride, silently accepting Shaun's criticism and getting on with his work. Then early one morning, the simmering antagonism between the two men erupted into an ugly scene. Laura had never seen David so angry.

'You hired me to do a job — and I'm doing it!' His expressive eyes simmered with resentment. 'Work like this can't be rushed. If it's to be done properly, it takes time!'

'And the more time you take,' cut in Shaun accusingly, 'the more money you make — '

'Stop it! Both of you!' Laura rushed

into the dining room to find them standing in front of the fireplace, which David had been painstakingly rebuilding. 'I could hear your voices from outside in the lane!'

They both turned to look at her.

'David would never cheat anybody, Shaun!' she went on crossly. 'Even you should know that!'

'Keep out of this, Laura,' he retorted warningly, glancing at her in annoyance. 'This isn't anything to do with you. Go to your office!'

Laura gasped in shock, and David made an almost imperceptible move towards her. She met his eyes briefly, before turning on her heel and leaving them alone. She walked quickly across the lobby towards her office, then hesitated at the open doorway. With a shake of her head, she went on past it and out into the cobbled yard. Standing in the welcome silence, Laura stared through the archway and along the winding lane. She was tempted to go straight home — and never come back.

No, that wouldn't be right. She sat down dejectedly on the edge of the old horse-trough, which Mrs Lancaster had planted with flowers and heather. How long Laura sat there, alone with her troubled thoughts, she wasn't sure. At length, Shaun came quietly across the yard and sat beside her.

'I was worried.' He took her hand gently. 'You weren't in your office.'

Laura didn't respond. Or look at him.

'That argument — don't let it upset you. It's only — '

'*Business?*' she demanded bitterly, glaring at him. 'Don't even bother saying it, Shaun! Because it really doesn't matter anymore, does it? I can't go on this way. All we've done recently is disagree and argue about business!' went on Laura unsteadily, vexed at the stinging tears threatening to spill over. 'What's happening to us, can you answer me that? What's happened to our being in love?'

'Stress is getting to us both,'

murmured Shaun, taking a handkerchief from his pocket and dabbing her wet eyes. 'It hurts me to see you this way, Laura. And I blame myself for being too absorbed to realise how unhappy you've been. We need time alone. Away from Sandford,' he concluded softly. 'We've talked about going away, but we've never got around to actually doing it. Maybe we should go now, because once Monk's reopens, there'll be no chance of our taking a break together for months.'

'That's true,' faltered Laura. 'But I don't know. I'm not sure . . . '

'We owe it to ourselves. To each other,' he persisted, stroking her face tenderly with his fingertips. What do you say?'

Laura gazed into his eyes. Then she nodded.

'I'll get on to Miles Weaver and make a few arrangements,' he said quietly. 'With luck, we'll be on our way to Stratford-upon-Avon by this time tomorrow.'

'So soon?' Laura asked as he rose from her side. 'Can we leave the inn unattended like that?'

'There isn't anything more important to me than your happiness,' answered Shaun simply. 'It may not always seem so, but you have to believe it's true.'

She smiled at him, warmed by the ray of hope. Perhaps they could recapture the joy and wonder of being in love . . .

Typically of Shaun, his idea became reality in less than fifteen minutes. He insisted Laura take the rest of the day off to pack and get ready. With an easier mind and lighter spirits, Laura dealt with the letters on her desk before starting home. She was at the edge of the village when a police car from the local station drew alongside.

'Laura!' John Hammond rolled down the window and leaned out. 'I'm looking for David. Someone said he was working at Monk's Inn. Is he there now?'

'Yes.' Laura was alarmed at this grave

urgency. 'What is it, Mr Hammond? What's wrong?'

'I'm afraid I've some very bad news for David . . .'

# 11

'Mr Hammond,' Laura began, cold with foreboding. 'Can I come with you?'

The police officer opened the passenger door and she got into the car.

'Can you tell me what's happened?' she blurted out as they drove back into the village.

John Hammond glanced at her, considering. 'Ah, I don't see why not,' he sighed heavily. 'It seems an old pal of David's is coxswain of the Polkerris lifeboat — '

'Martin Tregarth?' interrupted Laura anxiously. David rarely spoke of his past, but he'd mentioned his boyhood friend to her. 'Has something happened to him?'

'No. It's David's father, Joshua Hale,' the officer related bleakly. 'His fishing boat is missing. The lifeboat's been out since dawn. Helicopter's out searching, too, but . . . '

'Poor David . . . ' she whispered.

'Apparently David's sisters tried phoning him at Riverside Mill — '

'He's been working at Monk's Inn since first thing this morning!'

'Aye. Well, anyhow, when his sisters couldn't reach him, Martin Tregarth radioed a message through to Sandford Coastguard and they got on to me.'

They were approaching Monk's Inn. Laura turned to him. 'Let me tell David!' she implored. She couldn't bear the idea of David's hearing such dreadful news in cold, official language. 'You know how close we used to be, Mr Hammond. I'd like to be the one to — to . . . '

'All right,' John Hammond agreed quietly, adding, 'But are you sure about doing this, Laura?'

She nodded unhappily, then got out of the car and ran into Monk's Inn.

David appeared to take the news calmly enough, however Laura watched the colour drain from his face. She led him to her office and he sat down as she warmed the pot for tea. David had hardly said a word, but she recognised the turmoil of conflicting emotions in his eyes. What could she say or do to ease the searing pain he was enduring?

'I haven't seen my father since I was sixteen,' he murmured at last. 'Sometimes I've wondered if I was wrong to let the rift between us go on, but I could never bring myself to make the first move. Not after what he did.' David sighed, his eyes meeting hers only fleetingly. 'I suppose I thought there was plenty of time to . . . That one day, we'd . . . Now it's too late!'

'You don't know that!' cried Laura emphatically. 'They're still searching, David. Your father could be found. You *mustn't* give up. There's still hope!'

'Yes, of course there is,' he returned softly, looking up at her as she brought the tea. 'But remember, I know the seas around Polkerris. At this time of year it can be treacherous — particularly for a small boat.' David shook his head slowly. 'I'm afraid there's little chance of my father being found alive.'

Laura stood a yard or so from his chair, her hands clenched at her sides. She felt so close to David . . . felt the desolation and agony engulfing him, and longed with all her heart to comfort and sustain him.

'I'd better call Barbara and Joyce, my sisters. This will be terrible for them.' He distractedly pushed a hand through his tousled hair. 'Then I must go down to Cornwall.'

'Phone your sisters from here. And I'll come to Cornwall with you,' said Laura impulsively, any thoughts of her holiday with Shaun banished from her mind. 'You can't go down there by yourself, David.'

'Thank you, Laura.' His voice was quiet and very gentle, and he moved as though to touch her face. Then drew back. 'You're a good friend. You'll never know how grateful I am you were here today.' He reached out and gripped both her hands, smiling up into her eyes. The fleeting glimpse of their old closeness tore at Laura's heart. 'And thank you for offering to come to Cornwall — but this is one journey I have to make alone,' concluded David softly.

Laura took a quick unsteady breath, regretfully aware of the once-familiar tenderness of David's touch. Withdrawing her hands from his, she turned away with an effort. Choking down a rush of emotions, she managed to speak. 'You'll be wanting to telephone your sisters. I'll leave you in private.'

⋆   ⋆   ⋆

Sleep eluded Laura that night. When she got up, there still wasn't any news from Cornwall. Later, when she returned from walking Smokey along the shore, she heard Ken speaking solemnly into the telephone. She hurried through into the hall as he was replacing the receiver.

'The search for Joshua Hale has been called off,' he said simply. 'David says he'll be staying with his sisters until the end of the week. There'll be arrangements to be — ' Ken broke off at the sound of Becky's footsteps on the landing. The little girl loved David like another big brother. Why upset her by telling her what had happened? At least, not unless she herself asked why David had rushed off to Cornwall. 'So, Laura,' went on Ken cheerfully as Becky came clattering downstairs, 'got your bag packed and all ready for the off, are you?'

'Yes,' she answered reluctantly, mindful that her young sister was within hearing. 'But how can I possibly go away?'

'What reason is there for you not to go?' countered Ken practically, in a low voice. 'We're all thinking about David, but there's nothing we can do. You missing your holiday won't help — and David would be the first to say so.'

Several hours later, when Shaun

arrived at Spryglass, he found Laura sad and subdued. He'd already heard about David Hale's father; word had whipped around Sandford like wildfire. Neighbourly concern it might be, but Shaun regarded the local preoccupation with minding other people's business as one of the more irritating aspects of village life. Nonetheless, he appreciated Laura's distress, and was sympathetic and understanding. Gradually he coaxed her into conversation as the miles to Stratford-upon-Avon slipped away.

Finally, Shaun's efforts were rewarded. He saw Laura gradually beginning to relax, responding with the warm smile he'd come to cherish. She hadn't been to Stratford before and, although there'd be plenty of time for sight-seeing after lunch, Shaun couldn't resist taking her to see Anne Hathaway's cottage. Half hidden by thick green hedges, with its tiny leaded windows peeping out from beneath thick folds of undulating nut-brown thatch, the cottage glowed in the early sunshine.

'It's beautiful!' she murmured, entranced.

'So are you,' he returned simply, taking her into his arms and kissing her slowly.

Holding hands, they continued the last few miles to the Hearts of Oak, the secluded sixteenth-century tavern where they were to spend their holiday.

'I especially asked Miles to give us this room,' began Shaun, unlatching the low door and standing aside for Laura to enter.

She paused at the doorway to admire the oak-beamed bedroom with its creamy washed walls, open hearth and antique furnishings.

'It's got the best views in the whole place,' he went on, slipping his arm about Laura's waist and leading her to the bowed windows. 'Look, sweetheart. A lake! With swans.' Shaun broke off, sensing Laura's sudden tension. 'It's all right, isn't it?' His question was uncharacteristically tentative. 'The room, I mean?'

'Y-yes,' she faltered uncertainly, avoiding his eyes. Instead, she concentrated on the sweeping expanse of shining willow-fringed water with its gliding snowy-white swans. 'You're right, the view's lovely.'

'You know that isn't what I meant.'

Laura's gaze met Shaun's enquiring one for the briefest instant. 'It's just . . . Well, I hadn't expected — ' she began awkwardly, stumbling over the words. 'You didn't say anything, and I . . . '

He drew her to him, holding her gently. 'I took a few things for granted, didn't I?' he murmured ruefully. 'Look, I don't want to rush you, Laura. If you're not happy with this, I can easily make other arrangements. Whatever you want — ' He inclined his head so he might see her face properly. ' — it's fine with me.'

'Oh, Shaun,' she whispered brokenly, his gentle solicitude provoking her emotional response. 'I'm so glad we came.'

After lunch, they spent the afternoon

strolling hand in hand along the banks of the River Avon, going on to explore the picturesque market town of Stratford.

'Tomorrow we can follow the valley down into the Cotswolds,' Shaun was saying when they lingered at the lake to watch the setting sun spill paint-box colours into the still, shimmering water. 'Go on to Bath, if you like.' He pulled her near and kissed her as they turned their backs on the lake and started up towards the tavern. 'We'll decide over dinner.'

Laura had enjoyed their day, however now she had fallen silent, her thoughts troubled. 'Shaun — wait!' She caught his arm as they made to enter the tavern. 'This isn't right! I shouldn't be here with you!'

He turned to face her, reaching for her, murmuring reassurances. Laura wasn't listening. She couldn't hear anything but the thumping of her own heart. Her throat was dry, and it was all she could do to frame the words.

'I thought — but I was wrong! Now I know I — I — ' she stammered wretchedly. 'I don't love you, Shaun. I'm sorry! I'm so desperately sorry . . . For all of this,' she finished in a small voice.

'Not wanting to be with me is bad enough,' Shaun said savagely, staring past her to the darkening lake. 'Apologising makes it even worse!'

'I only meant I was sorry for hurting you!' she murmured in confusion. 'That's all I meant.'

'It's David Hale, isn't it?' demanded Shaun angrily, his hands gripping her shoulders so fiercely Laura was compelled to face him. '*Isn't it?*'

'No! No, it isn't!' she cried honestly. 'He and I are friends, nothing more!'

'Friends?' he challenged bitterly. 'Perhaps you actually believe that, Laura — but I don't. You're in love with David Hale . . . You've never *stopped* loving him!'

\* \* \*

352

The spring morning was dark and chilly. Ken got up first to light the fire in the kitchen ready for when Alison came down to prepare the family's breakfast. In the grey half-light of dawn, he watched small blue flames flickering over the salty driftwood. They'd been married for almost a year, and Ken had been planning a celebration. He wanted to take Alison on a holiday, and ever since they'd first met, she'd shown great interest in his native Scotland.

It was many years since he'd last been back there, and while Ken certainly didn't have any desire to return to the poor pit village where he'd spent his boyhood, he'd really been looking forward to touring the Highlands with Alison ... Perhaps it was fortunate he hadn't got around to booking or making any proper arrangements. Plans of that sort would have to wait. He'd have to keep a careful eye on every penny now.

Months of rumour, about staff

cutbacks and departmental closures at the college, had become hard fact during last evening's staff meeting. Ken now knew he might not have a job for very much longer. Hearing Alison opening the front door to take in the milk bottles, he got up and put the kettle on to boil.

Alison never ate breakfast herself, but when Becky and Laura's was ready and keeping hot on the stove, she brought her coffee around to Ken's side of the table. 'Why didn't you wake me when you got home last night?'

'It was awfully late. Hours of blethering — but not much was actually said.'

'Have the authorities decided to give your department the funds it needs to continue?' Alison's quiet voice was concerned.

'You've got to be joking,' he retorted derisively. 'No — they've appointed a committee to make a report! Funds will be allocated according to their recommendations. Which means,' Ken finished in annoyance, 'we'll all be kept waiting until the end of next month!'

Alison laid her head against his shoulder in a wordless sympathetic gesture. She knew behind Ken's anger and impatience was a deep-rooted fear of unemployment. She was scared, too. 'Darling, if you do lose your post at the college . . . ' She fought to keep the anxiety from her voice. 'Will you go back to sea?'

'The last thing I want to do is leave you and the family,' answered Ken thickly. 'But it wouldn't be easy for me to get another teaching job. Going back to sea might be the only way out.'

'There is another way,' ventured Alison softly. 'Me! My designing and dressmaking!'

'Oh, love. Making frocks for Nancy and Helen is a nice little hobby.' He smiled, putting his arm about her shoulders. 'But it'll never be enough. This old place costs a fortune to heat and maintain, you know.'

'Please don't patronise me, Ken. I'm

serious.' Alison moved away and began preparing Becky's packed lunch. 'There's a shop to let in the village. Next to the newsagent's. It has everything I'd need and the rent is reasonable.'

'You've already looked at it?' Ken asked curtly. 'Without so much as a word to me?'

'Beginning a new business isn't easy. I didn't want to raise any hopes until I was sure the proposition was viable,' reasoned Alison. 'Now, I'm sure.'

There was no reaction.

'Ken, I want — and need — your support!' she added after a long moment. 'Even a little encouragement . . .'

'If a shop is what you want, then I'll not stand in your way,' he responded stiffly. 'As to the rest — well, if you're interested in my opinion, I don't like the idea!'

'Why not?' Alison was dismayed. 'I think it makes sound, practical sense! If I can earn some money, you won't have to go back to sea. You'll be able to take as much time as you need to find another suitable post ashore.'

Ken's face set into a grim frown. 'And while you're earning all this money, what will I be doing? Sitting at home all day? Twiddling my thumbs, reading the paper and waiting for the right job to happen along? I'm sorry, Alison, but you've got me all wrong! That's not for me,' he finished vehemently. 'I've always worked and provided for my family — and I always shall!'

Alison tensed. It infuriated her when Ken overreacted like this! He was so obstinate and proud. Couldn't he at least try to see her side of things?

'You're being selfish, Ken! You're considering only yourself — not the family or me!' she cried. 'I loved my work and my shop. I miss the challenge and the stimulation — the sense of achieving something in my life!'

Ken had abruptly turned his back to her, so she didn't see the wounded expression in his eyes. 'I'd no idea you were so dissatisfied with our marriage,' he commented coldly. 'You've a home and a family — I thought that was what every woman wanted. It was always enough for Jeanette. She was never restless — '

He was interrupted by Laura and Becky coming down for breakfast. After that, there was neither the opportunity nor the time for further discussion.

* * *

During the weeks that followed, Ken was irritable and short-tempered. Alison became increasingly unsettled. Restlessly, she spring-cleaned Spryglass from loft to cellars. Then she made new quilt covers and, with Laura's help, painted and papered the girls' bedroom.

'Want to break for a cuppa?' Laura asked, noticing Alison running a hand wearily across her forehead as they fitted wallpaper around an awkwardly sloping corner in the attic room. 'You look shattered.'

'I'm a little tired, that's all. I'm fine. Really.' Alison smiled. 'Besides, you've been working at the hotel all day so *you* must be exhausted.'

'No, I enjoy doing this! And the room's going to look lovely,' replied Laura enthusiastically, straightening up and admiring their handiwork. 'Besides, although business at Monk's Inn is picking up steadily, now the refurbishment is all finished and we're fully staffed again, my job isn't anything like as hectic.'

'It can't have been easy for you to stay on there,' commented Alison mildly.

'I didn't think it could work out in the beginning,' Laura confessed, speaking for the first time about her break-up with Shaun Pembridge. 'I offered my resignation, but Shaun refused to accept it. He knew how much I enjoy my job, and told me I should stay. It was such a generous thing to do — I'll never think him self-centred again — because it really was awful for both of us when we first split up. I'm glad we persevered though,' she finished self-consciously. 'With each day, seeing each other and being together is becoming easier and less upsetting.'

Personally, Alison was less than convinced about the nobility of Shaun Pembridge's motives. Laura was a conscientious, hard-working girl and an absolute asset to any business. Nonetheless, she was genuinely pleased for her stepdaughter and said so. 'I'm glad it's all going well. You work extremely hard, Laura, and deserve every success!'

'Thank you,' Laura said with a smile. 'You haven't been inside Monk's Inn since we reopened, have you? It's really beautiful, with antiques and paintings and tapestries. Some of the fabrics are reproductions of traditional Elizabethan patterns. I think you'd find it interesting,' she continued diffidently. 'I'd enjoy showing you around. If you'd like to come, that is? Perhaps we could have lunch together afterwards . . . '

'Oh, that would be wonderful!' Alison

said, beaming, pleasure bringing a touch of colour to her pale features. 'I'd love to come!'

They arranged to meet at Monk's Inn at eleven o'clock on Wednesday.

★　★　★

Alison didn't arrive promptly, although she was usually punctilious about timekeeping. When she still hadn't shown up half an hour later, Laura became concerned. She telephoned Spryglass but didn't get any reply. Dad had the car, so Alison would be walking into the village. Laura left her office and went outside to see if she could spot Alison coming up along the lane. There was no sign of her. Laura was turning to go back indoors when she suddenly saw Alison sitting hunched and alone on the bench beneath the oak tree across the green.

'Alison!' she called, sprinting over the damp clover-strewn grass. 'I've been waiting for — ' Laura broke off as she drew near the distraught woman. Alison's shoulders were trembling, her ashen face wet with tears. 'Alison, whatever's the matter?'

'I'm going to have a baby.' She stared fixedly at the green, with its swathes of golden dandelions and tiny white daisies. 'I didn't even suspect I was pregnant. Isn't that silly?'

'But it's wonderful!' exclaimed Laura, perplexed. 'Aren't — aren't you pleased?'

'If only you knew how I've longed for a baby!' Alison paused, raising anguished eyes. 'But Ken and I had agreed, Laura. He doesn't want another child. He's made that perfectly plain, more than once.'

'Dad loves children,' replied Laura confidently. 'He'll be thrilled when you tell him!'

'Tell him?' echoed Alison, distress making her voice shrill. 'How can I? When he's already desperately worried about providing a home and future for his family? No, I can't tell him. Not now.' Inhaling a steadying breath, she met Laura's gaze resolutely. 'I must ask you not to say anything about this to anybody — especially not to your father!'

★ ★ ★

'Riverside's starting to look good again, David.' James gave the fields filled with flourishing vegetables a backward glance as he and David wheeled barrows towards the barn. 'Granddad was showing me the greenhouses earlier. You're growing more under glass than ever!'

'Thanks to Dan,' responded David with a smile. 'We're partners now.'

Since Dan's illness, David had taken care of all the heavy work on his allotment. Dan came out to Riverside three days each week to work in the greenhouses.

'Provided we're not flooded again this summer, and if there are no other unforeseen catastrophes or expenses, I should just about break even.' He

363

paused, reaching the barn's open doorway and standing on the threshold. 'I'm not afraid of hard work, James, and I never expected running my own place to be easy but . . . well, lately I've been wondering if it's worth it.'

'You're never thinking of giving up Riverside!' exclaimed James in disbelief. 'You can't be!'

David didn't reply at once. He gazed out across the meadows to the ribbon of river threading between the willows. 'Somehow, all the heart has gone out of the place.' His voice was a mixture of wry humour and sorrow. 'Or perhaps the heart's gone out of me . . . ' He raised a hand in response to Dan's wave and he and James crossed to the mill. Becky and Smokey were sitting like statues amongst the bluebells and hare's tail, watching the brown-and-yellow ducklings bobbing after their mother on the river. 'Tea break, Becky!' called David.

She tiptoed a distance away from the bank, before running towards him.

'I wasn't expecting visitors today — especially not a young lady,' he told Becky as they all trooped indoors. 'Your Granddad and I are used to roughing it at tea break, isn't that right, Dan?'

'Oh, aye,' he agreed gravely. 'Tin mug of cold water with a few bits of soil in, that suits us champion!'

'But I'll find something a bit tastier for you, Becky.' David went into the sparse, antiquated kitchen, with the small girl and her dog following him. 'Let's see what there is in the cupboard, eh? We'll have whatever's there!'

Becky shook her head indulgently. Rolling up her sleeves, she began to wash her hands at the sink. 'You've been working hard all day,' she said seriously. 'Go and sit down with the others. I'll make our tea.'

'I know another girl who used to say that to me,' laughed David quietly, handing Becky a towel. 'Funny — she looked a bit like you, too!'

Becky laughed with him, before bundling him from the kitchen and opening the bread crock.

'You're not seriously considering giving up here, are you?' persisted James as they settled in the living room and waited for their tea.

'Oh, I suppose not,' replied David, tilting his ladder-backed chair and rocking meditatively. 'Riverside Mill is exactly what I always wanted. And I do like being my own boss ... On the other hand, the notion of starting at nine, finishing at five, and collecting a nice, regular wage-packet every week is awfully tempting.'

'Hmm, *that's* not everything it's cracked up to be, either,' said James with feeling. 'Ask Dad.'

'Ken told me he might lose his post at the college.' David frowned. ''Report's due the week after next, isn't it?'

'Yes. I know how I felt when I was waiting to hear if I'd got a place at music college,' recalled James grimly. 'Goodness knows what Dad must be going through.'

'Aye, Nanny and I were saying much

the same on Sunday when we got home from having tea with you,' Dan put in thoughtfully. 'We don't want to interfere, but we'd like to help.' He looked at James directly. 'Do you reckon there's anything we can do, son?'

'I don't know, Granddad,' considered James, pausing reflectively. 'I don't think so. I've only been home a few days, but I get the feeling there's something else bothering Alison. Besides Dad's job, I mean. She just isn't herself somehow.'

'Alison is going to have a baby,' Becky announced matter-of-factly. She walked across the room, taking small, careful steps as she balanced the tray of tea and sandwiches. 'I heard her and Laura talking. Daddy doesn't know. It's a secret.' She looked sternly at each of them. 'I'm knitting bootees for the baby. And that's a secret, too!'

The men stared blankly at each other for a few seconds.

'Well, well,' Dan chuckled at last.

'Another grandchild, eh? Wait till I tell Nanny!'

'Granddad!' admonished Becky, holding the heavy teapot with both hands. 'You're not to tell!'

'Not even your gran? She'll chase me with her broom if I don't tell her news as exciting as this!'

'All right, you can tell Gran,' conceded Becky, passing round mugs. 'But nobody else!'

They'd hardly started stirring their tea when the telephone rang. James was sitting nearest, so he got up to answer it. The caller spoke rapidly and without pause. James made several attempts to interrupt. When he did, he asked the distressed woman to wait and turned to the others, his face grave.

'David, it's one of your sisters. She's awfully upset. Your father's b — ' James checked, aware that Becky was listening and rephrased what he had been about to say. 'They've found him, David.'

\* \* \*

David was grateful James went with him to Polkerris for Joshua Hale's funeral. After the service, he and James and Martin Tregarth walked slowly from the church down into the middle of the small fishing town. David and James had booked in at the Mermaid and Castle.

'My father didn't trust banks or lawyers. He doesn't seem to have left a will, and Barbara and Joyce can't find his insurance policies, the cottage's rent book, or the ownership documents of the boat. None of his personal papers,' David told them. 'There's an awful lot of legal red tape. I don't want my sisters to have to cope with it. I'll get as much as possible sorted out before I come back to Sandford.'

'Maybe this isn't the time to mention it, Davey,' began Martin. 'But the *Minnow* wasn't damaged much.'

David nodded. Joshua Hale's boat had been recovered weeks before.

'Me and a couple of lads have done a bit of work on her, so she's perfectly seaworthy now,' Martin went on. 'What I'm getting around to saying, is that you could do a lot worse than coming back to Polkerris and taking over your dad's fishing — ' He was interrupted by the shrill bleep of his pager. 'That's a shout! I got to go!' Martin was already running along the steep, twisting street. 'See you both later.'

'Take care,' David called after him, but Martin had already turned the corner toward the lifeboat station.

David watched him go, his gaze gradually drifting across the harbour to the calm sea. 'I'm taking Minnow out for a blow, James,' he murmured thoughtfully. 'Want to come?'

Within half an hour, they'd left the harbour behind and were out on the open sea. David was strangely pleased at how familiar Minnow felt. He'd forgotten that a boat became more than timber and metal once she touched water, suddenly taking on the vitality and spirit of a living thing.

'You look the part!' James commented with a smile, standing beside him in the wheelhouse and admiring his friend's confident handling of the vessel.

'This is what my father wanted me to do,' returned David simply. 'He expected me to take over the boat and the fishing after he'd gone. There's the cottage where I grew up!' He pointed along the coastline to crooked rows of houses and scattered white-washed cottages. 'The one at the end of the harbour road. My sisters still live there, of course.'

James nodded. He'd seen for himself how strained relations were between David and his two older sisters. 'They don't know about your father, do they?' he said evenly. 'What you found out about him? Before you left home?'

'I've never told anybody except you and Laura.' David pushed open the wheelhouse window so the fresh salt air rushed in. 'Barbara and Joyce worshipped my father. I couldn't hurt them

371

by telling them he'd been deceiving our mother for all those years. So I just left without giving any reason. My sisters didn't understand — and didn't approve. They thought I was letting down my father, and our family. As the only son, I had a duty to stay and take over the fishing.'

'Is that what you'll do now?'

'I don't know. I have thought about leaving Sandford,' David admitted frankly. 'But coming back to Cornwall? It'd never entered my head until today. Although with things so uncertain at Riverside, I'll have to give it some serious consideration.'

They discussed the subject again the following evening when they were driving from the West Country back to Liverpool. The roads were fairly quiet and they made good time, arriving in Sandford earlier than anticipated.

'Won't you come in?' invited James, when they drew up outside Spryglass.

'Thanks, but I'd better get home to the mill.' David smiled, but his eyes were weary. 'Things keep going round and round inside my head. I must sort out what's most important. Whatever I decide now, will alter the course of the rest of my life.'

\* \* \*

He drove on slowly, away from the coast and up through the woods to Riverside Mill. Leaving the van just inside the gate, David got out to walk the rest of the distance. He was stiff and restless after the long journey. When the mill-house came into sight, he wasn't particularly surprised to see lights glimmering and the chimney smoking. Dan had a spare key, and came and went from the market-garden as he liked.

However, when David was passing the window towards the door, he saw it was Laura working quietly in the kitchen. As he stood watching her, she checked a dish in the oven before going through to set the table with a single place. So she wasn't intending to stay and join him for supper . . . David felt the deepest disappointment.

Little more than a year ago, on the morning after the storm that had devastated Riverside Mill and all of David's hopes and dreams, Laura had rushed into his arms and told him she loved him. He'd loved her, wanted to marry her . . . but like a fool, he'd sent her away.

In despair, David ran a hand through his hair, still watching Laura as she moved about the mill-house. If only it were possible to turn back the clock!

# 12

Although Laura had occasionally visited the market-garden, she hadn't actually been inside the mill since that morning the previous summer when she and David had broken up. She hadn't expected that being here again now would affect her so painfully.

Unable to bear the thought of David coming back from his father's funeral to a cold and empty house, Laura had borrowed the spare key from Granddad and come to light the fire and prepare a meal. Moving distractedly about the kitchen, she checked the oven and glanced up at the clock. David wasn't due for another hour or so. Plenty of time for her to clear up and slip away before he got here. He might want to be alone, Laura told herself, closing her mind to the real reason she didn't want to still be here when David returned.

Meeting him was becoming more and more difficult. Not because Laura didn't want to see David, but because she *did* want to see him. So very much. She wandered into the living room and put another log onto the crackling fire. Kneeling at the hearth, she sat back on her heels, her gaze drifting around the large, comfortable room with its high-beamed ceiling. Riverside Mill was a warm, safe, homely place again after last year's flooding. It was easy for her to picture a family living here. The family she and David might have had together . . .

Laura bowed her head, closing her eyes tightly, but the memories would not be shut out. Why had she never told David she loved him? Why had she waited so long? Too long! If only she'd let David know how she felt, everything would have been different. A sudden knot of tears choked Laura's throat. Rising abruptly, she scurried to the kitchen to begin tidying up. She kept clattering and dropping things, and jumped violently when a foot scraped on the stone step outside.

Spinning around, Laura saw the door unlatching . . . And suddenly, David was there.

Instinctively, she moved to meet him. Then froze. For a moment that stretched out endlessly, they just stared at each other.

'I saw you through the window. You shouldn't have,' began David quietly, glancing around the warm, welcoming room. 'But thank you.' He smiled, closing the door and taking off his coat.

It was the very ordinary, everydayness of it that made Laura go cold with regret. David smiled at her, walked towards her, as though he were coming home to her . . . It reminded Laura of all that had so nearly been hers. Of everything she had lost.

'I wasn't . . . You're early,' she faltered at last, struggling to gain a grip on her feelings. 'How are you? And your sisters?'

'I'm OK,' he replied, but a concerned

frown creased his forehead. 'Barbara and Joyce have taken it awfully hard. Barbara particularly. She's not been well, what with the shock and . . . ' David sighed heavily. 'She's pretty poorly. The chandler's where she works have been understanding about her taking so much time off, but it looks as though Barbara'll have to give up her job.'

'Your poor sister! How awful for her,' Laura returned sadly. 'I'm so sorry, David.'

'Yes,' he agreed bleakly. 'Something unexpected came up just before we left Polkerris, too. It was Martin Tregarth who — ' He hesitated, looking down into Laura's upturned face. She was pale. Her blue eyes large and dark. David had been about to mention the possibility of his leaving Sandford and returning to Polkerris, but changed his mind. 'It'll keep, Laura. I'll tell you another time.' He shrugged dismissively. 'That wouldn't be one of your hotpots I can smell cooking?'

'It'll be another twenty minutes or so.' Laura forced a bright smile, gathering up her bag and jacket. 'But everything else is ready. There's a fruit pie — '

'Won't you stay?' he asked quickly, realising she was about to hurry away. 'And join me? Please?'

Laura paused, torn. Perhaps he needed somebody to talk to? She nodded slowly.

David's heart sank, immediately regretting having asked her. She felt sorry for him! Pitied him. He could see it in her eyes, and was infuriated at himself for placing Laura in a situation where her kind heart made it impossible for her to refuse his impulsive invitation.

'Supper will be another twenty minutes,' she repeated mechanically, turning back toward the kitchen. 'Can I get you a hot drink while we wait?'

David followed her, scraping back a chair to sit at the table. Laura bustled about, putting the kettle on, warming the teapot. Squeezing by his chair, she fussed with tea cups and set another place at the table.

'Laura — for goodness' sake, stop moving about in front of me like that!' he exclaimed, turning away from her. There was a tense silence, then he glanced up at her apologetically. 'Sorry.'

'Oh, David . . . ' she murmured sympathetically. 'Was it dreadful? Polkerris, I mean?'

'No, not really,' he answered frankly. 'I can't explain it, but when James and I took my father's boat out, I suddenly didn't feel bitter anymore. All the old hurts were gone. I started remembering Dad the way he was when I was a boy. I thought the world of him then!' David smiled sadly. 'Respected and admired him, too. Wanted to grow up just like him. He loved the sea, and we had some fine, happy times together aboard the Minnow. On summer nights, Dad, Martin and I used to go sailing. We'd sleep on deck under the stars . . . Oh, if only I could see him, talk to him, just

once more, Laura! Tell Dad I — '
David's voice cracked, and he swiftly
averted his eyes, swallowing convul-
sively.

'David,' Laura whispered his name,
reaching out awkwardly to pat his hand.
With all her heart she was longing to
wrap her arms about him and comfort
him the only way she knew how.
Instead, she merely said gently, 'It's all
right, David. It's as it should be.'

Supper was strained. There was none
of the easy conversation and comfortable silences of their old days together.
Laura guessed David was as relieved as
she was when the meal was eventually
over.

'I wish you'd let me see you home,'
he said as she picked up her jacket. 'I
don't like letting you go alone.'

'I'd rather,' Laura insisted, more
sharply than she'd intended. 'Really.'

'OK.' He expelled a resigned breath.
Laura obviously didn't want to stay at
Riverside — or with him — a minute
longer than necessary. He walked with

her to the door, standing behind her to help her on with her jacket. His hands rested lightly on her shoulders.

Laura's heart thumped in her chest, panic and apprehension welling up inside her. If she walked away now, without saying anything . . . would she be making the same mistake all over again?

'David — I love you!' she said very softly, without turning to look at him.

When he didn't respond, she wondered desperately if he'd heard her. Then she felt the pressure of his fingertips increase. Gently, he brought her around to face him.

'Then marry me, Laura,' he said urgently, drawing her close against him. '*Marry me!*'

\* \* \*

Laura had popped into the newsagent's during her lunch hour to choose a greetings card. She was reading the verse on one with a beautiful flower picture when she became aware of somebody sidling alongside her.

'If I tell you I love you — ' The low voice was close to her ear. ' — will you let me walk you back to work?'

'David?' she enquired innocently, still reading. 'Is that you?'

'Who else were you expecting?' he demanded indignantly, bending to kiss her lips.

'Not in *here*!' she hissed, giving him a push. '*Mrs Almond* is over there by the magazines!'

'You're right. I should be ashamed of myself,' he agreed soberly, his eyes twinkling. 'What are you buying, anyway?'

'Birthday card for Gran,' she answered, showing him. 'What do you think about this one?'

When they'd left the shop, David slipped his arm around Laura's waist. 'Are you sure you wouldn't like to go away somewhere after our wedding? I know we don't have much money, but Riverside is doing reasonably well now so we can afford to have a proper honeymoon.'

'It isn't because of the money, David — truly it isn't!' Laura glanced quickly around the lane before reaching up to kiss him. 'I just want us to be married. The only honeymoon I want is our being together in our very own home at the mill.'

'OK,' David gave in amiably, kissing Laura very slowly, despite her protests that the postie was cycling by. 'If you should change your mind, though, you've only to say and we'll pack our bags and go somewhere!'

Laura nodded, her cheeks pink. As they approached Monk's Inn, David paused, taking both her hands in his.

'You know how I feel about our working together at Riverside after we're married,' he began seriously. 'But it's a huge decision for you. Why don't you think it over a while longer?'

'I don't need to,' she replied simply. 'I'm going to hand in my notice at the inn today.'

'You actually expect me to accept this?' demanded Shaun later that afternoon, tossing aside Laura's letter of resignation. Thrusting his hands into his pockets, he strode across the office to stare out from the window. 'You expect me to be all noble and civilised; to just stand by and watch while you throw away your whole future?'

'I — I'll stay on,' she began awkwardly, Shaun's vehemence taking her unawares, 'until you can find a replacement.'

He swung around and glared at her. 'You think that's what I'm concerned about? A manageress for this place?' Shaun's tone was scathing. 'You're making the biggest mistake of your life, Laura. The only reason I've said nothing before now, is because I was sure sooner or later you'd come to your senses!'

'Please don't say such things, Shaun!' she implored miserably. 'If you go on like this, you'll hurt us both!'

'Hurt? You don't know the meaning of the word!' he exploded brutally. 'Try watching the person you love marrying somebody else. *Then* you'll know hurt!'

\* \* \*

Spryglass's garden was rippling with deep drifts of fragrant bluebells, and the late spring sunshine warm enough for Alison to take her sewing outdoors. She was letting down the hem of Becky's best dress so she could wear it at the weekend when Ken returned from Southampton. He'd been away on field trips with his students from the college before; however Alison had never missed him quite as keenly as she'd done upon this occasion. Part of her longed to share the wonder of these early weeks of her pregnancy with him; another part was anxious about how Ken would react when she told him about the baby.

More than once, Alison had been on

the brink of impulsively blurting out the news. Then she'd bite her tongue and say nothing. It wouldn't be fair to tell Ken now. He hadn't been sleeping well, and although he'd never admit it to her, Alison knew he was terrified by the possibility of losing his job. To prove his worth, Ken was pushing himself relentlessly. If he wasn't working late at college, he'd bring papers home and stay up till all hours working. And now, there was this field trip. Alison's concentration strayed from her needlework. Whatever the consequences, she'd be grateful when the college announced its decision on Friday. Ken would be returning home the following day.

If only he'd be pleased they were to have a baby . . . If only he didn't lose his job . . . If only he wasn't compelled to rejoin the Merchant Navy . . . Her needle and thread darted swiftly through the fabric. So many 'if only's! When the hem was finished, Alison went inside to press the dress. She was setting up the ironing board when the telephone rang.

'Ken — I was just thinking about you!' she exclaimed in delight. He usually didn't call until teatime, when Becky was in from school. 'Oh, it's marvellous to hear your voice, darling!'

'Steady on!' he protested, sounding pleased. 'I only phoned last night, and we talked for ages! This call will have to be quick. I'm on my coffee break.' Ken hesitated slightly. 'Everything is all right at home, isn't it? *You're* all right, Alison?'

'Of course. We're all fine,' she insisted reassuringly. 'I'm not missing you at all!'

'Good. I'm doing enough missing for both of us. I never realised I could be as lonely as I've been this past week. All I've done is think . . . ' He paused, a shade awkwardly. 'Anyway, since I was in this neck of the woods, I've been catching up with a few old friends from my Merchant days. If I do get the push from the college, there's a decent chance I can get a job down here in Southampton.'

Alison tensed, her fingers closing tightly about the telephone. Ken was going back to sea! He'd already decided. He'd be away for months at a time. She'd be without him . . .

'Are you still there, love?'

'Yes,' she murmured sombrely. 'I'm listening.'

'I'll explain properly when I see you,' he went on hurriedly. 'But basically, it's short European routes. I'd be home three days out of every fortnight. Far from perfect, I know, but it'll tide me over until I can get another shore job, won't it?'

'I suppose so.' Alison suddenly felt weak. 'I'll miss you terribly, but it's far better than I dared hope.'

'And it would be just temporary, remember,' he insisted, breaking off. 'I'll have to go, love. Somebody else wants to use the phone. See you Saturday.'

★　★　★

Very late on Friday night, Ken silently let himself into Spryglass. The porch light was on and the front door unbolted, so he guessed Laura was still at Monk's Inn. Leaving his suitcase in the hall, Ken went upstairs. Alison wasn't in their room, so he started up to the attic.

The door was ajar. He could see Alison sitting on the corner of Becky's bed, her arm around the little girl's shoulders. They were both fast asleep, the book they'd been reading together lying open upon the quilt. If Ken had had any remaining doubts, seeing his wife with Becky like this . . . Somehow, he knew he was right. He'd missed a great deal during his years at sea. Laura and Jimmy's growing up, all Becky's younger days. He hadn't even been at home when his children were born; he'd first seen their faces in photographs air-mailed to him halfway across the world. But marriage to Alison had changed everything . . .

Tiptoeing into the room, he closed

the storybook and bent to touch his lips to Alison's forehead. She stirred, opening sleepy eyes. 'Ken!' she exclaimed softly, trying to ease away from Becky without waking her. 'What are you — ?'

Ken beamed and took her hand. He led his wife out on to the landing before taking her into his arms. 'Soon as the lecture finished, I started driving home,' he whispered. 'I didn't want to spend another night away from you.'

To her horror and dismay, Alison started to cry. And couldn't stop. She fell against Ken, holding on to him with all her strength.

'It's all right, love. Just let it come,' he soothed, rubbing her back, resting his cheek against the smoothness of her hair. 'You're having a baby, aren't you?'

Alison raised wet eyes to him and tried to speak. When she found she couldn't, she nodded incoherently. 'I — I wanted to tell you,' she sobbed at last. 'When you came home. Tomorrow . . . '

'If you like, I can go away again and — ' began Ken cheerfully, trying to make her smile. Then he read the uncertainty in her troubled eyes, and understood. 'I'm *delighted* about the baby!' His voice was gentle, but his arms held her all the more securely. 'You do believe that, don't you?'

Alison stared up at him, a glimmer of joy appearing in her dark eyes. 'I want to believe it,' she whispered hesitantly.

'*Believe* it,' he responded simply, dabbing her face with his handkerchief. 'Oh, I know I said I didn't want to start another family . . . But I feel different about it now. During the past few days, I've sort of got used to the idea, you see.'

'Are you really pleased?' she persisted earnestly, the faintest smile touching her lips.

Ken grinned patiently at her. '*Yes!*' he mouthed silently. 'Yes — I'm thrilled to bits!'

'Well, I should be cross.' Alison sniffed, unable to suppress a watery smile. 'I'd planned my speech so carefully — and you already knew!'

'I didn't,' protested Ken amiably. 'But there's nothing like spending his evenings all alone in a hotel room for giving a man time to think. And mostly, I thought about you. The notion you might be pregnant sort of crept up on me.' He took Alison's face into his hands and kissed her. 'I guessed a bit — and hoped a lot.'

She stared up at him in wonder. 'Whyever didn't you say something?'

'Over the phone? No way!' Ken shook his head. 'I wanted us to be together. I wanted to be able to see you . . . hold you.' He paused uneasily. 'I'm no good at saying things like this, but I couldn't be happier — or prouder — than I am tonight!'

'Darling, you don't have to — ' Alison faltered as new and powerful emotions engulfed her. Her smile was now mingled with more tears.

'Hey, don't start that again!' murmured Ken, putting his arm about her shoulders. 'I haven't got another dry hanky! Come on, let's go downstairs and I'll make some cocoa . . . '

'Want a refill?' he enquired a little while later, when Alison was curled up beside him on the sofa. She shook her head, nestling closer.

'Just you.'

'You've already got me!' he joked. 'And that reminds me — I have some news, too. Not as good as yours, but I think you might be pleased! You know that seagoing job I told you about? I won't be applying after all.' Ken paused, smiling and watching Alison's expressive face. 'Just before I left Southampton, the college principal got in touch with the report's recommendations. There'll be voluntary early retirements and streamlining, but no department closures or job losses. My job is safe, love!'

'Oh, thank goodness!' She hugged him fiercely. 'You deserve it. You work incredibly hard, and you're a fine teacher!'

'Steady on!' he laughed, fending her off. 'You'll spill my cocoa!' Ken fished into the pocket of his shirt, and withdrew a small box tied with ribbon. 'This is for you.'

Alison untied the ribbon and opened the little velvet box, gasping as the soft lamplight gleamed upon a silver brooch set with a single richly glowing amethyst. 'Oh, Ken!' she whispered. 'It's beautiful!'

'It's a thistle. They grow in Scotland,' he commented gravely. 'Thought you might fancy a wee holiday, touring the Highlands and seeing the real thing — '

'*Daddy!*'

Becky and Smokey exploded into the quietness, the little girl clambering up onto Ken's knee and her dog trying to do the same. 'You're back! I've missed you! Are we *really* going to Scotland?'

'Who's got big ears, then? Yes, we're really going to Scotland.' He grinned at Alison, and winked. 'All four of us!'

'Five!' corrected Becky quickly.

'Five?' repeated Ken, looking anxious. 'Not expecting *twins*, are we, Becky?'

'No.' She shook her head solemnly. 'I meant Smokey. He can come with us, can't he?'

'Aye, why not!' Ken laughed, tousling Becky's fair curls. 'We'll *all* go — right after Laura's wedding.'

★  ★  ★

Spryglass was in chaos. James had been awake all night practising the piece he'd written for the simple service Laura and David had chosen at the village church. Ken was up a step-ladder, decorating the hall with garlands of fresh flowers Dan had brought from his allotment at dawn. Nancy, Helen and Alison were organising the kitchen, because instead of a fussy reception, Laura and David had asked for a quiet family celebration at Spryglass. Sadly, Barbara Hale's illness had prevented David's sisters from attending, but Martin Tregarth had travelled up from Polkerris to be best man.

'Alison!' Laura raced downstairs and burst into the kitchen, her face flushed. 'I can't find my shoes! Will you come and help me, please?'

'Of course.' Alison dried her hands, taking a quick look around the kitchen. Everything looked more or less ready. And the three-tiered cake Nancy had baked and iced was safely out of harm's way in the pantry. 'Becky! It's time you were getting dressed!' she called, hurrying through the hall. 'You too, Ken!'

'I'll fret about clothes when I've got these flowers right,' he muttered, leaning back a fraction on the ladder, squinting up at his handiwork. 'Are they straight — ?'

However Alison was already upstairs and following Laura into the attic bedroom. Carefully, she removed the ivory-coloured dress from its protective coverings. She'd hoped to design and make the wedding dress herself, but had also understood Laura's wish to wear the gown which had belonged to her great-grandmother and had been worn by Nancy and her mother, too.

The princess-seamed front bodice was laid on with delicate Victorian lace and the full fluted skirt fell to a gracefully shaped hem. Laura was taller than the earlier brides, and Alison had taken great pride and pleasure in making the alterations.

'It's an exquisite dress!' She smiled up at her stepdaughter. 'You look lovely, Laura. I wish you and David every happiness and blessing in your marriage.'

'Thank you!' Laura beamed, shyly giving Alison a little hug. 'If we're as happy as you and Dad — '

'Is anybody up there?' Ken's exasperated voice drifted up from the foot of the stairs. 'If we don't get to the church soon, David will think you're not coming!'

★ ★ ★

Laura was full of plans to grow herbs, cut flowers and a greater variety of soft fruits at Riverside Mill. And she was looking forward to planting wallflowers in the sheltered, sunny corners around the mill-house. The fragrant plants were David's favourite and as she watched him collecting the post, she was imagining their dark curling leaves and jewel-coloured velvety flowers in full bloom.

'Card from the family!' he called, holding it up and striding across the grass towards her.

'Hmm, Loch Katrine!' exclaimed Laura appreciatively, slipping her arm through David's as they walked together. 'What's your letter? It looks official!'

'It is,' he answered apprehensively, opening the envelope. 'From Boscombe's — the solicitors in Polkerris.'

'Not bad news?' Laura watched his expression become solemn as he read the contents, and gave his arm a comforting squeeze.

'No. Nothing like that. It's about Dad,' murmured David, rereading the letter as they wandered down to the seat beneath the willows. 'We assumed he'd never made a will, but evidently he had. Martin was doing some routine maintenance on the boat and found it — with all Dad's personal papers and a coin collection, too — squirreled away behind the panelling in the wheelhouse. My father didn't trust banks any more than he trusted lawyers!' he concluded with a small smile, passing the letter to Laura. 'It seems Dad actually owned the cottage, and he's left it to Barbara and Joyce, but he wanted me to have his coin collection. I didn't even know he was interested in old coins!'

'Oh, David . . . ' Laura reached up and put her arms about him, hugging him, as they sat together on the rough, sun-warmed bench. 'I know you've been unhappy, wondering how your father felt about you in his later years . . . ' She faltered, trying to find the right words. 'It's sad — I suppose legacies always are — but at the same time, it proves that your father never stopped thinking of you, or — '

'I know what you mean.' He smiled ruefully, gently threading his fingers into the soft waves of Laura's hair and drawing her closer. 'Apparently Dad collected those coins over fifty-odd years,' continued David at length. 'Boscombe reckons the collection will fetch a sizeable sum.' He exhaled a slow, measured breath, shifting slightly and leaning back. 'It'll come in very useful around here. And we can put some by for emergencies.'

'You and I share everything else, but this legacy is yours. You must use it in the way you feel is right!' Laura ventured after a minute, sensing David's disquiet.

He glanced at her quickly. Was she already aware of what was running through his mind?

'What would you have done with this money if you were still single?' persisted Laura mildly.

'I'm not — thank heavens!' he returned, pressing her hand to his lips. 'We are married and, after you leave Monk's Inn, Riverside will have to provide a secure future for us both.'

'We made our plans long before this came up,' Laura reminded him gently. 'You and I — we have everything. Our health and strength . . . and each other. We're already rich! But your sisters . . . ' She stroked his hair gently. 'Barbara's had to give up her job, and Joyce can only work part-time now. You're thinking of making over the legacy to them, aren't you?'

'I can't deny it. Dad meant well, but he couldn't see how things would turn out for my sisters,' David said quietly, gazing at her. 'I'd be uncomfortable if I kept even a penny of that money.'

'I know you would.' Laura traced the line of his strong jaw with her fingertips. 'And I'm proud of you because of it.'

⋆ ⋆ ⋆

Laura was working on Harvest Festival Sunday. She went into Monk's Inn several hours early so she could get away in good time for church. She and David were meeting the family and Gran and Granddad, and all going to the service together.

As summer became autumn, the inn's guest rooms were no longer fully occupied but business was still brisk, especially for dinner and weekend lunch bookings. So far, Shaun hadn't mentioned his plans for the Christmas and New Year season. In fact, he'd been delegating more and more responsibility to Laura, frequently spending days away without getting in touch. Going through the lobby, Laura saw a light under Shaun's door. It wasn't like him to be in his office at this hour on a Sunday morning! She knocked and looked in.

'Shaun, I'll need your signature — Mr Weaver!' Laura broke off, recognising the young man sitting there. They'd met once before, in Stratford-upon-Avon, where Miles Weaver owned the

Hearts of Oak country hotel.

'It's Laura, isn't it? Hello, again!' He rose, smiling warmly and shaking her hand. 'I'm just getting my bearings. Sorting out the important stuff, such as where the coffee and biscuits are kept! I was hoping for a chat, Laura, but didn't expect you in this early. Won't you take a seat? I'll be here for the next three days, but will try not to get in the way,' Miles went on briskly. 'I'm not planning any changes yet, so it's business as usual.'

'Mr Weaver, I'm sorry, but I don't quite understand.'

Miles Weaver considered her perplexed expression and arched an eyebrow. 'My apologies, Laura. I naturally assumed you'd be aware of the situation,' he began evenly. 'Shaun has sold Monk's Inn. I'm the new owner.'

'I see.'

'I want you to stay on, of course,' he added quickly.

'Thank you, but I resigned a while ago,' Laura quietly explained. 'I've only been staying on until Shaun found another manageress.'

'Ah, I understand,' he commented, recalling Shaun's fondness for Laura. 'Well, let me make a few phone calls. I'm sure we can sort something out.' When he was showing her from the office, Miles paused and remarked soberly, 'Shaun's a gypsy, Laura. I've no idea where he is now — or what he's doing. However, whatever — wherever — it is, it won't hold him for long. He's never been one to put down roots. I know he's pretty thoughtless and inconsiderate sometimes, but try not to think too harshly of him.' He grinned at her wryly. 'Shaun's not a bad sort, deep down.'

Laura went to her own office at the rear of the inn. The instant she pushed open the door, she saw the posy of flowers on her desk. Apricot carnations and tiny, creamy-white rosebuds. The flowers Shaun had always given her. They'd cared for — loved — each other once. Wherever Shaun was now, whatever he might do in his life, Laura hoped he would find happiness and contentment. Sadly, she held the posy in her hands. This was surely the loneliest way for them to part . . .

During the rest of that morning, Laura finished off all the work she had pending and cleared her desk. Miles Weaver couldn't have been nicer nor more accommodating, releasing her from her duties immediately. Leaving Monk's Inn for the last time, Laura paused in the lobby, looking round affectionately. Then she went outside and crossed to the green, already scattered with spiny green horse-chestnut shells, the glossy brown conkers spilling out into the thick grass.

The family were gathered there under the sprawling old trees, chatting to other folk from the village. David and Becky were shuffling with Smokey through crinkled, golden leaves, deep in discussion about Granddad's wood-carving skills. Laura fell into step beside them, slipping her hand into David's.

Becky was wide-eyed, bubbling with excitement.

'Granddad's finished making — ' she began, breaking off as she spotted the posy. 'They're pretty!'

'Yes, aren't they?' said Laura with a smile, offering the flowers to her young sister. 'Would you like to put them with yours, for the Harvest Festival?'

Becky nodded, adding them to her own bunch of colourful chrysanthemums and dahlias. 'Granddad's finished carving the cradle!' she continued enthusiastically. 'And Gran's made a frilly wee pillow and bumper. Alison said it's lovely, and Daddy said we're all ready for the Big Day!'

\* \* \*

Rose was born during the winter's first frost-spangled night. On the afternoon Ken and Becky set off to bring her and Alison home to Spryglass, the old house's gardens were white with a powdering of fresh-fallen snow.

Laura filled the dining room with bowls of freesia from Riverside's green-houses, then left David lighting the fire while she prepared a meal for the family. Returning to the cosy room a little later, Laura went to draw the curtains. She paused a moment to gaze beyond the garden to the shore and the distant grey thread of ocean. There was scarcely a breath of wind, and every-where was very still.

'It's starting to snow again.' She half-turned to smile at David, and he came to her side.

'The first time I ever saw you, you had snowflakes in your hair!' he said, moving his hands slowly up and down her arms. 'Have you given any more thought to that honeymoon you haven't let me take you on yet?'

'Mmm, as a matter of fact, I have,' replied Laura with a quiet laugh. 'I'd like to go to Cornwall. Meet your sisters and see Polkerris. Explore all the places you've told me about.'

'Sounds wonderful to me!' he responded,

his mouth finding the sensitive hollow behind Laura's ear.

They were still kissing when the garden gate creaked open. Alison and Becky with Smokey gambolling at their side came in first, followed very slowly by Ken, who was carrying the baby.

Becky broke away, racing up the snowy path and bursting in at Spryglass's front door. 'Laura! David! We're here! We've brought Rose!'

Shortly afterwards, Laura and David left Spryglass.

'Didn't you want to stay for tea?' David enquired with some surprise.

Laura shook her head contentedly, pausing at the gate to return a cheery wave to the little family before they all went back indoors. 'It's *their* day, David.'

He nodded, taking her hand and starting along the lane, but Laura pulled free, sprinting away from him.

'The tide's coming in!' she called over her shoulder, running across the snow-brushed sand. 'Let's go home along the shore!'

David caught up with her, swirling Laura into his arms. 'Say it again!' he demanded, his eyes shining. 'I like hearing you say that!'

'Let's go home, David!' Laura laughed breathlessly, standing on tiptoe to kiss him. 'Let's go *home* . . . '

## THE END